MOONLIGHT
THE JOURNEY BEGINS

PURABI SINHA DAS

Suite 300 - 990 Fort St
Victoria, BC, V8V 3K2
Canada

www.friesenpress.com

First Edition — 2021

This book is a work of fiction. Any reference to names, characters, places and events are products of the author's imagination, and any resemblance to actual events or places or persons, living or dead, is entirely coincidental.

Photo credit front cover - Kim Valenta

ISBN
978-1-03-910316-0 (Hardcover)
978-1-03-910315-3 (Paperback)
978-1-03-910317-7 (eBook)

1. FICTION, ROMANCE, HISTORICAL, 20TH CENTURY

Distributed to the trade by The Ingram Book Company

From the moment I read the first page I was pulled into Chandni and Kanta's worlds...characters woven so intricately together, leaving the reader in anticipation of the next puzzle piece…shift between space and time so beautifully crafted. I couldn't put the book down...a must read!
Nina Ganguli, Certified Life Coach, Author of Confessions of a Can't-aholic: How to go from "I Can't" to "I CAN"!

Purabi Sinha Das elegantly describes the struggles of two generations of women through the lens of a patriarchal Indian culture. The reader will be absorbed with Chandni Rai's journey as she peels back layers of family secrets to find her missing grandmother...finding the strength to cope with her own...reality. A complex and moving story. -
JF Garrard, Author of The Literary Elephant, President of Dark Helix Press

...two points in time... two lives that intersect...the two people never meet. We are drenched in the culture...climate...norms...women have lived through...continue to live through today. Purabi never lets us dwell on the characters' big decisions...life changing moments...instead moving us... facing forward. Every time I put the book down the characters stayed with me until I picked it up again.
Sandra Baker Director, Recruitment and Advancement at Hamilton District Christian High

For my constant:
Alak

Acknowledgements

I could not have written this story without the unconditional faith of my family. My husband, Alak, thank you for believing in me, reading the final draft and offering invaluable insights. Daughter Lolita for reading the first draft and subsequent ones, constructive feedback and unstinting encouragement. Son Rahul who was always ready with words of wisdom, and wit, when I was feeling down and about to lose confidence in my ability to write this story.

My gratitude to Heather Stephens, Manjari Thompson and Silvia Stekar for spending time reading the manuscript and asking discerning questions. Beverley Dowling for that gentle push that started the story at a Creative Writing class offered by the University of Toronto.

I am indebted to Barbara Kyle, author of the acclaimed series of historical novels *The Thornleigh Saga* and of acclaimed thrillers, for reading the first fifty pages of the very first draft and offering invaluable advice.

Thank you to my copyeditor, Holly Bennett, for enthusiasm, expertise, advise, support and meticulous care of the book.

Thank you to FriesenPress for professional support, guidance and hand-holding in bringing the book to its final stage before publication.

ONE

Chandni
Mauchak – 1970

The day after she turned thirteen, two things happened that changed the course of Chandni's life. Her father died suddenly. And she learnt something about her grandmother. She had never seen her. There weren't even any photographs, and her name was never mentioned in the Rai household.

As was the custom, in summer, the green shuttered windows of the white house remained closed through the long, glaringly hot afternoons. It was sometime after lunch. Chandni was supposed to be hard at work as second term exams were coming up. But she was tired, out of sorts, the heat sapping her strength. She wanted to talk, but her mother had retired to her own room. And Kunal? God only knew where her brother had gone. The three occupants of the house seemed almost alien those days, each in a world of their own, minding their grief.

She opened one of the shutters a tiny bit. She couldn't stand the *loo.* Hot, dry and dusty, it continued to rage outside. Everything had to be kept under cover, and even then, tiny particles of dust infiltrated wherever they could. The dust storm normally stopped around sunset and that's when the cleaning started.

They'd come, she assured herself, and was soon rewarded with the familiar sound. She leaned out further in order to get a better view, a wide smile flitting across her face. Tails twitching, a line of black buffaloes ambled along, sound of the *thunk dong* of the bell hanging on one of their necks painting the deserted road with a distinct quality all its own. They were on their way to the pond. A boy, she assumed no more than ten or eleven years of age, lolled on one of the broad backs, a thin switch stuck in one hand. He used it to swat at the beasts if they dallied too long. As Chandni watched, he tucked the ends of the cloth that had come loose more securely around his mouth.

She watched, a glint of envy in her grey eyes. The procession of beasts turned the corner, and was blocked from view by the high compound wall. At the same time, the clock struck the half hour.

Hands resting on the shutter, she hesitated for just an instant, then with a quick movement, closed it and turned back to the room. As always, the eyes from the photograph on the wall followed her, and as always, she tried to ignore them. The photo had been there for as long as Chandni could remember, her father's great-grandmother, or *Boroma,* another one of her ancestors she had never met. Encased within a black frame, the heavy-jawed face had watchful eyes, the *anchal* or headscarf half covering a domed forehead. It was a face that would brook no disobedience. This used to be their drawing room, where guests were entertained. It was now Chandni's. She hadn't wanted it, but her parents insisted she have a room of her own to study in. She had asked for the photograph to be removed. Instead, she had earned a lecture.

Not one to give in easily, she had tried another angle. Why weren't there any pictures of Kantabali, her own grandmother? She had asked her mother, not her father, fully aware even this tactic would not elicit a response, and she was proved right. She had been told to get back to the waiting books. Her parents' reluctance to answer any of her questions about her grandmother had given Chandni much food for thought. She had an inquisitive mind, fuelled by her sense of being wrongly done-by. Almost all her friends had a grandmother who spoiled them shamelessly. Why not her? Why was Kantabali's name taboo in their family?

She drew out the chair and seated herself at her study desk. When the sun had lost some of its bite, the wind went down. People began to emerge from their shuttered houses. The sound of rickshaw wheels bouncing on the uneven road was accompanied by clanging bells, the high-pitched tones of the ice-cream seller, the rumble of a lorry, all combined to convey that the world had not changed.

Yet, life in Chandni's home had. Permanently. Her father's funeral had happened the week before.

She was about to get a glass of water when the blue curtain lifted and Mrs. Basu, the town-crier, walked in unannounced. She never bothered to knock.

Suppressing the instant irritation, Chandni pushed the chair back and stood up in one fluid movement, offering to get her mother.

"Wait, wait, tell me how you are. Oh my, how thin you are, dear. My heart breaks to see you like this, fatherless…are you eating enough? Do you need anything?" The woman prattled on in this vein without pause as Chandni remained on her feet. Her entire being protested under this – intrusion – yes, that's what it was. She was certain their neighbour wanted only to delve for information at this time, and the cup of tea that she was sure her mother would provide.

Arrgh – Chandni hated her.

The beady eyes flicked over Chandni, then darted about the room, searching, for what? Chandni balled her fists and turned sideways, not caring if her gesture appeared rude, as her mother entered the room. Relieved, she headed for the door and was almost out when Mrs. Basu began once again, this time each word punctuated by long sighs and the clicking of teeth. Chandni hovered to listen. She had never done this – she knew listening at the door was rude. Yet she remained where she was, senses alert.

"It will be so-o-o difficult for you to look after this large house… and, two children also. But your husband has left you enough, I am sure. Oh dear, it's so sad to talk like this – he was here just the other day." Mrs. Basu paused to blow her nose.

Chandni's brows furrowed in concentration. She crept closer to place her ears to the wall, its cool touch like a soothing balm on her hot skin. She wanted to hear her mother's reply but it was too soft.

The nasal tone could be heard again. "Poor unlucky thing, you are a widow now. What will you do? You don't even have any family – not like your mother-in-law is here or anything. Of course, you can depend on us. We'll help you, dear – whatever you need, just come to me."

"Thank you so much, Mrs. Basu. We are all right." This time her mother's voice came out strong and clear. Chandni's mouth lifted in the familiar one-sided smile. Good for Ma.

But Mrs. Basu wasn't done. "As I was saying," she continued with a sniff, "you need to be careful, Mrs. Rai. You know how people talk. Of course, I don't ever listen to gossip, but I am your friend."

Chandni stuffed a fist in her mouth. Not listen to gossip, indeed. She was the epitome of a perfect gossipmonger.

But why should her mother have to be careful? Thoroughly intrigued, she had half a mind to stomp back into the room. But she was also prudent. It would not do to annoy her mother – especially at this time. Instead, she concentrated on listening. All feelings of guilt over eves-dropping had disappeared.

The voice went on, "You are alone now, no man in the house." (*What about Kunal?* Chandni wanted to shout.) "These strange stories about your mother-in-law – not true, I am sure. People talk, and you know that I am not one of them." She stopped suddenly with a rustling sound that could only be the re-arrangement of her raw silk sari. Mrs. Basu was always well-dressed. Then she started again. "Of course, you never knew her. Nobody ever saw her after they moved to that place. Tut, tut – oh, you, poor things. My heart is melting looking at you. Whatever happened to her, did you ever find out? When I came here as a bride, I was expressly told not to mention the name. My mother-in-law said that Kantabali had disappeared."

Chandni pressed closer to the door, making sure to stay well behind the long curtain. They were discussing her own grandmother. What did Mrs. Basu mean by saying Kantabali had disappeared? Absorbed in her thoughts and trying to make sense of what she'd just heard, Chandni had no time to move. Suddenly, her mother stood before her.

Her eyes, with their depth of hurt, and an ember of anger, bored into Chandni. "What are you doing here?" she asked in a low tone. Chandni stood with eyes downcast, guilt and shame turning her mute.

Without waiting to see Chandni off to her room, the tall, slender figure walked briskly towards the kitchen. Mrs. Basu would be served tea.

Mrs. Basu had left and Chandni was sitting at her desk. The fan whirred overhead - even the blades seemed to have succumbed to the heat and turned in slow motion. Snatches of the conversation she had overheard earlier buzzed through her brain. It was futile. She could not concentrate on dull books when there were questions to be answered. She wanted to speak to her mother, ask her about Kantabali. Why hadn't anyone ever said anything to her and Kunal? They had a right to know about their family history. She walked to the window and drew open the shutter to be greeted by the heat of the *loo*. She was about to close it again when the air in the room was rent with the unmistakable sound of shattering glass.

Chandni swung around. She stared at the smashed glass that had once sat within a picture frame, each jagged edge an accusation. *Boroma's* picture lay on the floor uncovered.

She hadn't even touched it.

She was already in her mother's bad books, and now, this.

With one quick stride, Chandni was on her haunches trying to gather up the shards.

"What are you doing?" With a violent start, she looked up only to find her brother standing at the door. His dishevelled hair looked even more so. There was a pencil stuck behind one ear and he was holding a book in his hand.

Relief washed over her. "*Dada*, I don't know how this happened, but I must clean it before Ma arrives."

"What happened?" Kunal had entered the room and was about to say something when they heard their mother's footstep, light and quick. Before either could speak, their mother had lifted the curtain and stepped in. For a moment, there was complete silence.

"How did it break?" she asked finally. She was well aware of her daughter's aversion to the photograph.

Kunal cleared his throat. "Ma, would you believe it? The picture just fell and broke." At their mother's look of disbelief, he tried again, "Actually, I had taken it down the other day, to sketch, you know, and guess I didn't put it back again properly." Chandni was staring at him but he avoided her eyes. Then she tried to speak but Kunal rushed on, "I have a frame that will fit this picture. I'll get it right away." With that, he ran out of the room.

Kunal shouldn't have spoken for her, and she shouldn't have kept quiet. But she also knew it would be hard to convince their mother to believe what had actually happened. She would make it up to her brother.

She still sat hunched over the broken glass, but now her hands got busy collecting the pieces. Her mother knelt to help.

"Don't hold them in your hand," she cautioned, spreading a corner of her sari. "Leave them here."

Chandni did as she was told, then picked up the photograph. As she did so, a piece of paper fluttered to the floor. It must have been in the frame behind the picture all these years. It appeared fragile. With thumb and forefinger, she picked it up, her eyes making a cursory check. An old letter, the writing faded, and written in Bengali. There were holes in places as though burnt. Chandni could only decipher a few words – "*please, come and get it, for surely this is Kanta...*"

Chandni's involuntary gasp brought her mother to her side. "Ma, this is a letter, I am sure it is, and it must be really old. But why was it behind the picture?" Her mother was holding out her hand, and reluctantly Chandni placed the aged paper in it.

Much to her disappointment, Chandni never found out how that piece of paper came to be stuck behind *Boroma's* photograph. Even the talk her mother had with them later that day was one-sided, her mother's disjointed sentences barely offering any information except that Kantabali had died young and *Boroma* had left Bundhpur Fort, bringing her grandson, Chandni's father, an orphan at seven months, to Mauchak. Kantabali's name was never mentioned in the Rai household.

Later, Chandni complained to Kunal, "We know nothing about our roots."

"Oh, you and your roots," Kunal threw his head back and continued to flip through a stack of records.

"Yeah, our roots -- we should know about our grandparents, both of them – don't you see?

"Chandni, don't be so sensitive." He had found the one he wanted. With gentle fingers, Kunal slipped the vinyl out of its cover and held it up. "This needs cleaning," and with a soft cloth, he began to wipe the record.

"Boys don't understand." Kunal waved her away. Seeing that he would remain engrossed among his collection, Chandni decided to leave her brother alone.

Their father was the son of Prince Kunjan Rai and his wife, Kantabali. Knowledge of her grandfather's conversion to Christianity at eighteen was something she held dear. This action had resulted in him having to leave home with his eleven-year-old wife to the fortress of Bundhpur in Central India. The young couple had been accompanied by Kunjan's grandmother, *Boroma*, a staunch Hindu and widow at the time. Why did she leave her own home to live with a pair of Christian converts in the wilds of Central India? Chandni didn't understand it.

Here she was, from the Christian side of the Rai family, possibly with hordes of uncles, aunts and cousins belonging to the Hindu faith, whom she had never met, and her imagination conjured up vivid scenes in which they all hemmed and hawed, sizing each other up, refusing to be the first one to break the ice. Suppose they didn't want to acknowledge her? What then?

Many times, she had been on the brink of asking her father about Kanta. But something about his detached air, the way he preferred his own company, had kept Chandni and Kunal from having a close relationship with their father.

Chandni's desire to be a writer, hidden jealously from the world, provided fodder for an abundance of prose, poetry, stories with a definite tinge of the detective in them, and simple observations. However, the idea of putting them together had not occurred to her until the morning of her twelfth birthday, when she was handed a notebook by her parents. She had clutched it with both hands while her parents looked on fondly. They understood, which was why they had given her the notebook as encouragement.

The notebook was five inches by eight inches, the cover embossed in gold with drawings of green ferns wrapped around an old, gnarled tree. A picture of a wooden swing tied to one of the branches exuded a sense of mystery. Turning it this way and that, she traced the tree with her fingers and under the gentle caress, the pages seemed to leap into life, inviting her to make entries. She would draw the figure of a girl on the swing. Yes, that's what she would do, decided Chandni, her imagination on fire. She couldn't wait to fill its pages.

Later, Chandni believed it was the notebook that had channelled her secret ambition into a concrete goal. Ever since then, she had burnt with a desire to write her family history, especially about Kanta. She had decided that her grandmother's name must be freed from the miasma of doubt and suspicion under which she lay hidden, convinced there was a good reason why she had disappeared. What gave her this conviction? Just a gut feeling, that's all. The mystery had to be solved. The family history would take some research, but then there was the chance she might stumble upon clues during the process.

Masjidpur – 1976

The heat of the day had abated somewhat, a soft breeze bringing a measure of relief. Even the old tree with its twisted roots reaching into the ground seemed to smile in anticipation. Chandni listened to the rustle of leaves. She had taken a proprietary interest in this tree from the first day of her arrival in her husband's home in Masjidpur. And that was just a week ago.

The street lights had come on, dispelling some of the gloom from the kitchen. They were frugal, the Ramsays, and Chandni knew better than anyone not to be wasteful. The table had been cleared of dinner utensils, and her in-laws had retired for the night. They were both getting on. Chandni sighed deeply, savouring this time alone.

Masjidpur was a small mill town, and not a pretty place. This house that she now was a part of faced the main street. She found the constant noise of traffic and people bothersome. It was at those times she thought of the city in England – Manchester – that would be home. It was much larger and probably noisier by comparison, and Chandni realized with surprise that she was changing, already becoming adaptable.

Her hands flew with urgency as she set the table for next morning's breakfast. In no time, she was done. She let her eyes wander over the round wooden table, making sure everything was in order, then pulled a chair closer to the window and sat down.

Her shoulders relaxed visibly.

Relishing the quiet, Chandni let her mind fly to the journal, tucked in a corner of the large suitcase that still lay unpacked in her room.

She hadn't written much lately. The past few weeks had been a whirl of activity flying by with the speed of wind during a cyclone. A slight tingle heated her cheeks. TJ had flown in from Manchester the day before the wedding, but they hadn't had a moment together. Always surrounded by family and friends, well-meaning, but like most Indians, intrusive. It was only the wedding night they could call their own. A short week later, TJ had had to fly back and here she was, in Masjidpur, with his parents.

Chandni stared unseeingly at the night sky. She wanted to, no, was dying to see her mother one last time before she left India. Mauchak was a two-night journey by train. But the passport work had to be done, so she had to remain in Masjidpur.

It was a waste of time, this endless waiting and thinking about it. Chandni's brows drew together. TJ should have been here to make sure her documents were ready. But no, he had to rush back to work. What sort of a boss did he have, anyway, who would not allow a man to spend time with his new bride?

Her slim form slumped further into the wooden chair.

In the chaos of last-minute preparations, she had forgotten to pack the folder containing her best essays and short stories, and the very first notebook she'd been given by her parents.

The wedding had been held in her childhood home in Mauchak. In the flurry of activities and a house full of guests, Chandni and TJ had only been able to exchange a few words. They were never alone until the wedding night, and then she had been overcome with shyness and found it difficult to put into words her innermost thoughts.

The festivities had ended late, the last guest finally departed, and around midnight the house had fallen silent, each exhausted member of the family in bed.

A room had been specially appointed for the young couple. It was to be their wedding night, a very special occasion. One of Chandni's cousins escorted the groom to this special room.

Not bothering to take off his shoes, TJ flung himself on the bed, linked his hands behind his head and surveyed the room. Arranged with great care, someone had looped garlands of flowers around the four-poster bed. The enormous bed itself was made up in pristine white sheets. A floor lamp shed muted light.

Trying to find a comfortable spot on the high pillows arranged behind, he pulled at them only to have his watch snag on the delicate lace. With a muttered oath, TJ yanked at the offending object. The watch was freed, but there was a large hole in the pillowcase. He flung the pillow to the bottom of the bed. Comfortable at last, a slight smile began to play around the full lips as he reflected on his accomplishment. He'd married Chandni, the girl who had seemed so distant at first, but who was now terribly in love with him. Knowing this, he allowed himself to gloat for a moment. Of course, he loved her too.

"What are you so smug about?" Chandni let her eyes linger on the dear face.

TJ started. He hadn't heard the soft footsteps.

She shut the door and pulled the latch to make it secure.

"I was thinking of you, of course."

"Of course," Chandni conceded, coming closer.

Too shy to change in front of another person, she had already donned a nightgown, its filmy folds draping her slim form becomingly. Her woman smell rose up, reaching TJ so that he grabbed her with both arms, giving up all pretense of nonchalance. Chandni felt her ribs crush, pain she welcomed as part of togetherness. This was the moment she had been waiting for – they both had. When they reached the bed, it was to fall into it with long sighs of contentment. The room, silent observer, took note of the passion of the young couple as they whispered endearments limbs wrapped around each other. The night was not for sleep. It was to make up for all those months of waiting. When Chandni hesitated, TJ showed her what to do. His desire was so great that he could not wait and had his way almost immediately. Chandni, eager to learn, accepted it as love.

Chandni looked around, at the small kitchen cum dining room, now her home also, and the ache of missing Mauchak and all that she had treasured growing up hit her with greater force. Soon, however, TJ's face loomed before her eyes setting her pulse racing. Afterwards, on that unforgettable night, TJ had kept her imprisoned in his arms. He spoke of his life in Manchester, the job he had found at a music store, the flat he was renting from a Mrs. Douglas. Chandni listened rapt and questioned at intervals. Food was important; she had to know about it.

"What do you eat? And most importantly, do you cook?"

"Oh no, Mrs. D takes care of it."

"Can she cook Indian food?"

"What Indian food?" TJ's eyebrows rose in mock ignorance. Then in a voice filled with laughter, he added, "Your Bengali fish, I suppose."

Chandni countered, "What do you know about Bengalis and fish? You aren't even one."

"I thank whoever is responsible." He gestured at the ceiling. "Don't want to smell fishy."

Chandni threw a pillow at TJ, which he swiftly deflected. "You are Anglo-Indian, so what do you know of Bengalis and their culture?" she blurted out, then wanted to bite her tongue.

There was silence in the room.

Had she offended him? Once again, she had let her tongue get away from her, something her mother was always cautioning against.

She rose on an elbow and tickled TJ's chest. He caught her hand quickly and kissed her on the mouth. She fell against him and let him hold her.

"At least this Anglo-Indian boy knows how to manage a Bengali girl."

Chandni unwrapped TJ's arms and sat up. "We are not going to fight about our backgrounds, okay?" TJ agreed readily, on condition that she give him a kiss. She complied.

At least there was someone to cook meals in Manchester, a relief for she had never been interested in the kitchen. Letting out a sigh of pleasure, she closed her eyes and let her hands wander over the slim body beside her. Instantly roused, TJ heaved himself onto her. Chandni's eyes widened in alarm. She could make out his face in the faint light of the moon filtering through the curtains at the open window, and it appeared different. Puffed up, as if he were holding his breath.

She wanted to talk some more, make up for those times when each meeting had made her feel like a thief stealing food from an unsuspecting vendor. But TJ was pulling her nightgown up to her knees, and not wanting him to feel rejection, she locked her arms around his back, silent and thoughtful.

The following day Chandni found herself on the train, on her way to her new home. Sitting between TJ and his mother, she listened to them. Mrs. Ramsay had asked her son questions, which were answered, always, with a dismissive joke. By the window, Mr. Ramsay's head rolled in keeping with the train's motion. No one paid any attention to the quiet girl whose only occupation seemed to be to bite her lips to keep them from trembling.

The thought of her own imminent departure from India brought her mother's face to mind. Careworn, yet still lovely, a face out of which shone a light that no amount of trouble had been able to erase.

With the sudden death of Chandni's father, there had been too many changes to contend with on top of mental anguish, which had to be carefully hidden. People of their lineage were not supposed to show their true feelings. The thing that most affected Chandni and Kunal was the sight of the table during mealtimes. In the past, brother and sister had turned up their noses at certain dishes; now, they had no choice but to accept what was in front of them, a direct result of depleting funds.

Looking back to those dark days, Chandni wondered if her mother had ever wanted to take a job, having three mouths to feed, including her own. She also knew the answer to her own question. Even in the twentieth century, society dictated how a widow was supposed to live, especially if she was unfortunate enough to have been married into aristocracy. Chandni's lips curled. She would have done things differently. She had a feeling Kanta would have too.

However, Chandni was nothing if not brutally honest with herself. TJ appeared on the horizon when she had been feeling desperate. Living hand to mouth, worrying where the next meal would come from, watching her mother do without so her children would have food, not knowing if she herself could continue with her studies. TJ's appearance offered a means of escape which she had taken willingly. To top it all off, it was about that time when Kunal had dropped his bombshell.

He told his sister, in confidence, that he was about to join the Order of Jesuit Fathers.

"How can you leave us, *Dada*?" Chandni had pleaded with him to reconsider. She reasoned that theirs was a close-knit family, each depending on the other for support. If one left, how would the other two carry on?

But Kunal's mind was made up. Before he left, he confided in Chandni it was their poverty that had helped him come to his decision. He just wasn't able to handle any of the consequences that followed.

"What about your conscience?" Chandni asked then, feeling betrayed by the one person she depended on to take her side no matter what, and now he was talking of leaving. So unfair. There was a tightness in her chest; she turned slightly and blinked hard to take the sting out of her eyes.

"What about it?" Kunal mumbled from the depths of the clothes closet, a pile of outfits lying at his feet. He seemed not to notice his sister's distress.

"Aren't you even ashamed of yourself, *Dada*? You are only doing this to get out of your responsibilities here." She was determined to stop her brother's foolishness. Chandni had pleaded, cajoled, then threatened, but Kunal had shrugged away all of Chandni's protests and continued with his preparations.

Determined not to display her own feelings, she had exclaimed with a laugh, "Well, once you are there in Australia, you'll disown us. You'll become a *Shaheb*. We'll never see you again." She coughed and swallowed the lump in her throat.

Kunal paused, stared a moment at the shirt on his arm, then turning towards his sister said, "I'll be back."

"When?"

"At your wedding, of course."

Chandni threw a sweater at him which he caught with a deft hand and a grin, then stuffed it into the suitcase.

One day when the sun was still struggling to reveal itself from behind the dark clouds and the air held the damp of approaching winter, Kunal, suitcase in hand, came to say goodbye. It was to his sister he had come. He said he couldn't face their mother's grief. And, then, as silently as he had appeared, he left. That had been five years ago.

They had heard from him only once since then – a few lines to say he was in a Jesuit seminary somewhere in Australia. He did not come to her wedding. Chandni would always wonder if he had received the note their mother left at the local Jesuit school. It was a major blow, something that must have affected her mother's health, for she began to appear, in Chandni's eyes, far too frail. Ma had assured her daughter that she was perfectly fine, just a bit tired after the wedding. She had blessed the married couple and sent them on their way with a smile.

Chandni was still musing when the sound of the clock striking the midnight hour jolted her back to the present. She had been sitting in the dark all this time. She supposed that she ought to go to bed, although all traces of sleep had long disappeared, leaving her edgy, unable to settle down. With another quick glance around the room to make sure everything was ready for the next morning, Chandni walked the short distance through the hall into her room. She changed in the dark and got in bed, pulling the pillow that TJ had slept on until the night before close to her. She wrapped her arms around it, and the smell of his cologne rose in her nostrils. How she missed him!

She tossed her hair out of her eyes with an impatient hand and blew air out of pursed lips. Here she was, stuck with TJ's parents. Only when the passport was ready, medicals taken, would she be able to join her husband. And the form, partially filled, was sitting in her purse. She leapt out, dug through the purse furiously until the form had been located.

Pen in hand, Chandni stared at it in consternation. Like all government documents, this too was officious in a most ridiculous way, meandering on about all kinds of things and asking endless questions. This should have been mailed already, but it had slipped her mind, what with TJ demanding her attention all the time. Promising to do it the next day, she returned to bed.

This was absurd, she, newly married, alone in bed. The small spark, lying dormant so far, rose now in a sudden conflagration filling her with anger and dissatisfaction with her situation.

Instead of wasting time here, she could be with her mother. Just the thought of her childhood home sent waves of rapture through Chandni. She would retrieve her notes, talk to Ma to her heart's content; but her thoughts suddenly took a turn she wasn't prepared for but knew had to be faced. She remembered the terrible row with her mother over her decision to marry TJ. She had a nagging feeling that her mother still wasn't too happy about it.

There will be a chance to talk things over, Chandni assured herself, pressing the pillow to her mouth. TJ's smell emanating from the damp pillow filled her with confidence. She had to convince her mother that they were meant to be together. A two-week getaway was called for. Her eyelids grew heavy. The deep languor spreading throughout her body brought in its wake a hunger that clamoured for satisfaction. She must have drifted off finally, and all of a sudden, her eyes opened into the night darkness, and she heard herself mumbling *I love you*, and found her hands within the warmth of her woman part. Fully awake, Chandni sat up in haste, a slow heat spreading across her face. She tried to marshal her thoughts into some semblance of order. There was planning to be done.

An hour passed during which she went over various plans. No matter which way she looked, there was one minor detail that could not be ignored. It cast its shadow over everything.

She couldn't travel alone.

Only when the first rays of the sun appeared on the distant horizon did Chandni fall into an exhausted slumber; but not before imagining what her grandmother's actions would have been in her place. Something told her that Kanta would have found a solution.

TWO

Chandni
Masjidpur – 1976

Chandni waited until lunch was over, when Mr. Ramsay retired for a nap. Mrs. Ramsay settled herself in the armchair across from the radio. Most afternoons were spent in this space in the corridor where wooden dividers had been cunningly used to give it the appearance of a separate room. Chandni took the opposite chair. The rain had stopped and a watery sun was trying to break through. Along with the sun, her spirits lightened.

"Auntie," began Chandni, still not comfortable to address her mother-in-law as "mother" or even "Mrs. Ramsay." The other woman didn't answer; she was searching for her spectacles. Chandni picked them up from a side table and handed them to her.

Chandni tried again. "It's so peaceful now, isn't it? The sun's trying to come out."

"What a relief." Mrs. Ramsay disappeared behind the newspaper.

"I want to visit Mauchak." Chandni paused, then rushed on, "You know, to see Ma before I leave India for good." She had Mrs. Ramsay's attention now. "It will be some time before the passport is ready, which gives me time to make the journey." Despite the wild beating of her heart, Chandni picked up a magazine and, opening it at a random page, pretended to read.

"Who will take you there?" asked Mrs. Ramsay. "You know I cannot travel again…these painful limbs won't allow me, and your father-in-law is almost bed-ridden."

From this response, Chandni concluded her mother-in-law wasn't opposed to the idea, only worried about who should accompany her on the journey. Mrs. Ramsay folded the spectacles and stood up saying, she would discuss it with her husband.

Later that night after the elder Ramsays had retired to their room, relieved she wouldn't have to make small talk, Chandni also headed to her own room. She pulled out the black notebook, the third volume. As was her habit, when she had to clear her mind, she settled cross-legged on the bed, and picking up a pen began to write, the words appearing fast on the lined page:

I wonder what Kanta would have done if she wanted to visit her Ma and was told not to, just because there was no one to chaperone her during the journey. Bet she would not hesitate to do just what she thought was right for her. Women should not be kept on a leash.

The lines had come of their own accord. She re-read what she'd written, a slow smile appearing on her face. She closed the notebook with a snap.

Nineteen and married. Time to take matters into her own hands. Masjidpur train station was a mere fifteen-minute walk from the Ramsay home. Now, to purchase a round-trip ticket. Chandni's face brightened at the thought of the wad of bills, their gift money, which she would use. However, the indisputable fact stared her in the face; the Ramsays would not allow her to travel alone within Indian borders, even though soon she would embark alone on the journey across the ocean, to another continent. The fuss about a chaperone made no sense, but it had to be respected nevertheless.

Chandni's shoulders sagged and she flung herself on the bed. *Think, girl*, she told herself urgently, squeezing her eyes shut to concentrate better.

Manisha…her best friend. Perfect. She must be convinced to help.

Chandni leapt up, eyes shining. Hands clasped behind her back, she began to pace. Somehow, she would have to contact Manisha, who had moved to Calcutta after marriage. It was also possible that Manisha was visiting her parents in Mauchak. What, then?

The floor-length mirror reflected an image of a girl whose very limbs seemed on fire, doubly reflected in the grey eyes glinting with an iron purpose. Turning to her reflection, she leaned forward and furiously whispered that to give in to doubts at this point was the mark of a defeatist. Then she opened the door and stood listening.

Only silence greeted her. Satisfied, she tiptoed to the corridor, feeling her way carefully in the dark. Reaching the spot where the telephone was kept, she picked up the receiver and dialled Manisha's parents' number in Mauchak.

As she had expected, Manisha was in Calcutta, but her mother told Chandni that her friend would be in Mauchak at the end of the week, an overnight train journey from Calcutta.

Thank God, Chandni mouthed silently, for a perfect solution had just been handed to her.

She thanked Manisha's mother and before hanging up jotted down her friend's telephone number in Calcutta.

The two friends spoke late into the night. They went over Chandni's concerns for her mother's health and the time she was wasting in Masjidpur when it could be spent in her mother's company.

"What about your paperwork? Is it done already?" Manisha sounded anxious. Chandni smiled in the dark. She knew her friend's nature, always thinking of the next step.

"Oh, it's in the mail, and I don't expect to hear from them anytime soon. I really want to get away from here, Mani. The waiting is driving me crazy. How could TJ leave without me?" The crux of Chandni's frustration; it spilt out now, but she could let her guard down with her best friend.

"Okay, let's plan this carefully. Don't worry, Chandni. Everything will be all right. You'll see." Chandni sat down, cradling the receiver to her ear, and allowed the familiar voice to settle her nerves. They spoke some more, then hung up with promises to keep in touch every day until they met on the train in Calcutta.

All that remained now was to work on her in-laws. Mr. Ramsay would listen to his wife, but Mrs. Ramsay might provide a stumbling block. Chandni was too truthful not to admit her concern. She was prepared for a confrontation, for there was sure to be one.

Timing was crucial. Trying hard to curb her impatience, Chandni waited until lunch was over. As soon as Mr. Ramsay retired to the bedroom for his customary siesta, and Mrs. Ramsay had seated herself in her favourite chair, Chandni presented her case, but first she arranged her features to appear humble.

"Remember our conversation yesterday, about visiting Mauchak to see my mother before I leave India?" she began, keeping her voice appropriately low.

At Mrs. Ramsay's nod, Chandni continued, "My friend Manisha is travelling from Calcutta to Mauchak next weekend."

Mrs. Ramsay looked questioningly at Chandni, who was considering the best way to continue. She cleared her throat. Here was the tricky part. Chandni would have to travel alone part of the way, from Masjidpur to Calcutta, half a day's journey. In Calcutta, Manisha would join with an aunt, and the three of them would travel together to Mauchak.

"Actually, Manisha's aunt has agreed to come with us and she is joining me from the next station after Masjidpur. I will only be alone for forty-five minutes." Chandni lowered her eyes to her hands. It was a slippery slope. Nonetheless, she carried on, determined to have her say. "Manisha will join from Calcutta, and then we'll travel together to Mauchak." It was not a complete lie, yet, the half-truth settled like a stone on her conscience.

"Have you called your friend?"

"Yes, last night." Long distance phone calls weren't cheap. Having confessed, she waited, hands twisting in her lap, for further questions.

At this point, the querulous voice of Mr. Ramsay drifted in from across their bedroom. He wanted his wife to search for his slippers; he needed to visit the toilet. Mrs. Ramsay nodded absently at Chandni, then heaved herself up from the chair. Limping slightly, she left the room as fast as her painful joints would allow. Chandni's eyes followed the departing figure. For a moment she was unsure of what had just transpired.

Had she received permission to travel?

She dared not move, or even breathe, until, gradually, realization made its way from mind to eyes that widened in disbelief. She would see her mother one last time before setting out for Manchester.

A decision made on the strength of her own belief, she had managed to sell it to Mrs. Ramsay; though there was the business of the half-truth, one she meant to deal with later. Now, there were important things to take care of.

Chandni's plan to visit Mauchak began to take off. She decided even to be packed and ready for the other journey, the final one, from India to England. The large brown suitcase, so lovingly packed by her mother, stood invitingly open. She remembered her mother's hands, the long fingers smoothing each item as if trying to transmit love by the very act, then folding them small and yet smaller so that every nook and corner of the case was filled. She had moved closer. Her mother had looked up with her serene smile, as if to say: *Courage, my love.*

There was the cosmetics case. Actually, this had come from TJ when he returned to marry her. She opened the red leather box, savouring its smoothness under her fingers. A scent rose to her nose; it came from the lipstick and compact nestling in a bed of satin. Reluctantly, she set the case aside. Then, she took out each item from the suitcase, methodically going through them, choosing some, discarding others on a pile set aside, until the case was emptied of everything, except a brown manila envelope. She guessed its contents, Pima's wedding gift to her; his letter was so filled with love, her eyes burnt. Pima truly had been like a father to her.

Chandni began to read the letter once again, marveling at her uncle's generous spirit; he explained that his executor would hold his will, by which Chandni would inherit his estate. Chandni knew the will wouldn't take effect until she turned twenty-four.

She smoothed the sheets of paper and returned them to the envelope. They would stay locked in the cupboard until her return from Mauchak.

She had changed her mind about taking the suitcase. The journey was only for a few days: a small bag to hold a sari, blouse, towel and some personal items would do.

Chandni remained seated on the floor. Along with spending time with her mother, the trip would be the opportunity to retrieve the notebook she had forgotten to bring. In Mauchak, there was an old leather-bound trunk in one of the storerooms. It contained legal papers, pitifully few and mostly in tatters, which belonged to the Rai family. Chandni, the bride-to-be, not allowed to do anything during the weeks leading to her wedding for fear of tiring her, had had time on her hands. Notebook in hand, she had been wandering around the house when she remembered the trunk. Opening it proved much more difficult than she had anticipated. She tugged at the latches until they came undone and one of her nails broke. Ignoring the damage, she turned her attention to the trunk. It was filled with cylindrical rolls of parchment paper tied with red thread. On the papers were old-fashioned looped letters in Bengali, difficult to decipher at first, but she had persevered.

The contents did not reveal anything dramatic, only financial accounts and estate inventories. She was about to return them to storage when her eyes fell on a line in one of the documents. It mentioned a place called Bundhpur, in Central India. As she had read, a growing sense of wonder began to take hold of Chandni. Her paternal grandparents, the prince and his wife, had lived in the ancestral fort in Bundhpur. Her own father was born there.

With the paper clutched in her hand, Chandni had flown to her mother. Her suspicion was confirmed. She wanted to know more; however, any chance of further conversation was put to an end by the arrival of Pima. Her uncle had arrived with workers from his own estate to help with last-minute preparations. She had returned to the store room to clean up the mess.

Now, she was convinced that in the rush her notebook had been tossed in the trunk by mistake.

THREE

Chandni
Central India - 1976

The brass hands of the round glass-fronted clock pointed to nine as the train began to pull out, slowly at first, then gathering speed, into the unknown dark, leaving behind the chaos and bright lights of Masjidpur station. It was headed for Calcutta, the point where Manisha was supposed to join Chandni, and the two would then continue on to Mauchak together.

Chandni had splurged all the wedding gift money on securing a berth for herself in a first-class compartment. Tucking the small case under the long blue seat, her berth for the duration of the journey, she settled beside the window taking in the scene in front. There were hurrying coolies, scolding parents shepherding their children to designated compartments, and the hiss of engines. A twinge of nervousness started its way up within Chandni. Was she doing the right thing?

Just then, a woman entered. The train started. The two remaining berths in the four-person sleeper remained empty.

"Made it," the woman said, wiping at the line of sweat on her forehead. She was wearing a green silk sari, and around her neck was a heavy gold chain. She looked to be about thirty years old. Chandni got up to help her with her luggage.

"Thank you, dear. Are you alone?"

After a moment's hesitation, Chandni said, "Actually, my friend is meeting me in Calcutta."

"Oh, I see. So, your husband isn't travelling with you?" She pulled a bamboo fan from her bag and started to fan herself vigorously.

"Well, he is not here; I mean, he lives in England," Chandni said and was immediately beset with doubts. Should she have revealed so much to a complete stranger? Ma always said it was impolite to ask questions.

"By the way, my name is Anita. Even my husband's in England right now. What a coincidence that yours should be there, too. My husband is studying medicine in London. I thought it was the perfect time for me to sneak in a visit to my sick mother."

Chandni had to know something. "Did you have to ask for permission to travel alone?"

Anita swatted at the air with the fan. "I told myself if my husband isn't here to accompany me to my mother's house, there's no way on earth am I going to ask for permission from my mother-in-law. I told her my plans. That was it."

Chandni undid her sling-backs and drew up her legs, glad to hear of Anita's independence. She let her eyes roam around the compartment. The beds had been made with immaculate white sheets, the pillows equally bright and white. The swaying motion of the train made her eyes feel heavy, yet she was conscious of its every movement – when it turned her body leaned to one side, then the sound of the wheels changed. *Dhatank, dhatank.* The unmistakably hollow sound of steel passing through a patch of space. Surely it was a bridge. Chandni leaned forward to peer through the window and made out the glint of water. They were crossing a river. She wanted to write in her journal, which reminded her that she would soon be able to retrieve her notebooks, and her heart sang with joy. Soon, however, lulled by the train's motion, her eyes began to close and she had to discard her initial plan to write. Switching off the reading light, she wrapped herself with the thin cotton sheet provided by the rail company and turned on her side.

Finally, she was on her way to Mauchak. Thinking of it brought a surge of happiness, and she smiled into the darkness. She imagined her mother's surprise, and this convinced Chandni, more than ever, that she had done the right thing. What did it matter she'd had to tell a few white lies to the Ramsays?

One needed to make one's own way out of a difficult situation.

Now, where had she heard that?

Take Ma, for example. Hadn't she also faced numerous difficulties after *Baba* passed away? Alone, a widow, without any knowledge of the outside world – she had struck out on her own, declining with great firmness help from certain men who would have exacted payment for their support. That was her mother.

Accompanied by the soft snores of Anita on the other berth, the noise of the wheels sounded loud, but to Chandni, it was a safe sound, and the continuous rocking motion brought comfort. She began to relax. The days leading up to this journey had been stressful, as she had constantly feared her duplicity would be discovered. But fate seemed to have conspired in her favour. She had been able to execute her plan.

It had seemed almost too easy.

Now, here she was, newly married, travelling unchaperoned.

An act of defiance against society. This alone brought her immense satisfaction. Instead of succumbing to helplessness, she had taken control of a situation, turning it to work to her advantage. She turned towards the sleeping form of her companion. How peaceful she looked, Chandni mused, grateful it was this woman and not someone else occupying that berth.

The train rushed through countryside that the night rendered dark and alien, except where pinpricks of light heralded a tiny village in the distance, or yet another station. Some of the rural stations appeared sad and neglected, like an abandoned wife patiently waiting for her husband to return, the train an errant husband who refused to stop, continuing on its rapid journey towards headier adventures.

Chandni's eyes flew open.

At first, she wasn't sure what had woken her. Gradually, however, as the last vestiges of sleep receded, her brain began to register the reason.

A sudden grinding of wheels, metal on metal, a terrible screeching sound ended in a colossal jolt, making the compartment weave drunkenly from side to side. And then, silence.

The train was standing still.

There was a tinkling of bangles as Anita picked up scattered clothes and bedding that had slid to the ground. Good time to visit the toilet, Chandni decided, leaving her seat. Standing up in a moving train had always made her nauseous. She helped tidy up, then made her way to the back towards a set of heavy green doors. A glance at her watch showed it was midnight – still five hours remained before she would reach Calcutta.

As she clicked shut the bathroom door, faint shouts from a distance reached her ears, and she also heard something else. It sounded eerily like the howling of hyenas. On some winter nights in Mauchak, the bone-chilling howl of a lone hyena would make her snuggle deeper under the bedclothes. At times, they had lost a hen or two when the predators boldly ventured into their fruit orchard and sneaked into the hen coop.

She tried to ignore the sound, but it grew stronger until the night air was rendered by a piercing scream, followed by another, and then another, sounds tumbling on top of each other, thick, fast, and frightening.

Somewhere out there, something awful was happening.

Thoroughly alarmed, she quickly fastened the latch up in its casing, thus double locking the door, at the same time eyeing the sole window in the toilet. Its shutter could be forced open and offer a means of escape, and she was determined to use it if she had to.

Other sounds, muffled at first, grew louder.

Five minutes later, the world she had known went berserk.

Long piercing cries, punctuated with loud yells and, then, the eruption of gunfire.

With shaking hands, Chandni managed to lift the window shutter. It was rusty and would only move a tiny bit, and she had to crouch on the floor to be able to look out. Her breath caught in her throat at the scene unfolding before her shocked eyes. The shutter jerked out of her hand and dropped on her thumb, but the pain went unheeded.

In that split second, she had got a quick glimpse of a group of horsemen brandishing whips and leaping into compartments from their galloping mounts.

The train had been set upon by *dacoits*, bandits. The screams came from their victims –passengers like herself and Anita.

Even the darkness of the night couldn't hide their white *dhotis* resembling jodhpurs, wound tight around their legs, tucked into calf-length boots. Dark turbans covered their heads with the ends wrapped around the faces, so they resembled headless ghouls on horseback.

The tiny toilet seemed to run out of air. She swallowed the bile rising at the back of her throat.

Chandni rose from her position by the window. How long had she been kneeling? She intended to get out, but her limbs wouldn't co-operate. A violent trembling spread across her entire body, forcing her to flop down on the toilet seat. She clenched her fists into tight balls and squeezed her eyes shut. This could not be happening to her orderly world. At the sound of a soft moan, her eyes opened, and with dread, she looked at the door. It stood solid as before. It was then she realized the sound had come from herself. She stuffed her fist in her mouth. She must be quiet. The men should not hear her.

The next moment, sounds, the likes of which she had been dreading, filtered through to the toilet to reach Chandni, who was rocking from side to side on the toilet seat, covering her ears with hands that would not stop shaking.

She shrank back into herself. The inevitable had happened.

The men had entered her compartment.

Her fists lay clenched on her lap, a tiny speck of blood on one where she had bitten it to stop from screaming. Chandni sat frozen. The slightest movement might alert the bandits. She forced herself to count to ten, taking deep breaths until her heartbeats slowed, ever so gradually, and, she was able to take stock of her situation. Holed up in this tiny space, she seemed to be taking an impossible risk.

Escape! Her mind screamed.

Where? And, how?

The bandits would be scattered throughout the countryside where the train had been held up, their garbled words were discernable even over the neighing of horses and the panic-stricken shouts of helpless passengers.

Against Chandni's ears crashed shouts of a male tongue spoken in an unfamiliar dialect. Then a long, drawn-out wail. And it came from their compartment.

Her heart beating wildly, she waited in her hideout.

Minutes ticked by. Ever so gradually, a silence arose, frightening in its finality. Chandni held her breath, her skin breaking out in a cold sweat.

Why was it so quiet?

As she waited, hardly daring to breathe, the truth gradually began to register in her tired mind.

The men had left their compartment.

She did not want to leave her refuge, afraid to find out what had happened to the woman. And yet, not knowing what was going on outside their compartment was driving her mad.

Instinct dictated she stay where she was, but for once, she was having none of it. Chandni opened the door a crack, then one foot at a time crept from the comparative safety of the toilet towards that place where she did not know what horrors lay. A few short steps and she was standing at the open door of the compartment. Only a few hours ago it had been a comfortable space, almost resembling a tiny room in a house.

With senses on high alert, she stepped inside, first with slow steps, which quickened until stopped by an open suitcase whose contents had spilt across the floor. On the seat opposite sat the motionless figure of the woman. Seeing Chandni, Anita spoke, in a hoarse whisper, barely audible, "Get out of here … the men … will be back."

Hearing the voice, so faint and full of pain, and yet with an urgency that could not be mistaken, a violent anger overtook Chandni. What had the men done to her?

She lowered herself on the seat and took the woman's hand gently within her own cold ones, and said, "Tell me, please, are you okay?"

"I gave them all I had…" a great sigh rose from her breast, but she didn't move. Chandni pressed her hand. A sense of bewilderment had arisen within her.

The woman was speaking, harsh rasping sounds, twisting together to create words out of a tortured mind, "They wanted more; I had no more. Only the chain around my neck…"

Chandni's fists balled, making her fingernails dig deep into the soft flesh of her palm. She saw the red streak across Anita's neck. One of the bandits had used his knife to cut the chain from her neck.

Once again, Chandni found herself mumbling; she bit her lips hard, making them bleed.

"I need to take a look at the wound," she said, appearing calm outwardly when in actual fact, all her instincts told her to leave the woman and get away.

Chandni made a bandage out of a towel from her case and tied it around the wound. Anita seemed to wake from a trance. "Stand in front of me so I can see you," she ordered Chandni, who got up immediately and stood before the wounded woman.

Anita's eyes had a strange glitter. "They don't know about you." She paused for breath, then continued, "I want to rest now."

Silence shrouded the space. Chandni continued to sit beside the woman. She did not know how long. A bunch of flies had invaded the compartment, and when a fat bluebottle began to buzz, she snapped to the present.

She stood up in a rush; the sudden movement jolted the immobile figure, and her eyes opened. "We have to get help."

Chandni's relief was so great that she wanted to hug the woman, but this wasn't the time for emotional outbursts. "You must go…now. Get help." Propelled by the woman's pain-filled voice, Chandni ran towards the open door and started to climb down the steps; in her hurry to get out, one foot became tangled in her garment and sent her flying down. The next instant, she was lying face down on the hard ground. Immediately, her ears had picked up the drumming of hooves. They had seen her and were coming to where she lay, exposed and helpless.

Trying hard to stay motionless, she slipped the large gold bangles from her wrists, thankful they had been made with a lot of years of usage in mind. The bangles came away easily. She scrabbled viciously at the earth with her nails only just managing to cover the bangles with what little sand, stones and dust the hard ground yielded.

The chain around her neck was another matter. Still with face pressed to the ground, she took a deep breath, gathered all her strength, then, with great care slid one hand under her body and up to her neck, and pulled with all her might. The chain remained intact.

Time was running out for Chandni. The horses were gaining ground.

She was filled with fury.

Chandni vowed she would not let them take the chain, a wedding gift from her mother.

And she wouldn't give up without a fight.

Her fingers with their broken and bloodied nails curled around the chain to continue pulling, until she felt her neck was on fire. She bit her lip from crying out. The gold chain slithered down, leaving a trail of wet, warm, liquid, to land inside her blouse where it lay snugly between her breasts.

There were two riders. They spoke to each other. Although she couldn't understand their dialect, it was obvious that they were arguing. They started to move away from her; the tension was just starting to ease in Chandni's limbs, when all of a sudden, there was the unmistakable pound of returning hoofbeats.

She held her breath. She must pretend to be dead.

The man was standing over her. With one booted foot, he turned her over.

Her hackles rose. How dare he touch her with his dirty boot?

She smelled his foul breath and felt the brush of hard skin against her own. Gesturing at her bloodied neck, he said, this time in Hindi, "Some motherfucker got to her first," and spat. The spittle landed within inches of Chandni's immobile face.

The second rider had joined him, and the two began to argue. This time, Chandni could not understand a word. She would never know what happened next. Her terror at the events had given way to anger, yet as the first rays of the sun began to be visible across the horizon, she could not move. Her body had gone into self-preservation mode and, thankfully, she blanked out.

Later, the sun rose, painting the sky in exquisite shades of red and orange, heralding the dawn of another day. Nature continued on as if nothing had happened.

People milled around, hopelessly seeking out lost property or speaking in muted tones. There was blood, plenty of it, from the wounds that had been inflicted by the thieves. Carrion birds, expecting a feast, were preparing to descend.

Later, looking back at the events of that day, Chandni would wonder why she had been spared. Except for the gash around her neck wrought by her own hands, she had come out unscathed. And yet, the violence and its aftermath would leave its own inevitable impression. That day marked the turning point in her life.

She stood up, resolute. A plan of escape was needed, away and out of this scene of devastation. The arched brows drew together as she forced her mind to think. Where would she go?

She had no idea where they had stopped. The distant mountain ranges indicated they were probably in a valley somewhere. A lonely spot, far removed from civilization, also perhaps favoured by local robbers. The infamous area of bandits was also, unfortunately, the regular train route from Masjidpur to Calcutta.

"Can you get me some water…please?"

The voice, close at hand, was hardly above a whisper, spoken in a dialect she did not understand. Startled, Chandni looked down to find an old man. He was trying to sit up, but kept sliding down until he gave up and sprawled full length on the hot ground. He lay there, too weak to move. On his forehead, there was a deep cut surrounded by dry blood. It opened, and before Chandni's horror-stricken gaze, began to ooze fresh blood. A thin line of red began to run down and into his eye. With a sigh, the man shut his eyes.

Tiredness and desperation had drawn new lines on Chandni's face, giving it a look of maturity beyond her years. She scanned the scene of carnage. Wasn't there a way out?

Cries from men and women filled the early morning air. The wounded lay amidst pieces of luggage, remnants of clothes, food, and drink. A sudden gust of wind, simmering and hot, blew through a pile of paper. A handwritten note fluttered from the pile, then settled on the ground where she stood. Even the mail van had been vandalized.

The sun stared down, merciless and uncaring, pouring heat and increasing the misery of the wounded.

She felt a tug at her sari and became aware of the old man at her feet. Oh, God, she had forgotten him. She guessed he had asked for water.

When their eyes met, there passed a message of mutual need, an unspoken promise to help each other. A deal was struck.

Chandni remembered her bottle of water. "I don't want to enter that death-trap," she muttered, tears of helplessness rolling down her cheeks. But the pain and pleading in the old man's eyes forced her back up the steps. And, she must check on Anita. It was because of this stranger that Chandni had been able to avoid the bandits' raid in her compartment.

Almost immediately, Chandni realized something had changed. Anita still sat in the same position as before but her open eyes seemed livelier. In fact, she had been waiting for Chandni to arrive. "Help me down, will you? I'll see what the train guards are up to. Useless fellows, I am sure they are hand in glove with the bandits." She held out a hand, which Chandni took and helped her to stand up.

"We need to be quiet," Chandni said. No one should hear. Both had managed to escape death. Chandni gulped air, trying to still her heartbeat. She must stay calm.

With shaking hands, she pulled at the water bottle still hanging above the window where she had hung it the previous night. When the straps became entangled, out of desperation, she pulled with such force the straps gave way, and the bottle fell to the ground only to roll away under one of the seats. Sobbing with frustration, she knelt, picked up the bottle; with lightning speed, Chandni jumped the few steps and on to hard ground. In her other hand was the overnight case. She could not recall picking it up. When she turned, meaning to help Anita down the steps, there was no one. Thoroughly confused, Chandni took a step forward when she felt a tug at her sari.

The old man must have sensed her presence, for he opened his eyes, shifted his weight slightly, and his mouth opened into a perfect O. He was ready, he seemed to say. Quickly Chandni leaned over to guide the bottle into the open mouth. The man drank greedily. His cracked lips pressed firmly against the spout like a child's mouth around his mother's nipple. Almost a third of the water was gone. Alarmed, Chandni stared helplessly, but didn't have the heart to stop him.

"Bless you, *Beti*," he wheezed, trying to ease back against the train, then stopped midway as if struck by a sudden thought. He peered at her curiously and asked, "Why are you alone? Where is your family?" He spoke Hindi.

"I am by myself," Chandni answered, realizing her mistake almost immediately. She shouldn't have told him the truth. Now, more than ever, she needed to be on her guard.

She need not have worried. The man's eyes were closed. He had already retreated into his world of pain.

From where she stood, she could make out some movement. Shading her eyes with a hand, she strained to see if help had arrived. A child's wail sounded through the desolation and was quickly hushed. A group of women sat in a circle; it seemed they were guarding something.

She needed to figure out the next step, and quickly. Would the old man help? He was her only chance. She was desperate and these were desperate times, so where was the harm in asking?

Chandni made her voice deliberately nonchalant. "*Dadaji*, do you know the name of this place?"

"Bundhpur," he replied.

The single word spoken so calmly yet had the power of thunder, sending waves of shock through Chandni until it reached her mind – and there it stayed, teasing and challenging her to action.

"Are you sure?" she asked finally, her voice sounding shrill to her own ears.

He nodded without opening his eyes.

Out of all the places in the world, how she could have landed in the very place that had belonged to her forefathers was unfathomable. It was as if someone wanted her to be there.

Was this the reason she had been spared?

Chandni knelt on the hard-packed earth. Now the old man would not have to look up. She knew that pained him. "*Dadaji*, do you know the way out of here? We need to get away." Speaking about what was uppermost in her mind only made it more tangible. But how could someone in his condition help?

She must remain positive.

His eyelids fluttered then and with great difficulty opened as he tried to focus on her face. "Yes, yes," he began in a voice laced with pain. It seemed to come from the depths of his rib cage. Chandni leaned closer until her ear was almost on his mouth. "I know. Not that way," a shaking hand pointed towards the thick forest covering the greater part of the area where the train now stood. "Another way, forest dwellers live there – they can help. Not *dakoo*."

His words brought hope. Chandni sat back on her heels.

"That's good to know, but how will you walk?"

"Don't worry about me, *Beti*. Look," he indicated his head, "this is not so bad." Chandni leaned forward to hear his plea and promise. "Please give me more water. I'll walk with ease. Not to worry, *Beti*. Those *dakoos,*" In spite of his condition, he cursed the marauders roundly. "They were too busy looting and wounding. They thought I was dead, but I only fainted." A sudden gleam of cunning lit his eyes. "They were looking for jewellery on you, but they got scared when the sun was starting to rise."

Ahh, so that's when she had fainted. Realizing that she had duped the men brought an involuntary smile, and she exchanged a conspiratorial look with the old man.

Her hand went up to her neck to touch the scraped skin and came away dotted with red. She recalled now in vivid detail the feel of that boot on her hip, prodding to find purchase on her still form as though she were some kind of animal or even a bag of grain. At the recollection, a violent shudder ran through her entire body. She felt defiled. How could humans be so vile?

"*Beti*, you can wear your chain and bangles now." At Chandni's incredulous look, he smiled slightly, then continued, "No one will harm you."

He had seen her desperate attempts to hide her jewellery. But his words also filled her with confidence and a sense of relief. By great good fortune, this man, also a victim of a train robbery, had been placed in her path, not only to help her out of the jungle, but also to show her the way to her ancestral home. In return, she would look after his wound and help him walk. With a start, Chandni remembered the other person who had also helped her. Anita. She must make sure that Anita was being taken care of.

A small voice, one she could not ignore any longer, had been nagging at her throughout: the complete folly of her hair-brained scheme, destined for failure, from the very beginning. Whatever made her embark on this journey? She who had never stepped outside the gates of her house alone?

Ma and Pima would be horrified when they found out. What about TJ? Oh, no, he should never know. And the lies she told her mother-in-law! Surely, she was now being punished for her actions, here in the middle of nowhere, completely dependent on a stranger. She must atone for her misdeeds.

Chandni's eyes fell on *Dadaji*. Strangers, until now. His wrinkled face, despite the wound on his forehead, seemed to hold its own, and where the turban had come askew, wisps of white hair showed. His eyes glinted with light when he spoke, the beard showing red specks. Without further delay, she set about taking care of the ugly gash.

They would help each other.

FOUR

Chandni
Central India – 1976

Even with all the odds stacked against her, Chandni refused to give in to negativity. Nor would she waste precious time on self-recriminations.

She suggested to *Dadaji* he must rest. It looked like a long journey through the jungle. She stood up, sweeping her gaze far and wide, trying to find signs of help. None had arrived, at least, not yet. She noted with relief the number of survivors, which seemed high considering the brutality of their attackers.

Standing under the searing sun in a place far from home, Chandni began to feel, way down in her gut, the first stirrings of something akin to exhilaration. Surrounded on all sides by cries of pain and loss, the fact that she had come away unharmed was incredible. Her thoughts running in this vein were brought to an abrupt halt when once again, she saw the robber's obsidian eyes, felt the power of his murderous hand around her throat. Almost at the same time, these thoughts were flung aside, and she pulled herself up to her full height, all five feet. She resolved never to give in to fear. She, who had cheated death, would fight for what was her own – life, personal belongings and family, if it came to that.

No longer would she allow others to decide what was good for her. She must trust her own instincts.

At this moment, her instincts dictated she help these people.

Earlier, she had noticed a group of women sitting in a circle, their keening piercing the air like so many knives. It was towards them that

Chandni headed. As she drew closer, two mounds covered with cloth, which she suspected were bodies, became visible. Thankfully, her suspicion proved incorrect.

One of the women, upon noticing Chandni, told her they were a newly married couple on their way home with family. The man tried to put up a fight but was shot at and his bride had to hand over her jewellery. Chandni had to walk away or break down; the rage building in her breast needed an outlet. She wanted to scream, shout obscenities, shake her fist at the Omnipotent, furious that He had allowed this to happen. What had that young couple done to deserve such a thing? They were just starting out on a journey together, just like TJ and herself.

But she did none of it.

A new rhythm had entered her life. Born out of her recent success at striking out on her own, she began to organize, with an ever-increasing confidence, some sort of rudimentary relief for the wounded and the stricken. In that desolate space, surrounded on one side by a threatening jungle and on the other, a forbidding mountain range, people huddled together, like sheep almost, without hope. Chandni's eyes swivelled back and forth absorbing it all. This, she knew, would be forever seared in her memory.

Suddenly, out of the crowd, a little boy came running. Stopping in front of Chandni, he stuck out a tiny hand to clutch at her sari. She saw that tears had made runnels down his dusty cheeks; snot ran out of the tiny nose and he heaved great sobs. She bent down and picked him up. The boy settled himself on her hip, as if he belonged there. No one paid them any attention. Where were his parents? When the child smiled, Chandni's heart beat faster. She had never been good with children, always tongue-tied. Wondering how to communicate with the boy, she smiled at him. He gazed at her wide-eyed.

Wondering what to do, she was about to walk towards the group of women she had stopped by earlier when an old woman hobbled up to them and began to speak. For the thousandth time, Chandni cursed her inability to understand. Eventually, she established, through signs, and also words, which neither understood, that the boy she held was the old woman's grandson. The robbers had taken everything from her, even the child's silver bangles. She was returning to her village after performing the last rites for her son, who had died of a lump in his head. Chandni surmised it must have been a tumour. The daughter-in-law took her own life after her husband's funeral. The old woman was returning to her village with her grandson. He would live with her.

Chandni hugged the child once more before handing him back to his grandmother. She lifted her face to the sky, sparks flying from her eyes. Was there any fairness in this world? Where was God when he was needed? Most importantly, why did He allow such horrible things to happen to innocent people? Soon, however, she calmed down, enough to hold a hand, tie a bandage, offer a drink.

Unbeknownst to her, Chandni was growing up. The helplessness she had felt earlier was being replaced with an energy, an eagerness to help people. She was starting to lose her inherent shyness with strangers.

She had been correct in her assumption. The robbers had only attacked the sleeper compartments. They must have fled into the mountains, but not before robbing their victims of jewellery and cash. When some passengers put up resistance, they were brutally beaten. Fear and horror writ large on their faces, some of the victims burst into loud lamentation. There were conflicting reports. Some said they had tried to pull the emergency chain, but the robbers held them at gun-point. Others said the driver of the train had been killed, which forced the train to come to a halt. Yet others said there were robbers riding with them as passengers and they pulled the chain.

"Where were the guards?" Chandni asked a young man who was kneeling before an open suitcase. It was torn and the belongings scattered.

"They hid," came the reply, then he spat with vigour into the parched ground.

The old Chandni would have flinched, affronted. She would have hurried away. But not this new woman. She asked, "Do you know if anyone has contacted the railway police?"

"Yes, the engineer has…he also has a wound from trying to fight the *dakoos*." He continued with his attempts to shut the suitcase. Chandni looked at the hunched figure, defeat painted in his very stance. She hesitated for a moment, then walked away.

She began to organize those passengers who were able into groups to make bandages out of bedding; there wasn't enough water to wash wounds, but this was a minor problem. Some of the wounded were too traumatized and needed to be held. Chandni surprised herself as she held a woman's hand while her husband struggled to breathe. He had fought to hang on to his money belt, and received a severe cut across the face. Chandni did what she could to ease his pain.

The day seemed endless, although her watch said otherwise. From time to time, Chandni paused, expecting Anita to show up. Her questions about the missing woman brought no answer. It seemed as if Anita had disappeared into thin air.

Chandni was tired of hearing the cries and moans of the wounded, and the curses from the robbed who had escaped harm only by giving in passively to the demands of the *dacoits*. The women, especially, needed help. They had been robbed and traumatized, many having had their earrings and necklaces ripped right from their bodies, as Anita had. The women rocked wordlessly, nursing their torn earlobes.

Some of the victims simply stared into space, hands hanging uselessly by their sides or folded into balls on their laps.

Chandni continued on her way, helping wherever she could. Nervous energy made her want to do something, anything. When her ears picked up the sounds of someone muttering, she followed it to a woman hunched on the rail tracks, only a thin sheet covering her body. She seemed alone.

When Chandni bent down to speak, the woman jumped up, and with a scream, landed a blow on Chandni's head. Then she started to run, the sheet fluttering behind her like a flag until it slithered to the ground where it lay, motionless. The woman disappeared into the jungle on the other side.

Chandni was so shocked, she forgot her own pain and stared at the trees that had swallowed the woman.

What had made the woman attack Chandni? She had only meant to help.

Just then, the sound of wheels on gravel reached her ears, and she turned quickly. A Jeep appeared, driving at breakneck speed. It screeched to a halt in the clearing around which most of the people had been sitting. This was the only shady spot where a meagre shadow had been cast by the compartments so early in the morning. As Chandni watched, a group of men jumped out, gesticulating and talking, their voices indistinct to her ears. Help had finally arrived.

There was a flash of green. Chandni's hand flew to her mouth. Anita had been there all that time, only she hadn't seen her. From the very beginning, Anita had wanted to report the incident to the police. Now was her chance.

Chandni retraced her steps, walking quickly to reach the old man. She realized in that moment that she did not want to get caught up for the rest of the day in the slow retrieval of all of the passengers to town. The old man knew the area, knew the forest dwellers.

"Bundhpur," she muttered aloud. Seeing Ma had been the sole purpose of this journey, but what if she had to find her grandmother first? If she was leaving her homeland for good, she had to do it now.

TJ
Manchester - 1976

When TJ reached Manchester, the sun had yet to make an appearance. All he carried was a light shoulder bag. He had given Chandni explicit instructions to bring the rest. Being married had its advantages, having someone to do what he asked. TJ laughed under his breath, a heady sense of pride filling him.

In this expansive mood, he hailed a taxi and gave directions to the house in Moss Side, where he was a tenant.

The taxi slowed to a crawl in the alley littered with dustbins, their garbage spilling out onto the street. All of a sudden, a cat emerged from underneath a parked van and almost got hit. The taxi driver swore loudly. A couple of workers shuffled past, their drab clothing melting in the grey dawn. TJ paid the driver and threw in a handsome tip; he had money to burn with his parents' wedding gift. Mrs. Douglas was sure to be waiting, but TJ did not ring the front bell. Instead, he turned left and quickly ran down the few steps that led to a door. Turning the key, he let himself in.

Dropping his bag on the floor, he lit a cigarette and took a long drag. Then, without bothering to take off his shoes, he sprawled on the bed.

He should call Amy. He was pretty sure there would be a temper tantrum. A warmth grew in his belly. He knew how to pacify Amy.

But right now, he wanted to be by himself.

It was still hard to believe that he was actually married. His forehead furrowed. Old doubts came crowding in, beating at his brain, suffocating him for a moment, calling him a fool.

TJ flung the cigarette towards the ashtray on the table beside the bed. It landed on the floor. Cursing, he bent to pick it up and bumped his head on the table.

Running nervous fingers through his hair, he tried to block his mind from the question hammering at it. Why had he got married?

TJ shut his eyes.

And, at that moment, Chandni's face floated across, imprinting itself on his closed lids.

That face, beautiful as a painting. He had wanted her from the first day he had seen her at the college library, sitting by herself. He had always wanted to date a Bengali girl. He had been told they were hard to please. But like every other girl he had dated, Chandni had also succumbed, though in a different way.

TJ remembered how he had desired her, begging her to love him the way he wanted. There was some fumbling, quick kisses, but when he tried to go beyond squeezing the tiny breasts, Chandni had stopped him, always. His lips tightened thinking how she had refused. Marriage or nothing, she had said.

What a tease! But Chandni had stood firm. Now, back in Manchester, the feeling that he had been manipulated returned with greater force. His jaw clenched. *Dammit, why was she such an innocent*? She needed to be taught the intricacies of lovemaking, he concluded. That would be fun. He hoped that by the time Chandni joined him, she would have got over her initial shyness and would be eager to please him. He had to admit that his wife's reluctance, while it irritated the hell out of him, was also exciting.

He let his mind wander. He remembered the day he had come across another girl in the college cafeteria. She was with a group of students, and he found himself sitting beside her. He couldn't remember her name now, just the bold eyes, inviting, challenging. That was quite something. He took a deep drag of his cigarette.

One afternoon, they had come across each other in the field that ran adjacent to the college. It had started to drizzle, which was the perfect excuse to take shelter under a hedge. No one was around, not even a stray cow or goat. And there, in the damp grass, they tore at each other, fast, demanding. As she straddled him, urging him to go faster, he had closed his eyes to imagine that it was Chandni he was making love to, and finished almost immediately. The girl had been furious. She had accused him of incompetence. TJ's lips lifted in an amused smile. He showed her how he could tease out the last bit of enjoyment, using only his mouth. The high-pitched sounds of fulfillment emanating from her open mouth had been drowned out by the thunder and lightning. When it was her turn to go down, TJ reflected, she had been like a pro. It made him wonder where she'd learnt it all. They had met twice more at the same place. Soon after, she'd married and left town. There were others after that. A man had to take care of things in his own way.

He had no reason to feel guilty. Chandni would never know. He would never tell her. If she had been willing to show her love, he wouldn't have strayed.

He lit another cigarette, piled a couple of pillows under his head, and blew smoke into the air. His thoughts returned to his wife.

He missed Chandni. Strange how she had never asked where he lived in Manchester. She was far too trusting.

Suddenly, his brows drew together. Mrs. D. She would have to be pacified, somehow. She had given him the cold shoulder the day he left for India. To get married, but that was a secret he guarded from everyone - Mrs. D and Amy alike.

A vision of Chandni rose before him - grey eyes fringed with dark lashes, the perfect oval face on a long neck. She was tiny. He could span her waist with half a hand. He loved the way she always pushed her hair back from her face, as if afraid of missing out on anything, her habit of tilting her head to one side while listening.

TJ stubbed the cigarette in the battered aluminum ashtray resting on his chest, then, sighing deeply, picked up the phone by the bed and dialled Amy's number.

FIVE

Kanta
Sarbogram – 1913

The outdoors held a special fascination for eleven-year-old Kanta. Their house in Sarbogram boasted an enormous garden, and it was here, it seemed, that the beauty of each succeeding season took root and stayed, almost like the jars of pickles that her mother made and put out in the sun. Flavours captured. Beauty preserved. She was especially fond of the old gardener who was pressed into service at the Burman household every year – planting potatoes, beans, onions, sweet potatoes and maize.

"Where do you live, Rameshwar?" Kanta asked when once again he appeared at their house.

He pointed a gnarled finger in the general direction of the path that snaked its way out of the village.

It was planting season. Kanta followed along behind him and his two oxen. She wasn't satisfied with his answer and asked once more, "No, tell me exactly where your house is…you know, in which village?"

"My village is smaller than this, behind *Devir Pahar* – the hill of the Goddess." Kanta had to be satisfied with this cryptic response since she had no idea where *Devir Pahar* was. With childlike logic, she decided he must live close enough, for how else could he arrive so quickly at her father's summons?

She watched as Rameshwar began to pull weeds. Judging by his tremulous voice, Kanta concluded that he must be very old. Despite his age, he did have strong hands. The weeds came out with ease. Once this ritual had been taken care of, she knew what was to follow. Sure enough, he got behind the two oxen, his prized possessions, and proceeded to till the rich soil.

What'll it be this time? Kanta always wondered. Row upon row of potatoes interspersed with carrots and onions? The maize had to be wonderful like last time. The taste of the previous year's sweet meaty bounty still lingered in her mouth. Sometimes she was allowed to fill a basket with peas and tomatoes for the kitchen. Most of it went in her mouth. She screamed with laughter at her mother's exasperation, then apologized profusely and offered to pick some more. And this had turned into a game between Kanta and Roopmala.

Sonalal, the *gwala*, came every morning to the back door, leading his milking cow by a jute rope. Kanta rose early just to be able to watch as he squatted on his haunches working the bursting udders of his star performer. As he worked rhythmically, thick streams of milk collected in the shiny copper bucket held between his knees. Kanta would creep closer, careful not to frighten the cow, and peer into the bucket brimming with the frothing liquid. How she would love to milk the cow! It seemed easy. All she had to do was grip the udders firmly and pull down towards the bucket. But her courage failed at the last minute. What if Ma found out?

During those months taken up with planting crops in their own garden, the Burmans had to depend on the vegetable seller for fresh produce.

In her eagerness to greet the woman, Kanta was sure to run ahead and unbolt the side door, which usually remained barred unless merchants and servants needed to enter the inner courtyard. This habit of hers never failed to annoy Roopmala, who gave her daughter a good scolding each time.

Kanta liked the vegetable woman, for she always seemed jolly, smiling at Kanta and asking her what she wanted to eat. Tomatoes, red and ripe, some small golden potatoes, green beans and sweet peas nestled among strong white cauliflowers – everything looked so attractive in the reed basket. There were onions, too.

Since nothing but the sweetest and ripest tomatoes would do for her mother, these and other vegetables were chosen with great care and placed on the weighing scale. Kanta's eyes followed the vegetable seller's careworn hands as they placed the mound of chosen vegetable on one disc of the weigh scale and on the other, a weight. There were weights of different sizes, some heavy, an inscription on each, with the smallest resembling a shiny yellow pebble. This one was her favourite, yet it was never used, which prompted Kanta to ask her mother, "Ma, why does the smallest look so new?"

Roopmala, whose attention was on the scale, answered absently, "Probably because people buy a lot so the little one is hardly used." The disc with vegetables was dipping to one side, it didn't look right in Kanta's eyes. Before she could speak, the woman had added the small shiny weight to the other disc. Excited that her special little weight was finally put to good use, Kanta touched her mother's shoulder and was rewarded with a smile. Her mother understood.

The woman was waiting for payment. "Oh, can I, Ma?" Kanta wanted to touch the woman's hand. Her wish granted, she placed the coins gently into the waiting palm and had a fleeting sensation of having touched a rock with sharp edges, almost like the one she had found once in the garden. Her mother had taken it away, though, saying she didn't want Kanta to get hurt.

She stepped back quickly, ashamed of her unkind thought. She should make up for it, but how? Chewing on the end of her garment, Kanta debated whether she should help lift the heavy basket on to the woman's head. That's it. She should help. However, her good intentions were thwarted by Narain, the kitchen help, who stepped forward, and with one easy swing, settled the basket on the woman's head.

Kanta watched the woman leave. Where was her home? How many people were there in her family? How did they cook their food and what did they eat? She imagined the vegetable seller hunched over the cooking fire, preparing a meal for her large family, each one hungrier than the next. It had to be leftovers from the basket, Kanta decided, tugging at her braid which was coming loose. Narain might know. But there was a problem. Kanta was not supposed to visit the kitchen, not without her mother's supervision. Shaking her head, she headed for the garden, hands clasped behind her back, when her attention was arrested by the unmistakable call of the charcoal sellers.

In Kanta's home, winter nights were rendered cozy by clay braziers filled with glowing charcoal. Each room had one.

When Kanta wanted to know why the charcoal looked different from the coal in the kitchen fire, her mother had given her a quick lesson in this wonderful commodity. Charcoal could not be bought from the regular coal seller, but from forest dwellers who chopped trees, then piled the wood and covered it under soil. This mound was then lit and left to burn slowly. Kanta had been enthralled.

When the charcoal was ready, it was packed tightly into enormous baskets woven out of *shaal* leaves, which the women carried on their heads and walked to town to sell to the townspeople. These women were usually adorned with silver jewellery; those who couldn't afford it simply displayed black markings on their skin to simulate jewellery.

"Why do you wear so many?" Kanta once asked, pointing at the beautiful silver wrapped around throats, noses and ears, even encasing arms and ankles.

"All that we own, we wear," one woman answered. She seemed friendly because she smiled a lot. The others listened. Kanta could tell they were amused by her curiosity.

One woman wore rolled up banyan leaves in her ear lobes, which had stretched the skin to such an extent that the lobes hung, almost touching her shoulders. Kanta's eyes were drawn against her will to the mutilated flesh. She was also quick to note the black markings on the woman's arms.

However, it was her ears that intrigued her, and she couldn't help asking, "Why are you wearing leaves in your ear?" She had to find out.

The woman's teeth gleamed white against the ebony skin as she replied with a laugh, "I am not rich, so I take leaves from trees to adorn my ears."

"But it must hurt so much. Why do you do it?" Kanta couldn't keep the distaste out of her voice.

The woman laughed again, this time with genuine amusement. The others tittered. Kanta was embarrassed, but she listened anyway, nodding her head, although it was hard to understand what she had just heard. It hurt a little at first, but they got used to it. Anyway, the woman said with a dismissive gesture of her hand, being poor didn't stop her from beautifying herself for her husband.

Kanta pulled her sari up to her knees, knowing well this could get her in trouble, and ran towards the edge of the garden to see if she could catch a glimpse of the charcoal sellers as they passed.

Narain was there already at the well. She had been warned never to go anywhere near the well; it was deep, and unlike others in the neighbourhood, did not have a cover. From a distance, Kanta watched, as Narain drew water. Maybe she could help. But the boy was fast, the bucket came up, water splashing down the sides, and he returned to the house, back to his post in the kitchen.

Mango and banana trees abounded in the garden, their tempting fruits begging to be eaten. The tall and majestic *neem* reached up with its canopy of thick green foliage. The robust guava tree provided welcome relief from the sun. The fruit was delicious, too – smooth on the outside and crunchy inside, without any bothersome seeds.

Kanta loved to watch the woodpecker going about its daily business. Sometimes even a couple of parrots would perch on a branch of the guava tree, their beaks making dents in the ripe fruit, dropping a lot as they pecked away. Kanta was positive that was where the saying originated: *pakhir moton khachho* – eat like a bird.

The one thing she loved the most and used almost every day was the swing hanging from the guava tree. This had been fashioned out of an old wooden seat made according to her mother's specific instructions. Whenever she could, it was here she came. She understood that she was very lucky. Most girls her age would be married and taking care of their own households. Not Kanta. Once, she had overheard her parents discussing her. She had stood silent, wanting to hear more. She was greatly relieved when her father disagreed with her mother about marrying her off. *Not yet*, he had said, *let her enjoy childhood.*

One December morning, Kanta was sitting on the swing, enjoying the peace and quiet of the early hours. She wanted to be left alone, for a while at least, from the ever-vigilant Asha, who nagged at her all the time. Don't sit in the sun. Walk gracefully. Cover your head. Ever since her older sister Menaka had married and left, Kanta became her *ayah's* sole responsibility.

Kanta heard Asha's footsteps even before her plump form came into view.

"*OMa, tumi ekhane boshe acho*? My goodness, you are sitting here? I have been looking for you all over the place." The faithful servant shook her head in annoyance. Beads of sweat ran down the sides of her face. She must have run to the garden, Kanta guessed, throwing the maid a shrewd look.

"Why can't I sit here?" she challenged, kicking at the grass with her bare feet.

Asha came closer and wagged a finger at Kanta's face. "Come, get up. I have to oil your hair."

Kanta's lips turned into a thin line.

Asha's voice softened. "You need to look good today."

"Why today?" Kanta's sharp ears had picked up the slight change in the other's voice. She fixed her maid with a penetrating stare. Asha was actually waggling her eyebrows and smiling. She was behaving very strangely. What was the matter with her?

Since her initial question had remained unanswered, Kanta tried a different approach. With arms crossed on her chest, she looked the maid straight in the eye, and said, "If you won't speak the truth, I will tell Ma you are bothering me for nothing."

Asha ignored Kanta's attempt to intimidate her. "Humph. Better come with me and get cleaned. Oh, look at your hair. I am ruined." The maid slapped her own forehead. "What to do? It'll take me hours to get those tangles out. Why are you so *dushtu*, naughty? And, if you must know, you are to go to the temple with your mother. So, come, no more fuss – you don't want to upset Ma, do you?"

Kanta's pitiful attempt at freedom had failed. She knew better than to argue when the summons had come directly from her mother. She jumped off the swing, and ignoring the maid's pleas to walk slower, began to run, stopping midway to throw a triumphant look over her shoulder.

She would run, if she wanted to.

That same evening, a stranger entered the Burman house. He was the village *ghatak*, marriage broker. The servants were kept busy bringing huge mounds of food for him. He ate everything that was offered, and even asked for more to take for his family. Kanta's parents sat with him in the outer chamber.

From her position behind the door, Kanta could just make out the muted hum of their conversation. The stranger was saying, "Kamal *babu*, the Rais are absolutely wonderful people. God couldn't have created any better, and their son, Prince Kunjan, is one in a million." The air filled with strange sounds at this point. Kanta guessed the stranger was eating with his mouth open, smacking his lips, slurping, licking at his fingers. Ugh, she had taken an immediate dislike to him.

Her attention returned to what she had just heard. Something told her that she needed to focus on their conversation. If her parents were sitting with a stranger behind closed doors, it was important.

Her mother's voice, the one she sometimes used on Kanta when she would brook no argument, was heard saying, "*Ghatak moshai*, our Kanta has just turned eleven, and this prince is eighteen."

Kanta stiffened. *Baba* and Ma were discussing her marriage. With furrowed brow, Kanta leaned forward to hear better, and at that instant felt the weight of a heavy hand on her shoulder, a blast of hot air blowing across her cheek.

Asha was whispering, her charge's latest misdeed almost making her stammer, "Come…come…away…at once." Without taking her eyes off the door, Kanta merely shook her head and put a finger to her lips. She had to hear the rest of the conversation.

However, Asha's arms had her in an iron grip. She was breathing hard. Kanta resisted with all the strength she could muster. The struggle took place in complete silence, like a pantomime. Kanta was now lifted away from the door. She turned with a sudden twist, fixing her eyes on the thin line of light filtering out from underneath the door of the room where her parents sat with the stranger. With desperation, Asha whispered that this time her parents would not forgive. She would be punished. Hearing the maid's dire prediction, all fight suddenly seemed to melt away from Kanta's rebellious limbs and she became limp.

"Let me go," she said. When the maid hesitated, Kanta spoke again, this time with the unmistakable tone of authority reserved for rebuking a servant. “I said, leave me.” The plump arms fell from her waist. Without a backward glance, Kanta walked away.

SIX

Chandni
Central India – 1976

Chandni and *Dadaji* set out towards the forest with the tall trees providing some shade, but not enough to bring relief. The searing heat enveloped the air, making it hard even to breathe. *Dadaji* clung to Chandni.

The heat was like nothing she had ever experienced in Mauchak, making those hot afternoons seem almost mellow in comparison. The red dust of the region clung to everything, settling in her hair, mouth, eyelashes, and even into the pores of her skin. She ran a parched tongue over her cracked lips, and the grit transferred to her teeth. They had walked silently for the most part; energy had to be conserved. When she coughed, *Dadaji* looked at her, sympathy written large in his wise eyes. They had not eaten anything since the previous night – fortunately, Chandni still had some of the cucumber sandwiches she had packed for the train journey. It was a good time to stop to eat and rest a while. The soggy sandwiches tasted wonderful.

"*Beti*, we must keep going."

Chandni started. Had she dozed off?

"Yes, I know – I was just resting my eyes for a bit." She smiled apologetically as she got up, brushing her clothes. They had been sitting under an old banyan tree, its gnarled branches reaching to the ground where they had taken root. For decades, these trees must have stood close, their branches intertwined like lovers' limbs, blocking the sun's rays so that only a faint glow could penetrate.

Chandni fancied that the trees stood sentinel, guarding who knew what secrets, and resented the intrusion into their private space. The dark shade, which before had seemed welcoming, now appeared full of threats.

She cast a quick, fearful look behind. As if reading her thoughts, *Dadaji* said, "*Dakoos* live here." When she put a finger to her lips, he dropped his voice to a hoarse whisper, "But don't worry, *Beti*, they are on the other side where the caves are."

Well, that was comforting.

Although it was becoming less frequent, newspapers would carry accounts of train holdups in this region, in which kidnapped passengers were held for ransom. If she were to die, her biggest regret would be that she did not get to see her mother and husband again. Also, Kunal. But she had escaped.

The short rest and food, meagre as it was, had done a world of good. They needed to get out of the jungle before sundown. Chandni stole a quick look at her feet. Red-painted toes, once so seductive that TJ had sucked on them on their wedding night, now looked incongruous under the film of dust and dirt. She eased her right foot gently out of its leather confine, biting her lip. It seemed the short rest had done more harm than good to her feet, turning the angry welts into painful blisters. Even the slightest movement made the inflamed skin scream in protest.

An image of the family car flashed across her eyes. She had never walked so much in city sandals. When they couldn't afford a car any longer, she had simply borrowed her brother's bicycle.

She trudged on, licking at her cracked lips, staring straight ahead, her feet a mess of torn skin and blisters. She had been sipping very sparingly from the dwindling supply of water, consumed with waves of guilt every time she did so. Her companion, it seemed, could do without. She should try to emulate him. There was a possibility they might have to spend the night there, in that frightful forest. Just for one second, her steps faltered, then righted themselves. If he could walk even with a head wound, then she had no reason to complain.

She had tied the end of her sari *anchal* to his left wrist so he would not fall, and he held on to it with both hands. They were careworn hands; years of hard labour had rendered deep grooves into the palms and bent the nails like talons. Calling him *Dadaji* had come naturally. Her paternal grandfather had passed away long before she was born. She had always known the males of the Rai family hardly lived beyond forty-five, and on occasion, they had passed on at an even younger age, like her father.

Her throat ached. She could not swallow for the lack of spit in her dry mouth. Her feet bled. The dense growth of trees obliterated the sun. In a perverse way, Chandni wanted the sun to shine on them. She would welcome even its glare, but not this darkness at daytime. Her mind whirled round and round, like a windmill, and in its wake, strange questions churned.

How long does it take to dehydrate from heat and lose consciousness? How did the POWs contend with their fate? What about the slaves that one read about crossing the desert in chains? How did they stave off hunger and especially thirst?

She was quite certain that she could possibly go without food. But without water? Impossible.

Yet, she and her companion had kept walking, after that brief rest, without touching a drop from their supply. Surely that proved something? She came from fighter stock, Chandni reminded herself, squaring her slim shoulders. Men and women who had fought hand in hand to protect their territories against their enemies. Her ancestors. The old man's perseverance against heavy odds also pointed to a similar ancestry.

Her mother's face floated in front of her – serene and dignified always. Her wavy hair gathered in a loose bun at the nape of her neck, and the unshakable spirit, so much a part of her, shining through. She could even smell the perfume that her mother wore. And there was the garden of roses, her mother's pride and joy. She was a child again, sniffing at the blooms, then plucking some to arrange in a vase that she would place on the coffee table, just so, in the drawing room. Her mother would not say a word at the sight; only the dimple at the corner of her mouth would deepen. That had been enough for Chandni.

Memories of those days – doing whatever she pleased in that dear old house in Mauchak, where each room came with its own distinct character, and the tiled courtyard where she used to play with her dolls – threatened to finally break through Chandni's self-control. She tried to swallow the lump in her throat. Her vision blurred. With an impatient hand, she rubbed her eyes and failed to notice the stone. With a cry of pain, she stumbled to the ground, bringing her companion on top of her.

For a few minutes, Chandni lay stunned. Gradually, however, she became conscious of severe pain in her big toe. Had she broken it? She pleaded wordlessly with God. When her eyes opened, they stared straight at the tops of trees, thinner by far, and the sun shone through. This could only mean one thing – the forest was ending.

Excited with her discovery, Chandni sat up in a rush, dislodging *Dadaji*. She apologized for her clumsiness. The old man dismissed her regret with a wave. He wanted to make sure that Chandni had not hurt herself. They checked each other, for they were a team, each person's well-being dependent on the other. He touched her toe, then told her to flex it. Thankfully, the toe wasn't broken.

After about half an hour of steady walking, they came upon a narrow path of mostly red soil snaking its way out of the jungle.

"Will it lead us to the village of Bundhpur?" she asked. What if…

Her query had brought *Dadaji* out of the stupor into which he had fallen. "Paths are many, *Beti*," he replied, not exactly answering her question.

She did not need an answer. She had been destined to come here. It all made sense now. Her plan to visit Mauchak one last time, the lies she had told to get her way, the train holdup, and how she had been able to save herself. Then her meeting with this old man, who would lead her to that very place she had dreamt of. Seeing it would certainly take away some of the disappointment of not knowing her grandmother.

She had to take care of this old man. A head wound with a blunt object was no small thing. Nevertheless, he was holding up well and even walking faster. She wondered where he was getting his strength. During the last half hour, he had appeared to float, eyes closed and resting more and more on her arm. Perhaps the thought of reaching home had given him a boost.

Not to be outdone, she determined to pick up her pace. She was her parents' daughter, with ancestors who had fought their way down from the deserts in the western valleys to the verdant plains by the river Ganges in the east. Here they had settled and ruled and had also forged alliances through marriage with the ruling houses.

They had never visited their ancestral dwelling, although plans to make that important trip had cropped up from time to time. Her mother had always been in favour of visiting her own father. Why travel to unknown places when they could have a comfortable holiday in her father's house that was in a town close to Mauchak? Travel time would be cut by half. Who could argue with that logic? So, the longed-for visit to Bundhpur had never taken place.

Chandni started to believe the suffering and pain of the last hours had not been in vain. They were simply means by which forces beyond her control had taken over, to guide her steps towards an important event. That the horrendous experience of the previous night had actually led her to *Dadaji,* and that he was a native of these parts, seemed destined.

"How much longer do we have to walk?" She tried to sound bright, but her voice squeaked like an old door with rusty hinges. She coughed. At nineteen, who was she to complain of tiredness?

"Just a few more miles, *Beti*," he panted. She liked the way he called her *Beti*, daughter, family to this brave man.

She threw a quick glance at the bandage round his head, noted it was still in place, but drew in her breath at the sight of fresh blood seeping through. Praying he would make it to the approaching village, she quickened her pace. A blue sky, seen at regular intervals also helped to lift their spirits.

They were now on a well-defined path, possibly used by the local villagers, reasoned Chandni. The red soil continued, and following the example set by her companion, she spat vigorously to dislodge what clung to her teeth. Awful. But it felt good to get away from those trees.

Chandni was filled with a burst of energy. She would see the fort of Bundhpur. And then, make the journey to Mauchak.

When her ears caught the faint strains of music, she feared it was her imagination. When it did not go away but grew louder, she slowed down, to listen. Lute and drums, and the unmistakable voices of women and children lifted in joyous melody. She stopped. As if in answer to her silent question, the turbaned head of her companion moved slightly, from side to side.

"My people are enjoying the *mela*." His face wreathed in a smile. They stood together to watch and listen. The path out of the forest that they had followed had gradually led upwards. To the right stood the village in the valley below, as if within the scooped-out hollow of a bowl, and from this elevation, the brightly clothed figures, busy with their celebration, looked like beautiful birds. Chandni's heart lightened.

"What festival is it?"

"Something women do for their families."

She had to be satisfied with that much. "*Dadaji,* who else is in your house?" She was eager to meet his family.

"Just me and my oldest son, my daughter-in-law and their daughter." He fell silent after this and began to walk faster, and so did Chandni.

After some time had elapsed, he suddenly stopped and pointed a finger at the distance. Chandni, whose concentration was taken up by the stony ground, looked up to follow the pointing finger. What she saw stopped her dead in her tracks.

"That's Bundhpur Fort," he said. "*Beti*, they come."

At Chandni's raised eyebrow, he elaborated, "People, you know? To see that fort. *Ram, Ram*, how untidy it is, not too many – *sarkar* cares nothing." His voice rose to a pitch at this point, out of his mouth tumbled words fast and furious, and from the disjointed phrases, Chandni made out the man's distress at the present condition of the fort, and his dissatisfaction with a government that refused to help. All of a sudden there rose within Chandni annoyance at her parents. Why had they let go? They were partly reimbursed for their losses when the government began to take property away from the aristocracy after their country gained independence from the British. In Chandni's mind, however, owning family history in the form of property far outweighed any kind of monetary gain.

They reached the fort in silence. It had been a hot climb.

She put up a hand to shade her eyes. A look of wonder spreading slowly across her face, Chandni stood silent and motionless. She had reached the home of her ancestors. Forgetting her exhaustion, she hurried forward, and the old man followed.

Most of the structure was in ruins. Its bones bared to sun, wind and rain; it had managed to maintain an indelible air of dignity. Weeds grew everywhere, choking the steps leading up to a massive wooden door. This door seemed to have withstood the ravages of time, for it still displayed intricate carvings of warriors on horseback with banners flying and soldiers following on foot with sword and shield. It opened to Chandni's push. She entered, hesitant at first, then with eager steps walked forward until she was standing in a courtyard.

The *rajbari* was built in a square, and even to Chandni's inexperienced eye, the Mughal influence was apparent in the multi-faceted arches at the entrance. The centre of the structure was divided into two courtyards. The main courtyard, facing the walls of the fort, housed four floors of apartments. The second courtyard, leading out of the first and visible through an open door hanging on its hinges, attracted Chandni's attention. As if pulled by unseen hands, she entered, letting her eyes travel with increasing wonder at the five floors of apartments.

The home of her grandparents stood lonely, sick, neglected. Eyes misting over, she swallowed hard. She was angry also, directed at her parents for never giving their children a chance to see the place.

Gradually, however, an unknown dread began to creep into her mind. Like entering a darkened room in a strange house, she did not know what she would find.

The hot desert sun beat down on her, so she pulled the end of her garment over the top of her head. A low parapet made of stone offered a shaded spot. She headed towards it with thankfulness. Here she sat down with a long-drawn sigh. With her legs drawn up and her chin resting on her knees, Chandni looked around. The arid surroundings had a beauty of their own, bottomless and infinite. It drew her into its bosom, offering rest. The wind had picked up, the red dust lifted and swirled into a circle. Through this red haze, her eyes caught a hint of movement.

Was it a group of horsemen in the distance?

She leaned forward to get a better view. At this point, to her amazement, the faint outlines of a *palanquin* became visible. Every sense in her body was tingling with anticipation; her eyes squeezed into slits in an effort to look into the distance. Once again, there was the sound of drums. Only this time, it came, not from the village, which was left far behind, but from the direction of the *palanquin*. Bare bodies glistening with sweat, the *palanquin* bearers sang and played the drum while their load swayed to their marching feet; the horsemen slowed down to trot alongside.

All of a sudden, the wind shifted, lifting the curtain at the window of the *palanquin.* In her eagerness to see the face behind, Chandni overbalanced and nearly fell, but her fingers managed to grasp an edge of the parapet and draw her back. The renewed pain from her broken fingernails went unheeded. However, the face behind the window drapery had disappeared. Fighting waves of disappointment, she was able to discern voices which, even from this distance, sounded unmistakably happy. They belonged to the horsemen.

Chandni drew in her breath at the splendid sight.

The men were clothed in brilliant-coloured tunics with matching turbans glittering with jewels, and long swords hung by their side. It was hard to see the faces through the curtain of red dust the wind kept swirling up, but their nobility was easily recognizable from their stance. She was filled with a sense of elation, and something else. Kinship?

One of the horsemen detached himself from the group and cantered over to the *palanquin.*

The air trembled with joy and promises of more to come. This was the moment she had been waiting for. All her life.

Instinctively, Chandni recognized the leader among the horsemen. And, the one behind the curtain? She knew her too, although, her face was hidden. These two made up an integral part of who she herself was and where she came from.

They had appeared to her on purpose. It was up to her to find out why. She must speak to them. But she couldn't move. She had become one with the stone parapet.

"Don't leave me," Chandni cried out. Her desperate plea was picked up by the wind and tossed aside, like loose paper out of a torn book. She tried, unsuccessfully, to raise a hand, gradually becoming aware of a hazy shape that wouldn't stay still, so she tried to focus hard with her eyes, the rest of her having turned to stone.

"*Beti*, are you alright?"

The sound of the old man's panic-stricken voice pulled Chandni out of her trance; she emerged bewildered. What had just happened? Had she fallen asleep? Was it a dream? No, her heart refuted peremptorily, although in her mind there grew a doubt. Yet, the figures had been life-like. How was that possible?

She looked around. Everything was as before: the ruins, the silence and heat from the sun above. She, who had always scoffed at the supernatural, had been subject to an unearthly experience. She wanted to lay her body down on that broken parapet and shut her eyes tight, as if by doing so she could conjure up the scene again. Maybe they would speak with her next time.

She struggled to rise, heart thudding against her rib cage, beating a wild rhythm.

The old man was waiting for a reply, curiosity lurking in his eyes, and also concern.

Hastening to reassure him, Chandni said, "I must have dozed off for a second, *Dadaji*," and looked away, afraid he might detect the irritation she felt. She wanted to be left alone, not to have to worry about food and drink, or plan another journey. Her mind was seething with questions and she desperately wanted those people to return. They would have the power to make right from wrong. They did not belong in this world. Yet, they had appeared to her as clearly as the old man standing in front of her.

Was there a message in their sudden appearance, something of grave importance? Sometimes people, long gone, would appear to their loved ones. To relay a message, perhaps. Then, why had they disappeared without giving her a sign? Was it because they felt she was not ready? At that moment, she would have given anything within her power for a chance to journey to the past and get acquainted with her father's family, whom she had never seen.

Reality, on the other hand, was hunger pangs - so acute they could not be ignored any longer. She looked upon *Dadaji* to bring relief, as he was of that region. Chandni wiped her eyes with knuckles caked in red dust. She straightened her shoulders and gathered up her belongings.

"*Beti*, I'll bring you to safety. Don't worry, I promise."

She smiled at him. He was a loyal friend. "*Dadaji*, this place seems deserted. Food and shelter will not be possible and we need them badly." There was urgency in her voice.

"*Beti*, my village is not very far from here." Seeing Chandni's face brighten, he was quick to add, "But how can we reach it in our condition?" Chandni nodded. As anxious as she was to reach the village, she knew they wouldn't be able to walk far, not without a rest and some food.

Dadaji's next words were encouraging. "There is a hut, over there," he pointed ahead. "Shepherds, like me, stay there under storms and rain. We will rest there for some time."

"Great idea, *Dadaji*. Let's go." It felt good to share some of the burden of thinking and planning.

They walked in companionable silence for another hour as the sun travelled further to the west. Chandni wanted to tie him to her *anchal* once again, but he insisted that he could manage on his own. She took this as a good sign.

It was about one o'clock in the afternoon when they reached the hut, just a simple shelter with one room made with closely packed mud and a roof of woven twigs. A crude hole in the wall provided ventilation. By the door, there was a short wooden post, which Chandni guessed was meant for tying a dog. A shepherd would always have a dog. The one door was made of woven straw and twigs. It was shut by means of a tree branch tied across it. *Dadaji* untied the branch and they stepped in.

The last occupants had left a couple of potatoes and onions in a blackened pot. A bundle of twigs, some dry dung cakes for fuel, and a box of matches lay beside the fire pit, which had simply been dug straight out of the mud floor. *Dadaji* busied himself lighting a fire.

While engaged thus, he motioned with his head at the water bottle, saying, "*Beti*, I need some." When Chandni hesitated, he explained, "These potatoes need water to soften. They can't be cooked in the ashes as I'd wanted."

With great care, she let a few drops dribble into the pot. Responding to the pointing finger, she poured some more until the potatoes were somewhat submerged. Twisting the lid closed, she set the bottle away.

With reversed roles, *Dadaji* gave the orders, which Chandni followed with alacrity.

Orange flames licked at the black pot, and in less than a half hour, a meal of boiled potatoes and onions awaited them. Chandni watched *Dadaji* dip his right hand in the pot, scoop up some of the mixture, roll it into a ball, then toss the whole thing into his mouth.

She followed his example.

The hut was soon filled with the comfortable sounds of slurping and smacking of lips. Both had enjoyed the meal, scraping the bottom of the pot and licking their hands when done. Then, they sat in peaceful silence, feeling the tensions of the past hours slowly fade, making way for a strong urge to sleep.

Chandni smiled fondly at her companion. This old man, whom chance had thrown in her path was now looking every bit his age, whatever that could be, but would not let on how tired he was, and that he required a change of bandage.

She touched it with the tip of a finger and frowned. "This needs to be looked at."

He was having none of it. "Don't worry about me. When I reach home, my daughter-in-law will look after it." He wouldn't meet her eyes, keeping his head lowered.

Chandni was adamant. She was going to take care of it. All he had to do was sit still. Why wait until reaching home? Didn't he have a daughter, right here? She knew she had won, for he looked up then; the eyes under the bushy white brows had a definite hint of brightness in them.

"*Beti*, you know how to get your way." In a split second, they had become equals. She, educated city girl, and he, unlettered shepherd, they were partners on this journey.

She unwrapped the bandage carefully. Without any knowledge of first aid, even she could tell the wound had not festered. It had a healthy pinkish tinge. Without antiseptics or even water to clean the wound, Chandni tried to think how best to help. She had promised and must not fail. Light from the weak fire cast shadows on her face as she turned to it, as if for inspiration. One incident from her childhood came to mind. She had once seen the milkman in Mauchak make a paste of mud and cow dung, which he had spread on an ugly gash on the hind legs of one his cows that had innocently walked into a barbed-wire fence.

She explained the procedure to *Dadaji.* When he laid a hand on her head, she acknowledged the blessing. He raked some of the dung from the fire. She sprinkled a few drops of water on it and made a paste. This she placed on a leaf plucked from the door. Holding her breath, she picked it up with her left hand and, with great care, spread it on his forehead.

There were two reasons she did not wash the wound. The first was that their water ration was dangerously low and in this dry region, it could be hours before a fresh supply could be located. The second reason was her knowledge about the disinfecting properties of cow dung. If people used it to mop their living quarters and the cooking surface of their hearths, then, concluded Chandni, it had to be good.

Soon, the hut was filled with the smell from this concoction, bringing to her mind images of the garden in Mauchak. During the monsoon season, when grass grew to luxuriant heights, the milkman was allowed to bring his herd of cows to this veritable cornucopia of delight. The gentle beasts feasted on the succulent grass, then showered appreciation by dropping heaps of dung along the way.

She settled on her haunches, her chin resting on her knees. The smell of her sweat mixed with the dung rose in waves. She was filled with longing for a long, cool bath. Happening to glance at her abused fingers, she made a quick decision. With thumb and finger of her right hand, she drew out a piece of soap from her bag, poured a few drops of water, lathered, and quickly cleaned up. If there was heaven on earth, then this was it. Chandni closed her eyes, taking an almost sensuous pleasure in her toilet.

And guilt be damned.

She had been through enough already, so spending a bit of water on herself was no sin. The dust-laden sari and blouse would have to do. The blisters on her feet had burst, mixing red dust with the red of her blood. "Oh, Lord," she groaned. Whatever was she going to do about her feet? Wearing sandals was out of the question now, and she could not imagine walking barefoot on this rocky ground. She leaned against the mud wall, trying to ease the darts of pain that shot through her neck and shoulders. There was a dull ache behind her eyeballs.

She glanced at *Dadaji*, fast asleep in the opposite corner. The noises coming from his mouth didn't sound good. He coughed, then began to choke on his spit. Hurrying over to his side, she lifted his head, cradling it in the crook of her arm to help him breathe easier. His eyes stared at her face without recognition. Some anxious moments later, during which Chandni sat motionless praying hard, his breathing eased and he closed his eyes. She laid him down gently.

Once again, she leaned back, and with hands clasped around her bent knees, closed her eyes. A bit of rest was all she needed. Just enough for the blisters on her feet to settle down.

SEVEN

Kanta
Sarbogram – 1913

Once again, Kanta jerked awake. She had done it twice already – every time her eyes closed and she felt herself floating, something happened to her legs and she jumped up. She was sharing the bed with her older sister, Menaka, who was there for the wedding.

When she did it again, jerking and sitting up, Menaka burst out, “Stop it, Kanta. I am so tired and you won’t let me sleep. What’s the matter with you?”

“Don’t know. It’s just that my legs won’t stop moving.” Kanta was huddled under the bedclothes at the foot of the bed. She did not want to be close to her sister, who had a habit of slapping her when annoyed.

“You are stupid,” her sister snapped, then throwing aside the bedclothes, she rose on an elbow and called out to the maid, who was sleeping on a mat just by the door. “Asha *Mashi*, you better light the lamp – keep us company, will you?”

Asha held a match to the tip of the oil-soaked wick, igniting a tiny flame that turned into a golden paisley. She set the clay lamp carefully on a brass holder in the centre of the room. A golden pool of light surrounded the lamp, while the shadows receded to the far corners of the room.

“Well, now are you satisfied?” asked Menaka. She yawned to draw attention to the absurdity of it all.

At the first sign of light from the lamp, Kanta had brightened. “*Didi*, this is like old times, isn’t it?” She drew the thick quilt around her body, ready for some serious discussion. Tomorrow she would leave her childhood home forever to live amongst strangers. Her hands, clasped around the knees, gripped together until they almost turned white. The long hair fell in playful tendrils across Kanta's face, hiding the tear-filled eyes. She rubbed them with her knuckles. She wouldn't cry. She had to be brave. *Didi* had done it. She must, too.

Her bravado, however, was short-lived. With a strangled sob, she burrowed back underneath the quilt. Why, oh, why, would the Rais choose her? They were royalty and she was not. And, the prince was so much older. Why hadn't they chosen Menaka?

She flung aside the quilt, and breathing hard, shook her sister. "If the prince is already eighteen years old, why didn't they choose you? You got married a long time ago." Her sister's marriage had taken place when she herself was only two, so Menaka would have made a nice bride for the prince, she reasoned.

"I don't know and it's not important." With a big sister's vast knowledge of the world and its conventions, Menaka threw her a deprecating look, closed her eyes and then turned so that her back faced Kanta. Her attitude said the girl talk should cease, immediately.

The unsteady flame from the lamp threw shadows on the walls, flickering, insubstantial, not to be trusted. Kanta's eyes followed their movement, her mind in turmoil, refusing to be still – just like the shadows. She chewed on her lower lip. She felt her sister's annoyance, although the reason eluded her. Menaka's husband belonged to a rich landowning family that allowed her to dress in fine clothes and jewellery. She was free to do as she pleased. There, the true reason for her own fear now became clear – she was terrified of losing her freedom. At home, she was able to plan her day, safe in the knowledge that mother and father would always love her, no matter how often she got into scrapes. She could order Asha around, most of the time, and could play with Monoroma whenever she wanted.

Would she be able to do as she pleased in her husband's house? The sense of fear that had had her in its grip all this time suddenly began to lessen. In its place was now a feeling of rebellion. What if she refused to get married? What if she ran away?

At this point, Asha, who had been sitting quietly, began to speak. "I am not supposed to tell you this, and don't you go repeating it to anyone," here the maid's voice dropped to a whisper, "but I know the Rais didn't want a rich man's daughter for their son, or even one from the aristocracy, of whom I am sure they know many." She paused, making sure the sisters were listening, then continued. "I also know the bride had to be young, but not so young that she would be a bother, you know, crying and all that." She threw a shrewd look at her young charge.

Kanta was listening intently, her eyes enormous in the small face, and even Menaka had stopped pretending to sleep and was alert.

When she was certain she had their full attention, Asha continued, "I heard the *ghatak* tell your parents." Here, Kanta sat up with a start and opened her mouth, but the woman lifted a hand. "Yes, you remember the day, don't you? The day I caught you listening at the door." Kanta nodded mutely. She lowered her eyes quickly to avoid Menaka's surprised look, who, after a few moments, said with impatience, "Asha *Mashi*, what are you trying to say? Hurry up. We need to get some sleep."

The maid, feeling important, was only too happy to repeat what she had heard from the marriage broker. The Rais had said the bride would remain under the care of the prince's grandmother until she was considered old enough to take up her wifely duties.

At this announcement, Menaka said with a smile, "Well, looks like these are nice folks you are going to live with, Kanta." Her voice had a touch of wistfulness.

Asha interrupted, "Oh, there's more – they also said they didn't want a dowry."

Both girls gasped in unison. No dowry? Such a thing had never been heard of.

"They have said – you know, the Rais – that a dowry was not important. They are filthy rich so why should it matter? Anyway, they said they are only interested in a young girl from a middle-class family who would be easy to mould." Having delivered this piece of information, the maid got up to blow out the lamp and returned to her mat. Soon the room filled with sounds of the soft snores and deep sighs that come from peaceful sleep.

For a long time afterwards, Kanta remained awake. She was trying to fight a growing panic that threatened to overcome the little self-control she had managed to hang on to. What did Asha mean by the Rais wanting to mould the girl? What were they planning to do to her? Now, she had given voice to her deepest fear. After getting married, she would spend all her time with *Boroma*, the prince's grandmother. That's what the maid had said. She should know she was a gossip.

At that point, Kanta's thoughts teetered to a more urgent matter – would she be beaten if she made mistakes? She couldn't imagine what it was she was supposed to learn. Why did she have to get married, anyway? Her eyes darted to the sleeping form of her sister, who was snoring, blissfully unaware of Kanta's inner turmoil. No, help would not come from her. It had to be her mother. She would get up really early and talk to her mother. Everyone seemed so busy, always demanding her parents' attention, that she hardly saw them anymore. As she planned on how to get to her mother next morning, she realized that she had no idea what to ask.

An itch had started at the nape of her neck. She scratched at it violently, drawing blood, and continued to sit deep in thought. Finally, with a shiver, she lay down and pulled the quilt over her head, like a turtle hiding under its shell.

The December morning seemed especially bright. A few puff clouds, resembling so many carefree children, floated about the blue sky; a breeze, in which a faint chill lingered from the previous night, danced through the trees. Everything appeared fresh as though smiling in anticipation and the very air crackled with an intense excitement. This was the day of the wedding. Kantabali was to be married to Prince Kunjan, of the royal Rai family of Golapdanga.

Neighbours had shown up early at the Burman household so that Kanta awoke to the sound of excited chatter and general commotion. She had lain awake a long time, for the information from the maid had unsettled her. But there was precious little she could do. Kanta decided not to worry any more. Swinging her legs off the high bed, she opened the bedroom door, just a bit.

The sight of women, their neighbours, sitting in close groups peeling and chopping what looked like mounds of vegetables – an age-old tradition proudly upheld and looked forward to – drew a frown from Kanta. Her grey eyes, surveying the scene, assessed the situation. The matrons, busy laughing, gossiping, downing cups of tea and chewing *paan*, did not notice the girl hiding behind the door. Someone started singing a ditty, something about a mother-in-law and her greed for gold supposed to be paid by the bride's family, which did not arrive, resulting in the verbal abuse of the father of the bride. Screams of laughter followed this colourful song.

This would go on all day. Kanta stood fidgeting at the door, precious minutes ticking away when she should have been talking to her mother. How? She blamed the wedding, notwithstanding the fact that she was the chief player at this event. And there was the other problem. Even if she did get to her mother, then what? What would she ask?

Kanta was stumped only for a moment; then the usual effervescence, so much a part of her character, rose and she made a quick decision. The garden. Her chin went up, and her head lifted. She stood tall, shoulders back. She would spend the entire morning in the garden, away from grown-ups, all on her own. She placed one foot forward, carefully brought the other one across the threshold, then bending almost double, she was out and running, like a hare out of its hole, towards the garden door.

It was the season of roses and the garden was filled with their perfume. Kanta sniffed appreciatively. The stone bench, her favourite spot, beckoned. Moisture from the early morning dew came off on her fingers when she touched it. She sat down. Her eyes gleamed. Her damp garment would get her in trouble. But, no, wasn't it her wedding day? Surely no one would scold her today? The sudden movement of green and blue high above the tree caught her attention. She set her sight on it, wishing she could also be as free as the parrot.

Without warning, Kanta's vision was blocked by a pair of soft hands. She removed them and turned to find her best friend Monoroma behind the bench.

"Roma, you are here," Kanta shouted, bouncing off the bench.

"You know, Kanta, I almost ran back. So many people at this hour – but they were too busy to notice me, so here I am."

The two friends sat down.

"What about your parents? Do they know you are here?" Kanta didn't want her friend to get in trouble.

Monoroma gave her a playful punch. "Oho, look who's talking! You sound very grown-up – I guess because you'll be a married lady soon."

"Let's not talk about that, I'll stay here as long as I want, and you can, too. Do you want a turn on the swing?" Then she remembered her friend's fear of heights and slipping an arm around her shoulders, she said in coaxing tones, "Roma, this will be the last time we will be together like this – without grown-ups."

"All right – but promise you won't go too high."

"I promise," Kanta said. She made the gesture of a binding oath by pinching her throat with thumb and finger

This was their favourite place, away from everyone, playing house, eating the ripe fruits, running through the trees, and screaming with laughter at nothing in particular. The garden also possessed another quality. It could, by the power of its beauty, subdue even a couple of talkative eleven-year-old girls. During those times, Kanta and her friend did not talk. By their very quietness, they blended in as if part of the garden itself.

Kanta, ever resourceful, had even managed to filch a couple of fresh *rosogolla* from one of the giant earthenware pots, left to cool on the shelf by the kitchen door. More sweets, of the hues of the rainbow, were cooking for the wedding feast. Biting into the warm spongy sweetness, the girls' mouths seemed to fill with liquid sugar. They devoured the rest, then ran to the wooden swing. Kanta straddled the broad seat and waited for her friend to climb up. When they had settled themselves comfortably, she used her bare feet to push forward.

"Today, I'll reach the very top." Kanta's boastful announcement rang loud and clear.

"You promised!" reminded her friend in a small voice. "You know heights make me dizzy."

"Don't worry. It'll be fun. You'll see."

In no time, her efforts had them up in the air. Kanta's braids tumbled out of their ribbons and flew every which way. Wild excitement had taken hold of her. She could do anything, anything she wanted.

A flock of sparrows, disturbed at their meal, rose in a dense blur while a *bulbul* sang its throaty song, as though urging the about-to-be-wedded girl to make the most of the day, for her childhood was about to take flight as surely as the birds. Her eyes rested for a moment on the red-whiskered bird, envying its freedom as it came and went.

She thrust out her hips as if in defiance, and, with the increased momentum, the swing creaked back and forth, rising higher until it appeared to reach the very top of the guava tree. That's how she would gallop on her mare, Lattoo, through the dense forest. The wicked demon could never catch her. Kanta felt free as the wind and quite ready to conquer the world. Her delighted laughter rose to embrace the trees, to travel in waves, upward, towards the sky, then to echo back until it was lost in space, and the garden fell quiet again.

Wait a minute. Why did the seat feel so light all of a sudden?

She looked down. The space between her feet where Monoroma had been seated was empty. Immediate realization of what had happened filled her with such terror that she screamed, once, then stopping the swing, jumped out. And there, among the dead leaves and rotting fruit, lay her dear friend.

"Roma, Roma!" Kanta's cries filled the air as she tried to wake her friend. "Don't just lie there; say something, please! I am so sorry; I should have listened to you instead of showing off."

With an impatient hand, she dashed the tears from her eyes and drew her friend's head onto her lap. After what seemed an eternity, when in fact it was only a few seconds, the fallen girl opened her eyes. At the sight of her friend's tear-stained face, she even managed a weak grin. "I am sorry, Kanta." She sat up. "I started to feel dizzy, and before I knew it, I had slipped from the seat."

Kanta was so relieved that she forgot to scold her friend for not having spoken up before fainting like that, and draping an arm around her waist, she helped her to their seat. Both needed to recover, one from fright, the other from anxiety.

"Tell me, Kanta," asked Monoroma, swinging her legs, "will you miss me when you are in your husband's house?" Her own wedding was to happen the following month.

"Of course, I'll miss you, silly," answered Kanta with a touch of impatience, then continued with greater calm, taking Monoroma's hand. She had noticed her friend's downcast eyes. "And anyway, I'll be coming home to visit everyone, from time to time. So, it's not like I'll be gone forever."

"But your husband may not allow you to visit us." Monoroma turned away and started to chew at her *anchal.*

Kanta placed both her hands on her shoulders. Now she had her friend's full attention.

"You listen to me, Roma," Kanta said. "Can you imagine anyone trying to stop me from doing something I want to do? Anyway, Ma tells me that Prince Kunjan is a kind and thoughtful person. Who knows, he may even agree to play with us. That'll be nice, won't it?" She turned the full power of her incredible eyes on the quiet figure sitting beside her. For her friend had doubts, and rightly so.

"Your husband will laugh if you ask him to play with us."

"Maybe," Kanta replied. But she wasn't about to give up. "I'll make his life miserable if he does." At this declaration, Monoroma choked with laughter. Kanta grinned. Both knew it was possible.

Absorbed in their conversation, the two friends had failed to note the sun's gradual ascension. Meanwhile, word had got around that Kanta could not be found, which put the Burman household into an uproar. Everything had to be ready by noon; where was the bride-to-be?

"Oh, where can the naughty girl have gone off, now?"

When Kanta heard the unmistakable voice of the maid, she dragged her friend by the hand, and the two crouched behind the bench. Soon the disgruntled Asha came into view. The girls tried hard not to giggle. That proved unnecessary, for a gust of wind caught Kanta's hair and blew it outwards.

Asha pounced on them. "There you are, naughty girl. Everyone is looking for you and you sit here, in the sun, turning brown by the minute, and…*O Maa*…look at your face, what have you been eating?"

Kanta stood up and tried to wipe her mouth where the sticky syrup from the sweets was still visible. She knew it was now the end. A sigh escaped her lips.

Her friend had risen at the same time and was standing quietly by her side. She gave Kanta a quick hug.

Kanta blinked rapidly. With a sudden movement, she disengaged herself from her friend's arms.

The garden had grown quiet, the birds were gone, and the trees drooped. Without a backward glance, Kanta started forward, her legs striding so fast that the old servant had to run to keep up. She could hear the woman muttering, "Eleven hours gone, nothing done yet, oh these old bones of mine – how much more. *Durga, Durga*, help me."

Kanta's sharp ears caught the lamentations. With chin jutting forward, she walked even faster. She wasn't sorry, not one bit, for what she had done. Serves them right for worrying. They were all in it together…her parents and sister, and the maid.

They'll regret sending me away, she consoled herself. I'll make sure I am sent home.

Up the verandah steps she ran, and at the sight of the dishevelled girl, there rose a collective gasp from the matrons. She kept her face averted until the safety of her bedroom was reached. There, under her sister's stern supervision, Kanta was hauled to the bathing room.

Two hours later, scrubbed clean with perfumed soap, hair washed thoroughly then dried with a long cloth, Kanta returned to the bedroom. A squeal of surprise escaped her lips. Piled high on the bed were various things. Her mother's work, when she herself had been hiding in the garden.

The bed was draped with a heavy spread of blue satin, exquisitely embroidered in silk threads of yellow and green. Small round pieces of mirror sewn at regular intervals between the embroidery made the colours jump and reach the four corners of the room as nothing else could have. At its centre was the wedding trousseau. Five intricately designed jewellery sets made of gold and embellished with rubies, emeralds and pearls, including a separate set of gold bangles inset with diamonds, seeming tiny and fragile, perfect for delicate wrists. An exquisite tiara filigreed in gold with a design of dainty flowers set with rubies rested on top of this splendid display.

The red wedding sari, commissioned to one of the leading weavers in Varanasi according to Roopmala's personal design, was of the softest silk, with gold motifs the size of a *rupee.* Milky pearls, sewn in the centre of each motif, lay in gorgeous profusion through the entire six yards. The sari border, a broad swath of gold, had hand-embroidered lotus flowers intertwined with leaves in pink and green thread running along its entire length, each leaf outlined in diamanté. There were also numerous saris of hand-woven silk and cotton, cashmere shawls, dainty shoes and slippers, silk undergarments edged with the finest lace and even Kanta's favourite dolls.

Roopmala had thoughtfully added a box of watercolours, a packet of paint-brushes and some drawing paper. The real meaning behind this gesture wasn't entirely lost on Kanta – this was another one of her mother's ploys to keep her from running wild – but she did like to draw and paint when the mood came.

Kanta started forward, but Asha was faster.

"Oh, no you don't," she said, steering the girl to a cushioned seat in front of the dressing table.

"Let me just see everything properly." Kanta tried to run back to the sparkling mound.

This time Asha picked her up with both arms and returned her to the seat before the large mirror. Menaka, who had been watching, laughed with merriment. Her job was to help the maid get her little sister into her wedding finery. The bride had to be readied for her wedding ceremony, which was to start in a few hours.

Kanta shot her a look that spoke volumes. "*Didi*, why are you two treating me like a child? Am I not to be a bride today?" She pouted.

"If you don't sit still, we'll never be able to dress you up. And then, what'll Ma and *Baba* say to your groom when they are told the bride is late because she was behaving like a child?"

After a moment's silence, Kanta turned to her sister. In a voice that could not hide the tremor, she whispered, "*Didi*, please don't say anything to Ma. I'll be quiet as a mouse, I promise." Menaka nodded, her expression soft.

Her hands twisting continually on her lap, Kanta bit her lips and blinked rapidly. Out of the corner of her eye, she watched her sister walk to the bed, pick up some items, and begin to pass them to the maid who would do Kanta's hair. This proved difficult; black and curly, it sprang from her scalp with a mind of its own. No amount of fine oil or pins could hold it down for any length of time. A look of amusement passed between the two older women.

Then, Menaka picked up diamond-studded hairpins from a silver-filigreed tray to hold in readiness as Asha braided and twisted the unruly mane into some semblance of order.

Once the hair had been coaxed into a bun and pinned, Kanta's head felt twice its size; she had a sudden urge to tear it all off, and run fast, and far away. Maybe she could live with the charcoal sellers. Their life appeared so much more exciting. Many times, while playing, Kanta had actually practised calling out like they called their wares. Getting dressed for her own wedding, she somehow wondered if they weren't the ones better off – they did not have to wear heavy clothes or have pins stuck into their scalp. Their skin with intricate black paintings intrigued her more than jewels. With careful attention, she assessed her own skin, her face scrunched in concentration. It did not pass the test.

Then, she brightened considerably. She had another idea, which seemed easier than the first. If she offered to carry the heavy basket, the vegetable woman might agree to have Kanta live with her. She squirmed with excitement. The pin Asha was pushing through the braided hair went deep, making Kanta yelp.

"That hurt, Asha *Mashi*."

"No, no, I didn't – it's this silly pin." The flustered maid held up the offending object, a pin of gold, on top of which was attached a pearl and ruby peacock.

Kanta yanked it out of her hand. In a flash, she had tucked it under her bottom. Out of reach.

At that precise moment, her mother entered the room. Kanta looked up eagerly. Here was her chance, but how to get the others out so she could be alone with Ma? She took in the tiny line between her mother's eyebrows, the overly bright eyes, and decided to hold her peace, for the moment.

"Kanta, my dear," her mother put out a hand to lay it gently on her daughter's shoulder. "Can you be still for one moment while I fix this veil on your head?" She held out a yard of gossamer tissue, bright red, with tiny gold dots scattered throughout.

Kanta wanted to throw her arms around her mother, but Asha continued to slip more bangles onto her arms. Never one to stay quiet for long, she said, “Ma, please tell Asha *Mashi* to stop poking pins into my head. She’s hurting me…” Evading the maid’s hand, she stood before her mother, looking absurdly vulnerable, in spite of the finery. The gold pin lay forgotten on the seat.

Her mother made as if to pull her young daughter into her arms, but the moment passed, and she said, “I have decided that you will keep your hair down. Are you happy now, my pet?”

Kanta was triumphant. Her mouth stretched into a wide grin. Ma had listened to her. She threw herself against her mother’s body with all the force she could muster, to be enveloped in a tight embrace.

The tender moment ended within seconds. Placing her back on the seat before the mirror, Roopmala cautioned her daughter, “Now, that’s enough. Sit still for a moment while I fix the veil.” After the task had been accomplished, she held Kanta’s chin in her hand and gazed at the young face as if etching it in her mind; then, placing a soft kiss on her forehead, she left the room.

All was done. Menaka stood ready to escort her sister out of the room – this room they had shared until her own wedding day. From underneath the draperies, a small hand emerged, and Menaka took it in her own.

Today, Kanta also was leaving her father’s house.

Countless memories jostled against each other. Cool winter nights when the two girls snuggled under the comforter; hot summer afternoons when the room became a haven behind the *khus*-scented bamboo matting that covered the windows. Kanta, with Ma and *Didi,* would lie on the cool floor to rest after lunch. She would plead with her mother to read aloud her favourite story, the one about the greedy jackal and the moon. She never tired of hearing her mother’s voice reading it.

She swallowed hard, the unshed tears rushing back to rest in her throat, giving it an ache that wouldn’t leave. She disengaged her hand from her sister’s grip, and staring straight ahead, stepped across the threshold on to the verandah. Here, just for an instant, she hesitated, as if to say something;

the entourage behind came to a halt. Kanta took a deep breath, then, with her customary quick steps, began to walk down the curved staircase.

With one foot on the last step, once more the bride hesitated, eyes behind the veil scanning far and wide. Where was her mother? She wanted to see her, talk to her. She had a sudden urge to shout, to run and look for her mother. But Menaka's hand was on her back; the poking fingers implied she should keep walking. Kanta turned to face her sister.

Menaka was whispering, "You know Ma can't be present at your wedding."

"But I want to see her," Kanta said, her voice rising.

"Shh – don't you know that's not possible?" Menaka was gripping her arm, making it impossible for Kanta to move. Everyone was familiar with the bride's ability to run like the wind. Menaka was not taking any chances.

"Stupid rules." Kanta's chin went out. She said, "I'll speak to *Baba*." With one quick movement, she had flung aside her sister's arm to rush down the sleek stone stairs; however, the headlong descent was hampered by the heavy garment she was wearing, and by Menaka's next words.

"Behave yourself, Kanta. Do you want to shame *Baba* in front of everyone?"

The quick retort on the tip of her tongue died. With a sudden finality, it had come to Kanta – she was about to leave her parents. The childhood home was no longer to be hers. Once the marriage vows had been taken, she would belong to another family.

Though still too young to understand the full implications of marriage, Kanta had got the gist of it. In her opinion, it did not portend well.

Baba was waiting in the hall downstairs.

Trying hard to move with decorum, Kanta gathered the front pleats of her sari in one hand, and holding the banister with the other, she began the long descent. Her eyes fixed on her father, who was looking up with a small smile, and she let herself relax. Surely *Baba* knew these people and liked them. What was there to fear? Then, she noticed the throbbing vein and the sadness clouding his features. He stretched out his arms, and Kanta flew into them as if taking refuge from a storm.

Kamal Prashad held his daughter for a moment, then, slowly disengaging from her clinging arms, he led her to the wedding dais.

EIGHT

Kanta
Golapdanga – 1913

Kanta jerked awake. An unfamiliar sound, something between a baby's cry and the hoot of an owl, had reached her ears. She was tired, and very uncomfortable. The heavy sari and jewellery poked at her body from odd places. Yet the steady gait of the bearers carrying her *palki*, and their combined voices singing in rhythm, had been able to lull her to sleep. But she was awake now, and miles away from Sarbogram, her childhood home. The mere thought of what she had left behind made her eyes smart, and forgetting her resolve not to cry, she let the fat drops course down her cheeks.

She was feeling sorry for herself. At this moment, back in Sarbogram, the family would be going about their business, Ma and *Baba* chatting with Menaka, Asha *Mashi* cleaning the bedroom, while she had to sit quietly in a stupid little *palki*, sweating in heavy clothes. She blew her nose on her garment, and, at that point, became aware of a change in the gait of the *palki* bearers.

She prepared to lift the leather curtain, just a bit, for a quick peek. But the red veil covering her face and hanging down to her chest was heavy – her arms in their load of bangles struggled to free her face.

Then a voice from close by asked, "Are you wondering about the noise?"

Kanta's hand flew to her mouth. The curtain flopped back in place. She knew she had done wrong, for hadn't her mother said a new bride kept her face covered at all times?

But who had spoken? She must find out. Once more, the curtain rose, a little. This time she was careful to keep her face covered, and through the veil scanned the face of the young man smiling down at her.

It was her husband, Prince Kunjan Narain Rai, astride a horse.

He seemed to understand her curiosity because he was saying, "The peacocks scream when they see something they are not familiar with. They mean no harm. I hope they didn't scare you?" This last sentence was more a question than a statement.

"No," began Kanta hesitantly, searching for the best way to respond. She didn't want to be laughed at, but then plunged right in by confessing, "Well, yes, a little, because the noise woke me."

"Don't worry, I will stay close to you," he said. Then, as an afterthought, he added, "Why don't you go back to sleep? I will wake you when it's time." She noted how one corner of his mouth lifted, and the eyes crinkled at the sides. She was sure he was laughing at her. With the curtain held firmly between her fingers, she nodded mutely. Sleep was farthest from her mind. Kanta was taking no chances.

They had reached the gate to the Rai estate. Her wondering eyes fixed themselves on the thick wooden planks closely screwed together with copper studs and sharply conical at the top. She had quite recovered from her initial fright and was now burning with curiosity to see the place that would be her home for the rest of her life. So, this was the bastion of one of the ruling families of Bengal. She imagined the Rais going to battle on horseback, family banner fluttering in the hot breeze. Perhaps the raja, in full battle regalia, had sat under a swaying howdah atop the broad back of a caparisoned elephant on his way to fight the enemy. Kanta sat up straight, stirrings of a feeling of pride filling her with a great longing for her family to witness the splendid sight.

Another man from the group, who she would later learn was manager of the estate, headed to the gate. He rang a bell set in a recess in the wall surrounding the outer perimeter of the mansion. Its loud clamour brought the gatekeeper, who opened a smaller gate to the side through which they entered the premises.

Forgetting her earlier resolve, she pushed aside her veil with an impatient hand and stuck out her head to drink in the strange sights and sounds. They were now proceeding up a wide avenue lined on either side with enormous *neem* and *jaam* trees, their tops almost touching to make a canopy of blessed shade. Good for climbing, she assessed, letting her eyes run over their spreading branches. Dainty fountains appeared at intervals between the majestic trees, and droplets of the cool spray, resembling iridescent beads, fell on the hot and dusty group. The splash of water from the fountains mingled with the cooing of doves from the dovecote to make for an atmosphere of heavenly peace.

The *rajbari* was set well back from the gravel path, only springing into view at the last moment. Built of white marble, the structure sparkled in the afternoon sun, almost blinding the eye. Wrapped within the arms of a wide verandah, porticoed columns rose gracefully, reaching up to the terraced roof. An unmistakable aura of dignity marked this place, mingled with a sense of welcome, seemingly directed at her.

Kanta counted twelve windows on the main floor alone; they were tall and covered with glass, the likes of which she had never before seen. The windows in her father's house were made of wood with nothing in between. These windows opened onto the verandah. She had to drag her eyes away to watch open-mouthed at yet another fantastic display – this time it was a line of peacocks ranged on the lawn with fans wide open, as if to welcome her. It was their cries she had heard. She had never seen such magnificent creatures, and Kanta, with a young girl's delight, was about to clap her hands when a frown from the person opposite stopped her. This was Bina, assigned by the Rais to look after the new bride. The older girl had mostly held her peace throughout the journey, only making sure that the bride was comfortable. Kanta's hands returned to her lap.

The distant cooing of the doves continued adding to the fairy-tale quality of the place.

Retainers, clad in white high-necked *kurtas* with red *cummerbunds*, brilliant red turbans on their heads, stood on the wide steps leading up to the verandah, two to each step.

The bride's *palki* had been set down at a distance. Craning her neck, Kanta was just able to make out what was going on in front. The first two servants greeted their prince with folded palms, then offered what must be cool rose-scented water, she guessed, to Kunjan to wash his face, and soft white towels to dry off. Shanti Ram, the manager, did the same but from a respectful distance.

Kanta had been primed well by her mother. She continued to sit in the *palki*, waiting to be carried to the back of the house by another entrance, through the inner courtyard and then to the women's section. Never, ever to leave, and if for some unforeseen reason she had to go out, which was not likely, she, like the rest of the women, would use the back stairs - never the front.

With the sudden realization of her changed status, Kanta's previous excitement seemed to evaporate – her head drooped.

Meanwhile, Prince Kunjan had come to check on his bride. He lifted the leather curtain and whispered, "We will talk later, Kanta. Don't be afraid." Kanta's spirits lifted immediately. She nodded. He was gone, just as quickly as he had appeared.

The bridal *palki* entered the women's courtyard through a set of doors carved with flowers, fruits, animals and people. Here waited the women of the household for *Bodhu Boron,* welcoming the bride. Kanta followed their instructions, gently kicking a pot full of rice signifying abundance, then standing on a plate of *alta* so the bottoms of her feet took on its red hue. She was blessed, then taken away to one of the numerous rooms along the verandah.

Her toes curled inwards as she walked slowly, leaving red footprints on the cold marble floor. Her feet felt strange, alien almost, and not part of her. Her whole body felt as if it belonged to someone else – she had to obey instructions directed at her while jokes flew back and forth amidst a lot of laughter and giggles, the new bride the brunt of them all.

She wondered if her sister had had to undergo such rough treatment. She herself had been too young at the time, didn't understand enough to ask her sister when later Menaka came to visit. If anything, she had been envious of the attention heaped on her sister and had wanted to be a bride herself. Her mother had smiled gently, chucking her under the chin, and told her to enjoy her childhood as long as she could. What if she had the power to turn back the clock?

The procession came to an abrupt halt. A pair of hands lifted her veil, and Kanta found herself looking directly into a pair of eyes, black and glittering. The face belonged to an older woman, almost ancient by Kanta's standards. Dressed in white, her head was covered and her hands bare of any jewellery. Wordlessly, the two stared at each other.

Kanta was the first to look away. Without waiting to be told, she bent to touch the woman's feet.

Strong arms raised her up. "Welcome to your home. I am Kunjan's *Boroma*. From this day onward, you will stay with me at all times, sleeping, eating, learning household duties. I will tell you when you are ready to live with your husband." Each sentence was spoken in a deep, steady voice.

Kanta's heart plummeted to her toes. She would be a captive in this house, this stern woman, her captor. What about the prince? Her eyes darted here and there – surely, he hadn't forgotten his promise. Should she ask? She opened her mouth, then shut it. *Boroma* had turned away, and she herself was propelled forward by numerous hands.

The child bride had arrived.

Kunjan, who was still a student when he got married, had to return to St. Paul's school for boys, in Calcutta soon after the wedding. In the days leading up to his departure, he tried to spend time with his wife. He was a great storyteller. Kanta's favourite was the one when Father Aloysius, the Jesuit priest from St. Paul's, lost his way and ended up at the Rai household. Not only did this priest charm Kunjan's father into sending his son to the Christian school, but he also spent long hours playing cricket with the estate's children, becoming somewhat of a hero in their eyes. Then the day arrived when Kunjan would leave for school. When he came to this point, Kanta's sensitive ears picked up the marked sadness in his voice. *Boroma* had retired to her room, and when Kunjan arrived for his grandmother's blessing, the door remained closed.

At this point in the narration, Kunjan fell silent. Kanta gave him a moment to pull himself together. She was puzzled by her husband's sadness. If *Boroma* was acting like that, then Kunjan should not waste time thinking about it.

She pulled at his sleeve. "Don't stop – please, tell me all the stories of your school." Her husband emerged from his thoughts to look directly at the small figure in front of him, sitting on a chair too high so that her feet remained off the ground. She was waiting, eyes bright with anticipation as if entering a forbidden world, legs swinging back and forth. A burst of laughter erupted from him.

"If only you could see yourself now, Kanta. Your face is so open it mirrors all your thoughts, and I think I know now that you are a very impatient girl." He continued to talk about the time when Father Aloysius took the boys on a trip to an area of Calcutta that housed poor people. Here they had played out The Prodigal Son.

Kanta stopped him at this point, "What is this story? I don't understand."

"It's like this, Kanta," Kunjan said. "It's from the Bible, the Christian holy book, and it has so many stories. Father Aloysius chose this one because we read it during class and liked it."

"Can you teach me to read it, too?" Kanta would not give up on the chance of learning to read books her husband seemed to enjoy.

"All right, but you must promise not to breathe a word to *Boroma*." Kanta nodded, eager to comply.

The two spent long hours together, Kunjan teaching her the English and Bengali alphabets. She picked them up fast, storing information like a squirrel storing nuts and wanted more; soon, however, it was time for her husband to return to school. He set her daily lessons for the time he would not be home.

Kanta missed him and took to roaming through the rooms, although her favourite would always be the drawing room, elegantly arranged with red velvet draperies covering long windows that actually opened out to a terrace.

Kunjan had brought her here one day under the pretext of a meeting with his father, except that he knew the raja was holding council with the village headman, somewhere on the estate.

On the polished marble floor of this room was a mosaic of stars in muted shades resembling twilight. The walls sported gilt-framed photographs of ancestors long gone and, between these, lamps in shining bronze, wall sconces appeared at regular intervals. The ceiling was covered with what at first appeared to Kanta to be a diaphanous covering the colour of dusty roses brought from the four corners of the room and tied into a knot in the centre, from which hung a crystal chandelier. She pointed at it mutely, turned speechless by its sheer beauty. Kunjan picked her up in his arms and held her high. To her amazement, the thing she had thought was fabric was actually revealed to be something else entirely. Plaster of paris, her husband explained, placing her back on the ground. Light pink in colour and appearing soft, it reminded her of the pink shawl her mother had packed for her with strict orders to wear it only for special occasions. It weighed next to nothing and she could fold it into a tiny square.

It was in this magnificent room that Kanta's father-in-law, Raja Mohan Lal Rai, entertained guests, both Indian and European. Kanta had planned to hide behind a sofa during one of these meetings. But ever since Kunjan's departure, *Boroma* had been keeping a strict eye on her movements, and Bina the maid had been ordered to accompany the new bride at all times.

Two months had passed since his return to school, and just when the other students were talking excitedly about summer holidays, Kunjan fell ill. It started with loss of appetite followed by aching muscles. He preferred his bed to any kind of activity. For someone who loved sports and the outdoors, it appeared strange to everyone; when his temperature started to rise and wouldn't come down, the fathers at St. Paul's became concerned. Soon after, he was diagnosed with the dreaded typhoid.

An incident occurred at this time that would have far-reaching consequences in both their lives. Kanta, however, would remain unaware until much later, when she heard it from her husband.

Father Aloysius, Kunjan's teacher and mentor, spent long hours by his patient's bed bathing the hot forehead with cool water and coaxing a few spoons of thin gruel down his throat. That was the best that could be done. One day, Kunjan opened his eyes to the strains of a melody. To his utter amazement, he found the priest kneeling on the floor, palms pressed together in the act of prayer. Even more astonishing was the sound of a song being sung, softly, yet with such intensity that the room seemed to throb and pulsate. Kunjan could not understand what was happening, so he lay quietly, keeping his eyes closed. Soon, however, the sound began to fill Kunjan with an exquisite force, an energy that he had not felt for over a month, and he sat up. Abruptly, the song came to an end. Father Aloysius returned to his position on the chair beside the sick-bed. The two never mentioned this incident.

From that day on, Kunjan's temperature began to come down, and by the end of the week he was able to eat and sleep in a normal state.

But he hadn't forgotten the care he had received during his illness. "And, the song?" Kanta asked, leaning forward. Well, her husband replied, he wasn't sure afterwards if he had heard right. Maybe it was his weakness making him hear and see things. Kanta wasn't satisfied with such a banal answer. She was sure Kunjan was hiding something from her. She meant to find out later. Now, she wanted to hear the rest, "Carry on – there's more, isn't there?"

Grinning at her, Kunjan had continued with the story. His inquisitive mind forced him to talk to this saintly priest, by whose ministrations it seemed he had stayed alive. He wanted to know what compelled someone to sacrifice his own well-being for another.

"The Christian religion is based on the tenet that everyone on this earth is born equal. Since we are all children of God, we should love one another just as He loves us. This means taking care of each other in times of need," Father Aloysius said.

This was something completely new to Kunjan, whose world was clearly defined by strict caste rulings. Everyone had a specific place in society, dictated by birth. No one would dream of crossing these boundaries set up by society from time immemorial.

It was agreed that instead of making the journey from Calcutta to Golapdanga, Kunjan would spend the summer holidays at school. He was considerably weakened after the long illness that occurred just before his marriage.

The school was quiet with the boys gone home for summer. Bored out of his mind, Kunjan had walked out of his room to sit under a banyan tree in the grounds. He tried to read but gave up after a while. He set aside the book and looked around. One question that kept appearing in his mind was: Why hadn't he died? Wasn't typhoid usually fatal?

Kunjan did not know that the boys and teachers had been praying for him when he lay sick, close to death. He found this out from his teacher, who also explained that his recovery was the direct result of prayers. How could God not hear so many voices praying for Kunjan?

During those early days of recovery, when he could only take short walks in the school garden or sit in a shaded corner of the verandah in front of the sickroom, Kunjan gave much thought to what Father Aloysius had said. This Christian religion where there was no caste, it taught love for all. What a completely new idea! This love and caring for fellow beings, irrespective of caste or creed, appealed to Kunjan. He was at the threshold of manhood, with life's endless possibilities ahead, but he also possessed a nobility of spirit, an inborn spirituality that yearned for fulfillment.

He borrowed a copy of the Bible from the school library, reading with great concentration, understanding what little he could on his own, but for the most part finding it too difficult to follow. He did not know what he was looking for in this book. But the feeling that there was something waiting for him persisted, a fulfillment only to be brought by in-depth understanding of this most difficult subject. For unlike the Hindu religion, where there were images to pray in front of, Christianity did not offer any such comfort. It was the Word and belief in Resurrection. He asked to be included in Bible study class.

After his marriage, back at school, Kunjan reached a decision.

Kunjan would have a discussion with Father Aloysius. If he had expected accolades from his teacher for wanting to convert to Christianity, then the words he heard disappointed him.

Father Aloysius had listened to him in silence, then said, "Kunjan, I understand your feelings. But think hard and deep. Once you commit yourself, there's no going back."

Kunjan rose from the straight-backed chair and walked to the open window. He stood there, looking out, for a long time, then turned and sat down once more, hands clasped together, a line between his brows. When the priest said, "Take your time, you don't have to do anything today," Kunjan's head shot up.

"So, you don't think I am serious?" he said. His eyes burnt in his thin face.

"I did not mean that, and you know it, Kunjan. I only want to ensure that what you propose to do has not been brought on by emotion alone, rather a hungering of the spirit." The priest made as if to get up, but Kunjan leapt forward and stood in front of him, blocking his way.

"Father, you have to believe me –if I didn't want to change my religion – and I should know how big a step that is – for me, a born Hindu..." He wiped his face with a shaking hand, for the weakness had come over him suddenly. "I also have a wife, as you know, and I will need to make arrangements to get her out of the house." His shoulders slumped and he fell silent.

Father Aloysius said, "Kunjan, if you really want to do this, then take care of your health first. We can talk more when you are feeling stronger." They parted then, each going their separate way.

Two days later, Kunjan converted to the Christian religion.

That night, Kunjan lay awake. Thoughts passed in and out of his mind, doubts and fears about an unknown future. He should not tell his parents, his mind advised. They would never understand the principles that had prompted his conversion.

Finally, giving up all efforts to sleep, he paid a visit to his friend, and rousing him, confided his secret to Mohan.

The two sat up working on a plan that just might afford a chance of bringing Kanta out without having to confront his parents. It was imperative that *Boroma* not find out.

Fate had another plan.

Kunjan begged the school's gardener to carry his note to Kanta in Golapdanga. He had written instructions to his wife to meet him behind their house, where he would have a horse and carriage waiting. However, a curious chain of events befell this man. When he had reached his destination, and was in deep conversation with the gatekeeper of the Rai household, who should chance upon them but the estate manager, Shanti Ram himself. The messenger was escorted inside, the note taken from him, and he was told to wait in the servant's hall. After he had been left waiting for some time, Shanti Ram returned. He told the poor man, who was worried sick, that he should return to the school.

That same day, Kunjan received a visit from his father's manager to escort him home. Having learnt of the failed mission, he had been waiting for the summons.

A lengthy discussion ensued between father and son. Instead of a wrathful father, he faced the true magnanimity of Raja Mohan Lal Rai. He received his share of the family property in Bundhpur in Central India. There, Kunjan would be able to make a home for himself with his new bride. He was being given a chance to move out of Bengal. He understood this was his father's way of protecting him from future repercussions, if any, from their Hindu relatives. In his father's actions, he recognized his generous heart and farsighted wisdom. Not only had he been forgiven for his transgression, but he had also received what was rightfully his.

Boroma surprised everyone by choosing to accompany Kunjan and Kanta to the Rai estate in Bundhpur. When her son, Kunjan's father, demurred, she simply stated that it was a chance to bring under control their property in the wilds.

NINE

Kanta
Bundhpur - 1913 - 1921

Kanta had been awake for some time. She watched *Boroma* leave the room and close the door softly behind her. Fourteen-year-old Kanta could not wait for the day's activities to begin so she could join Prince Kunjan in planning their own games. They were going to have a picnic at nearby Basket Hill, so called because it resembled a human form with a basket on its shoulder.

Three years had passed since their move from the Rai mansion in Golapdanga to this castle in remote Bundhpur. Winters were colder here. She swung her legs from the high bed to the ground, the stone floor making her toes curl. Biting her lips, she tiptoed to the door and opened it a crack. She wasn't supposed to leave the room before seven.

She saw smoke come out of her mouth as she breathed. Wrapping *Boroma*'s brown woollen shawl around her shoulders, she quickly stepped into her slippers by the door and walked onto the verandah. The smell of burning wood, wafting in from the kitchen fire in the morning air, assailed her nostrils. Like a deer, she loped along the length of the verandah until she reached the room at the very end. Holding her breath, she lay one hand on the carved teak door; it yielded, and she stepped in. Putting her entire weight on her toes, she moved noiselessly towards the large bed that was to one side of the room. She tugged at the mosquito net until it came loose, and bending down, lay her hands on Kunjan's sleeping face.

Startled awake, Kunjan opened his eyes to the beaming face of his wife, who wasn't supposed to be there. But, with her usual love for fun, she had managed to do just that.

Kanta's legs, under the thin cotton sari, had been feeling the chill, while her hands had turned to ice. She looked with longing at the warm bed, and ventured to ask, "Can I get in with you, please? I am so cold."

A sound that could have been yes or no came from the depths of the thick quilt. Kanta chose to accept it as yes and scrambled in under the net. Pulling the thick quilt up to her ears, she turned on her side, longing to fit into the warm contours of Kunjan's back. Just for a moment, she hesitated, then throwing caution to the wind, crept closer until the warmth of her husband's body reached her cold limbs. Her eyes closed, she sighed a few times, and in a few minutes was fast asleep.

"*Bowma*, O *Bowma*, are you here?"

Boroma announced her presence in the room by the jingle of keys that hung at her waist. She had seen Kanta. Pointing a finger at her, she said in a voice throbbing with anger, "What are you doing here? Hope no one has seen you. Get up and return to your room immediately." Then she turned on her grandson. "And, Kunjan, I expected more from you. You are as much to blame as this little minx. She's nothing but trouble, and I'm counting the days when she can come to you as your wife and you will be completely responsible for her." She lowered her voice. "Actually, now that I think of it, I will arrange for a small function at the end of the week, after which you and Kanta can live as husband and wife. It's time for you two to start your lives together."

Kanta had been listening, round-eyed, to this tirade, but safe in the knowledge her husband would speak up on their behalf, it hadn't concerned her. What surprised and offended her was that Kunjan left the bed to stand with hanging head, like a culprit. Unable to remain quiet any longer, she spoke up, "*Boroma*, I only came to wake him up," she indicated her husband with her index finger, "and I only got in because it was too cold to stand while he slept," she finished, with an accusing look at her husband.

The entire situation suddenly appeared too much for him, and his shoulders shook with silent mirth. *Boroma* glared at her grandson, then turning to Kanta, said, "Get up before I lose all patience with you. Bina is waiting to help you with your bath. Now go." She pointed at the door with a finger stiff with authority.

With great reluctance, Kanta left the warm bed; with one last look at her husband, who refused to meet her eyes, she left the room, dragging her feet. At the door, she came upon her maid, who stood with eyes downcast. Kanta would have spoken; she did not want the maid to get in trouble, which was sure to happen, for *Boroma* was a harsh mistress. Bina, however, put a finger to her lips. Kanta understood. Head held high, she sailed down the verandah, maid in tow.

Kanta was well aware she could not share her husband's bed until it was time to do so. *Boroma* had said as much. This was a tradition of the Rais, in complete contradiction to the prevalent custom, where the bride and groom were expected to consummate their marriage, even when the bride was still just a child of eleven or younger. Kanta wished this could be her lucky day. The day she would be allowed to share her husband's room, talk about so many things, share jokes, play carrom, read aloud to each other; just imagining the possibilities made her all shaky with a kind of strange excitement that was hard to explain. But according to *Boroma,* they needed to wait until the end of the week.

Divesting herself of her sari, she sat down gingerly on the wooden stool in the bathroom. It was cold and her arms went around her chest, trying to ward off some of the chilly air. In this act she happened to glance down. Suddenly the two bumps sprouting up and out on her chest looked strange, yet alluring, the twin brown nipples standing erect. A pleasant shiver coursed through her entire body, and Kanta had a sudden urge to touch herself, but the servant's presence stayed her hand. She stole a look at Bina from underneath her lashes. Good, she was busy mixing cold water from the cistern into a brass bucket of hot water.

Kanta's hand strayed to her belly, gently touching skin that seemed to shiver on contact. Then she let her hand stray further down until it met the thatch of hair springing vibrantly from her secret place. Stealthy fingers moved, stopped for a second, then continued on until they came in contact with that part from which arose sensations overwhelming her at times. Just then, cascades of warm water began to flow down her back. Bina had just started with the soap. With a guilty start, Kanta folded her hand on her lap. Had Bina seen anything?

She tried to appear nonchalant. "Bina, did you read the two pages I told you to?" Eager to pass on her own knowledge, she had begun to teach her maid the Bengali alphabet, thus committing the ultimate crime. She had dared to obliterate an age-old boundary between mistress and servant. Her own education, received at the hands of her husband, she hid from others, especially *Boroma*.

Bina wrapped a towel around Kanta's head, then, with a coarse cloth began to rub her skin with vigour to bring out a pink glow. She said, "Mistress, I don't think we should continue – I'm afraid."

"I know why you say that. Just because we were caught doesn't mean it'll happen again."

Boroma had come upon them during class the previous day. She demanded to know what they were up to. Drawing pictures, Kanta was quick to reply. Sure enough, the open notebook showed various drawings in pencil. If *Boroma* had looked through it, she would have been surprised. For, at the very back were handwritten pages – lessons that Kunjan had set for his wife, as well as Bina's attempts. Still suspicious, but lacking time to question the two girls, she sniffed her disapproval and left, but not before delivering a final admonishment to the maid to take greater care of her mistress, and that failure to do so would cost her job.

This had left the would-be teacher fuming in frustration. Why could she not share her knowledge with Bina? Kunjan had shared it with his wife. Why should women remain illiterate? Didn't *Boroma* see the injustice of it all? Being a woman.

Kanta continued to teach Bina everything she herself learnt. This required a certain degree of cunning. Here, Bina proved a willing accomplice, for she too did not want her husband, Shanti Ram, to find out.

They were on their way to Basket Hill, chosen destination for the much-awaited picnic. The three women – *Boroma*, Kanta and Bina – rode in the family carriage. Kanta, who was sitting beside *Boroma*, shifted slightly; they had been on the road for close to an hour. Under pretense of fixing the *anchal*, her hands tucked the sides behind her ears, thankful for the little freedom it afforded. The window shades of the closed carriage were down, ostensibly to protect the female occupants from curious looks.

Kanta put up a hand, trying to suppress the yawn. How much longer would they have to sit in the dark? Beads of perspiration began to roll down between her shoulder blades, tickling the skin beneath its covering of lace and cotton. This time, in spite of the stern presence seated beside her, she pressed herself back against the leather seat, trying to stop the itch. The movement shook *Boroma* out of her reverie. "Sit still," she snapped. "I don't know what you used to do in your village, but here you have to behave like an aristocrat. Remember that." She shook a finger in the offender's face, to emphasize her point. Having delivered her speech, she moved a little farther down the seat.

The unperturbed Kanta, seeing that she now had room to move as much as she wanted, lifted one corner of the canvas shade at the window. A whole different world was rushing by – there was the sunshine, green fields, and gnarled tree bottoms – a kaleidoscope of colour. Kunjan was there, as well, on his horse, while she wilted inside the hot prison.

Why should she be in while her husband stayed out?

Unable to keep quiet any longer, Kanta spoke, "*Boroma*, it's quite hot inside, so may I ride with…"

There followed a moment of silence. If Kanta had been more attentive to the older woman's sentiments, she would have felt the sting of the deep disapproval her request had elicited. Bina bent down to retrieve a bundle that had rolled out of her lap to land between the two seats. In that instant, Kanta, seeing the light of laughter on her face, knew she had an ally.

"How can you even think of such a thing, *Bowma*?" *Boroma's* scandalized eruption resounded in the close confines like a cannon. And at that moment, there was a knock on the window. Kanta, sitting closest, pushed aside the curtain. She was spared more vitriol, for it was none other than her husband, sitting astride a black stallion and indicating with a smile that he would like a word. The carriage slowed down.

"Little girl, would you like me to break open the door and carry you off on my horse?" Kunjan whispered, careful not to let *Boroma* hear of his nonsense.

"Oh, could you do that?" she whispered back.

"Actually, no," came the disappointing reply, "but when we get to our picnic spot, be prepared for some fun and games." Spurring his horse, Kunjan rode off in a swirl of dust. Kanta smiled happily, eyes gleaming, as she threw a conspiratorial look at Bina.

The horses had picked up speed and the curtains had been rolled up. Kanta guessed that her husband's grandmother also wanted the breeze to fan across her face. The countryside flew alongside, showing the villagers at their tasks. They looked up and joined their palms in recognition of the Rai carriage from the wheat and gram fields, crops to be harvested next spring. There were mango groves, the sight of which brought an ache of homesickness to Kanta's breast. She had never returned to her father's house, not even for one day. Impossible now, due to the distance. When she sighted women washing clothes and bathing their children in the ponds, an image of Asha *Mashi* rose sharp and her eyes welled up.

Soon the villages were left behind; they had entered the last stretch leading to the hills. Gazing out of the window, Kanta caught her breath, imagining herself running to the top. No sooner had they stopped than Kanta, throwing open the carriage door, jumped out. The men on horse-back had arrived before them; she spotted Kunjan's mount tied to a tree and headed towards it.

There was no sign of her husband. The horse lifted its head, snorting and flicking its tail, eyeing her nervously. Soft-footed, she approached the animal, humming the same tune that she used to croon into her own mare's ear back home. It seemed to work, for the horse now stood still, allowing Kanta to come closer; she could see his eyeballs under their spiky eyelashes. Putting out a hand, she ventured to pat his face. The horse did not shy away.

Where was Kunjan? She turned towards the group in the distance, but he was nowhere. She was supposed to help the cook. This was *Boroma's* way of educating her in the ways of the kitchen, but Kanta had other ideas. Moving away, she chose a shady spot under the spreading branches of a tree and sat down. Dry leaves proved perfect for crushing between the palms, something to do while she waited. It was quite pleasant. Discarding shoes and socks, she wiggled her toes, then patting the dry earth, she spread the end of her sari and lay down, wriggling her bottom and smiling.

She shut her eyes, determined to enjoy this new freedom, but when after about fifteen minutes, in Kanta's calculation, there was still no sign of Kunjan, she became restless and sat up. Flicking dust from her garment, she started towards the horse, once again humming the same tune. The horse's ears cocked back, his neck stretched, and he puffed breath through his nostrils. The horse snorted. At the same time, she saw the bee headed towards them. Kanta was afraid of bees, having been stung once in Sarbogram and suffering from a painful swelling of her throat as a result. She flung out an arm, only to trip on her garment and lose her balance. She landed within inches of the horse's hooves.

The animal reared up on its hind legs, but before the hooves could come down on her, strong arms had seized its reins. With lightning speed, Kanta rolled over and out of harm's way.

She watched with horror the scene unfolding before her. Muscles straining, Kunjan pulled at the stirrup with all the strength he possessed, until it seemed that his arms would be ripped out of their sockets. Yet he hung on and would not give up. Gradually, and after what seemed like an eternity, when the horse was breathing easier, he began to ease up on the stirrup, at the same time continuing to whisper in the horse's ear, until, finally, the animal placed his forelegs back on the ground. The knots inside Kanta's stomach started to ease; she took a deep breath and wiped at her eyes. She stood up slowly.

Realizing that both of them could have been killed or horribly maimed had sobered Kunjan's playful manner of the morning.

Kanta's lips trembled. "Thank you for saving me." She knew it had been her fault for trying to befriend a strange horse.

Kunjan wiped the sweat off his face looking exhausted. Ashamed of her actions, Kanta opened her mouth to speak. She must not lose the friendship of the one person who was starting to mean so much to her.

"I was very foolish and did something for which I have no explanation," she said, her voice low. "I wanted to make friends with your horse, so I came close to him, but there was a bee." She looked up, her eyes imploring for understanding, then dropped them to her hands, twisting the end of her garment. After a slight pause, she tried again. "The bee distracted me. I tried to get away but tripped and fell near the horse. I guess I frightened him…" Her voice trailed away and her shoulders slumped while, her right toe continually dug into the ground.

When moments passed without any words of recriminations from Kunjan, she dared to raise her eyes for a fleeting second, only to drop them again. Kunjan was gazing at her bare feet, a faint smile playing around his lips.

"Don't feel bad, Kanta. I am so relieved that you are not hurt. So, shall we go for a ride?" Kanta's face brightened. He wasn't angry, after all. She happened to glance down and noticed the muddy ends of her garment, where bits of grass still clung.

"Now, like this?" Her smile faded.

Surprised, Kunjan asked, "Since when did you start to worry about how you look?"

"I'm not worried about this," she said, indicating the sari, "but *Boroma* – what about her?"

Kunjan laughed, "You know, when *Boroma* would have sent out a search party for you, I told her you were out collecting plums for her famous chutney. She'll be waiting, so we better get going." He swung her up, her laughter filling the air as her body became weightless before settling on the leather seat on the horse's back.

Kunjan leapt up, took the reins and signalled. The animal began to trot in the direction of the trees that lined the circumference of the field they were in. Held within the circle of Kunjan's arms, Kanta leaned back against his chest with a smile. Safe and secure. And happy. He belonged to her; there would be no one to interrupt their conversation and no distractions. Just the two of them.

Her hair, which had long since tumbled out of the gold-filigreed netting, was now flying free, sometimes on Kunjan's face when the wind blew it there. With one hand holding the stirrup and the other around Kanta's waist, he said, "I'll have to ask *Boroma* to have your hair cut short like those *memsahibs* in Kolkata."

"I don't mind at all!" She twisted around so that she was facing Kunjan, and began to remove the strands that were playing around his mouth. "At least, then, I won't have to waste time on it."

Kunjan hugged her close. "Mm - you smell good." He was smelling her special scent, a mixture of hair oil, soap and sweat.

Their eyes locked together, in an embrace, in which no words were required, only recognition of a feeling, shared by both, as primal as the day man knew woman.

Even the horse, sensing a sudden change in the air, had slowed down.

Kanta looked wonderingly at the man whose breath came ragged from his chest, as though he had run far. Sweat on her upper lip made her raise a hand to wipe it, but the hand became Kunjan's prisoner as he bent his head to touch her lips with his own. At the touch, a sensation, almost an overwhelming desire to cry, overcame Kanta, and a soft sound escaped her lips. She leaned sideways and laid her head against his chest.

Time seemed to stand still.

The silence was suddenly broken by the hammering of a woodpecker as it went about its business.

The moment had ended.

Kanta moved away, a slow flush rising up her neck. Her heart was going at a rate that was not normal. She opened her mouth to speak, compelled to break out of this new feeling of shyness towards her best friend. But Kunjan had put a finger to her lips, so she lapsed into puzzled silence.

Kunjan's hand was pointing to the left, where, almost hidden by a dense growth of shrubs and tall grass, meandered a stream, flowing to its own destination, wherever that might be. Through the tall grass walked a deer.

Kunjan pulled at the stirrup, signalling his horse to be quiet. Reaching the water's edge, the animal stretched its neck in one graceful motion and began to drink, oblivious of the two pairs of watching eyes. After it drank its fill, the deer walked away, as silently as it had appeared.

Being witness to such a simple yet beautiful act filled Kanta with tremendous awe for nature and her creatures. Eager to see more, she leaned forward precariously and would have fallen but for the strong arms around her waist. With one sweep of his leg, Kunjan stepped off the high saddle, Kanta held securely within his arms.

Once again, she was suffused with a strange feeling, and to break out of it, took a step forward. "Oh, could we follow the deer – I want to see his home."

"We could, but that would make us late for lunch, you know…" Kunjan's unfinished reply hung in the air. Both were aware of the consequences of such a daring act. However, Kanta would not give up. She tried again.

"At least, let's get a drink from this stream – I am so thirsty I can't think straight." To prove her point, she licked at her dry lips.

"We can do better than that." Kanta's face brightened. Looking at her, Kunjan lost his train of thought for a moment, then continued, his voice tender. "I can take you to the mouth of the stream, my love. Yes, I'll show you wonders today."

"Oh, yes, please!" Her eyes crinkled.

"All right, but you must promise to listen to me." At her vigorous nod, Kunjan continued, "This stream actually comes from between the rocks on the top of Basket Hill. Would you like to go up to that point?"

Clapping her hands, she hugged her husband. In the next instant, a shadow fell across her face. "Are you quite sure we won't get in trouble with *Boroma*?" she asked, adding in a low voice, "I am supposed to help with lunch." Would she be beaten? Like the last time when she'd climbed a tree and torn her garment? Even that time she'd been late for lunch.

"Stop worrying," her husband was quick to assure her. It was as though their roles were reversed. Where once she was the one to rush into a game, flinging caution to the winds, now it was Kunjan.

"I cannot wait to see your face when you witness the wondrous beauty of the spring," Kunjan said, taking her hand in his own. He examined the palm as though reading it, then giving it a gentle squeeze, added, "I can just imagine you cupping your hand, filling it with spring water, then bringing it to your mouth. Ah, what a picture – if only I could paint."

Kanta blushed. She withdrew her hand. Her husband was a poet, and she was sure he could draw and paint, as well.

They set out. The horse had been tethered securely to a stout tree branch. When they reached the grassy bank, Kanta lifted her sari to her knees and tucked it half-way around her waist. She had learnt her lesson. They walked for some time, until the woods thinned and gave way to a narrow path. Here they stopped while Kunjan got his bearings. Turning left, he led her through the path that weaved its way through a short stretch of land where the grass grew waist-high on both sides.

"Looks like people lived here once, but have since moved on," he observed. Kanta nodded in agreement. She was strangely affected by the place. The brooding silence and wild beauty infused her with a feeling verging almost on reverence. Her naturally exuberant spirits were quiet for a change. Should she open her mouth to talk, it would break the enchanted moment, and Kunjan would certainly start the trek back. Sunlight filtered through the trees, but the grass was damp under their feet. In silence, they walked until they reached the end of the woods.

"Can you hear it?" Kunjan broke the silence, glancing at his wife.

Kanta stopped and looked with wonder-filled eyes at the quiet landscape. It was a magical land, and any minute the fairy queen, followed by a train of fairies, would pop up.

Kunjan was claiming her attention. He had draped an arm around her waist, the other pointing to the right at a distance. The shining thread of water, flowing swiftly downwards between craggy rocks, was undeniably the most gorgeous thing she had ever seen. Her involuntary gasp brought a smile to Kunjan's face.

This was the starting point of the spring they had come across earlier.

As her ears grew accustomed to the stillness, the unmistakable sound of rushing water became apparent. Her eyes wandered again, until they alighted upon the water tumbling down the steep slopes of the hill; it bounced quickly down rocks made slippery through the ages, then slowed, creating mini-waterfalls to reach the bottom and become one with the stream. This stream was a long stretch of water, flowing sometimes narrow and at times broad, until it disappeared into the countryside.

They climbed the rocks as far as was possible, then Kunjan led his wife to the spring. Kanta's gaze rested on the scene before her; it was simple yet beautiful, inspiring veneration. She disengaged her hand and walked forward until reaching the stream, calling out, "*Ekhane esho*, come here."

Without waiting, she plunged into the pool, then waded towards the two rocks from whence the cool liquid gushed forth. Cupping her hands, she received the water to drink deeply. Simple water, the true essence of life, had never tasted so good, and she looked up to share this discovery with her husband – only to find him watching her intently.

She pretended not to have noticed his silence and began to climb out of the stream. The wet sari clung to her body, carving out the curves hidden underneath. Damp tendrils of hair framed the flushed face. The distant cooing of a dove suddenly broke the silence, a silence that had all of a sudden turned into a pulsating universe of unspoken words and desires that had lain dormant all this time, now preparing to spring forth, to envelop them.

Later, much later, Kanta looked up at the sky through a tangle of curls. Everything appeared the same. Yet the girl who had started out that morning intending to only have fun at the picnic was no more. In her place was a young woman, every pore in her body tingling with a myriad of sensations.

She had never felt so alive; although contrary to this feeling of vibrancy, she was also assailed with a sense of delicious inertia. Her husband's arms imprisoned her tightly, making it impossible to move. She did not want to leave this heaven on earth, but it was getting late. She felt a slight movement, and seizing the moment, sat up.

Kunjan's eyes, made luminous by love, rested on his wife. He said, his voice deep with desire and regret, "We'll have to get back before a whole troop arrives for us."

Kanta nodded, hands fluttering about her flowing tresses. Several times she tried to twist the lot into a bun, but without her hairpins, which were lost in the grass, there was not a thing she could do. She sighed in exasperation, at the same time becoming aware of her husband's watching eyes. This just added to her confusion. Giving up her attempts to tame her hair, she slipped on her shoes, then tried to brush out her crumpled garment.

Kunjan, still prone on the grass, extended a hand and caught one corner of her *anchal* just as she was preparing to stand up.

"Here, let me help you with your hair," he offered.

"You, help me with my hair? But you are a man!" was the surprised response.

"Trust me." Kunjan whipped out a comb from his pocket, and gathering her hair in one hand, proceeded to apply the comb through it with quick, deft strokes. Together they managed to braid Kanta's hair.

It was time to leave.

Holding hands, they started the walk back to the tree where Kunjan's horse was tied.

Kanta's usual chatter was missing. A new phase had opened for her. She held on to her husband's hand tightly, trying to match her steps to his longer strides.

TEN

Kanta
Bundhpur – 1913 – 1921

On her sixteenth birthday, Kanta discovered she was with child.

She was an early riser, leaving the bed at the crack of dawn, as if determined to get as much out of a day as was humanly possible. There was a lot of work, with help in the kitchen taking up most of the day. Her own education continued to make good progress. Having discovered a new world within the written word, she couldn't get enough of it and spent long hours at night, the only private time she was allowed, reading the volumes Kunjan provided. She was learning to quilt, which *Boroma* insisted should be done by every woman. It was not an onerous task for Kanta. She had developed a love for the art, for art it was – creating a kaleidoscope of colours and design by stitching old *saris* with lengths of yarn of a contrasting colour. They were then handed out to the estate workers. Kanta's quilts, made especially for the newborns, became a great favourite with them.

But there would be no quilting that day. Her mouth puckered as bile rose at the back of her throat. Her stomach felt like a gaping hole; she had been retching since she awoke.

"Congratulations." Bina had entered the room.

"Why?" Kanta swallowed. There was nothing left to bring up.

"You are pregnant," said Bina with a sly smile and turned to leave the room, obviously to get *Boroma*.

"Oh, wait!" Kanta called out to the departing figure. She tried to rise, and was immediately dizzy. She caught hold of the bedpost, her face white. Bina hurried to help her back to bed, then left.

Boroma was ecstatic at the prospect of a baby coming into the household. All her conversations were now about the yet to be born great-grandson. Of course, it had to be a male child, she said forcefully to everyone within hearing. And, of course, she herself would be his chief caregiver.

Outraged at the assumption, Kanta also felt the first stirrings of apprehension. Her baby would be taken away. She was sure of it, for who could fight against the powerful old woman?

She shared her fears with her husband, who comforted her, saying, "Our elders know how to care for newborns, and it is best for you, anyway. You will need to rest to get your strength back."

This failed to satisfy Kanta. She knew by instinct what lay in store.

Could she tell her husband about the numerous times she had been scolded and demeaned, even to the extent of having her arms pinched and hair pulled? But Kunjan would never know, for she could not tell him. He would not believe. Bina had applied a cooling herbal paste, and the welts disappeared in no time. *Boroma* knew how to hurt without leaving a telltale mark.

Once Kanta had dared to ask why. This earned her a heavy punch on the side of the head, and a muttered curse. To Kanta's ears, the curse had brought more pain. She had just heard her parents being damned for having sent their daughter to the Rai family without a dowry. She had crawled back to bed to weep. That's a lie, she wanted to shout. Kunjan's father had not wanted a dowry. But, how could she?

Kanta observed a certain change in her husband. He was no longer a mouth-piece for his grandmother; Kunjan was very much involved in the daily running of the vast Rai estate.

It was at this time, when the household was basking under the glow brought on by the expected arrival of an heir, that the terrible drought began. Famine stared them in their faces, affecting villagers and townsfolk alike. The paddy fields had sprouted only stunted brown shoots out of the dry soil; people lined up for hours at a time at the wells, their levels of water at an alarming low. Some had dried up completely, so that people of those areas walked miles to find water. Ugly fights broke out – and water, if found, was being sold at exorbitant prices.

The situation was beginning to turn desperate.

Temples resounded with the collective sound of songs, prayers, gongs and conch shells while priests performed the worship on behalf of their congregation. All day and all night it went on. Yet, with the lack of food and the gradual disappearance of water, people began to die. At times, the relatives of the stricken were too weak from hunger and thirst to perform last rites, so dead bodies lay where they were, bloated and decomposing, food for greedy flies. When a family did manage to somehow crawl with their load to the burning *ghats*, they didn't wait to see it finished; staggering back to reach their homes as quickly as possible, many collapsed by the wayside, never to get up again. Carrions circled above constantly, their raucous cries piercing the hot and stifling air. Village after village reeled under the heat, and rivers and streams dried up.

Each day, the sun continued to shine. People crept out to peer up at the blue sky, desperately seeking, hoping and praying for a bit of cloud that would promise rain. But none appeared. The sky remained a brilliant blue. Now the dead bodies of animals could be seen strewn along the narrow lanes, their bellies distended, skinny legs pointing skywards as if in supplication. Fish lay on the sunbaked river bed, flopping in desperation until they too perished. The stench of rotting flesh filled the air, for no one had strength left in their starving bodies to clean the streets.

Cholera, the scourge of civilization, arrived, waving its flag of victory and grinning in triumph. Fangs bared, it rushed on with merciless abandon and wicked glee, striking down man, woman, child and animal. Catastrophes like this had happened before, but they always started in the city. This time, however, it started in a village, was carried forward like a good deed, spreading in such haste that towns and cities did not find out until too late.

The poor villagers needed to see their master. They needed assurance that this evil phase would pass. Perhaps they were being punished for some wrongdoing. Only their master would be able to protect them and make it alright.

News of the epidemic was received with grave consternation by the Rais in Bundhpur.

Boroma conferred with her grandson, "Kunjan, it might be a good idea to visit the villages at this time so they get to know you, and you will see first-hand all that you own. Of course, Shanti Ram will go with you. You will start from the north, circle the villages, talk to the elders, then carry on to the west and east and finish your journey in the village of Gauribagan." Counting on her fingers, she concluded it would take about four months.

"*Boroma*," began Kunjan hesitantly, setting aside the notebook where he had been taking notes, "do I really have to go at this time, you know, with Kanta…"

"What about Kanta?" She set her piercing eyes on him, and when he would have spoken, she raised one hand, stopping him. "You know she will get the best possible care here. But you," she pointed a finger at him, "you need to be with your tenants at this time, for never shall it be said that a Rai hid like a coward while they suffered."

Kanta, who had been resting, heard the raised voice; she crept forward and with thumping heart, listened from behind the half-open door.

She wanted to interrupt, to demand why her husband should be sent on a journey when her time was near. Surely, the manager could go instead? But she kept quiet. She knew *Boroma* would have her way. No one had ever argued with her and won.

"I am not afraid," Kunjan denied passionately. "I will set out immediately to see for myself the devastation laid out where my tenants live, and I will do my best to mitigate their misery."

Hearing the vehemence in his voice, Kanta knew her husband would make the journey.

Kanta's labour pains had begun in the early hours the same day Kunjan's body was brought back to Bundhpur. He had succumbed to cholera, miles away and in the midst of strangers, with only the estate manager for company.

The pains increased gradually and continued through the day. Yet, there was no sign of the child wanting to come out. *Boroma* and the midwife exchanged glances; this would not be an easy childbirth. When the midwife suggested taking a few turns around the room, Kanta turned to *Boroma* for confirmation, but none was uttered. Supported by the midwife, Kanta took a faltering step forward, then another, all the while aware of the eyes boring into her back.

Minutes elapsed. Kanta dragging her swollen feet across the floor, leaned more heavily on the midwife's shoulder until a desperate cry rose in her throat, but she shoved her fist into her mouth and stumbled to the bed. There she lay, staring straight ahead, her eyes mirroring the hopelessness in her heart. She had heard the whispers when they thought her asleep. Nobody had said a word to her – not even Kunjan's grandmother.

She had felt Kunjan's presence during the night, only then she had thought it was a dream. Overjoyed, she had wanted to walk out holding his hand, but the image was gone in an instant, leaving in its wake unfulfilled longing and a whiff of Kunjan's perfume – a blend of attar of roses and musk. She had woken with a cry to an empty room, the lamp in its ledge shedding soft light amidst the shadows. *Boroma* had appeared soon after.

It would be easy to give up on life at that moment, Kanta reflected, but no, she had to live on for the sake of their baby. The baby, however, showed no inclination to arrive, as if it knew to remain in its mother's womb was infinitely safer than to come out into a world without a father. *Boroma* and the midwife busied themselves with meaningless little tasks around the birthing room, anything at all, just as long as they did not have to watch the young girl lying still and dry-eyed.

Towards evening, Kanta's pains increased. The water broke while the midwife snored in a corner. *Boroma* had just left the room. She said Bina should be with her mistress when the baby came – the maid had given birth to a baby girl the previous week.

Finding herself alone except for the sleeping midwife, Kanta sat up slowly, not daring to breathe for fear of bringing on another spasm. Then, with great difficulty, she managed to lower her heavy body from the high bed. Her bare feet met the marble tiles and a moment later, she was standing up, one hand supporting her belly. She ignored the wetness spreading through her garment and on unsteady feet, staggered to the door; usually a lamp burnt before each room, but not this evening. She made her way down the corridor where the shadows had grown deep, seeming to swallow everything.

She reached Kunjan's room. Holding on to the doorpost for support, she stood, her eyes fixed on the motionless form. They had dressed him up, her prince, in fine silk and laid him out on the teak bed; garlands of rose and *beli*, heady with their joint perfume, draped him. He appeared to be sleeping peacefully.

Kanta waited for her husband to stretch out his arms and pull her to him, as he always did when he caught her looking at him. Why does he not open his eyes? He must know she was in the room? She must tell him she had not cried of her pains, that should make him proud. She felt a touch on her elbow – it was Bina, pleading for her to come away. Then, Kanta became aware of the others gathered around the bed. Her eyes darted wildly, and she wondered aloud, *why are they here? Don't they know the master is back after a long journey and now needs to rest?*

Just then, *Boroma* appeared. With unmistakable authority, she took the girl by the elbow and escorted her out. Kanta could hear the muted voices from the room she had just left.

At one point, her ears picked up a steady hum, which appeared to come from the verandah. She found out from Bina they were getting ready for the funeral procession that would take Kunjan's body to the cremation ground outside the village. In spite of her weakened state, Kanta put up a fierce fight, insisting on a Christian burial for her husband; to everyone's surprise, *Boroma* agreed and personally asked the estate manager to fetch Father Aloysius.

Although she had won the battle and achieved what her husband would have wanted, Kanta knew it would cost her dearly. She had made an enemy for life.

There was nothing more to do but wait for the birth to happen. She had no tears to shed. Her entire world had now turned into a desert. The well of life, her husband, from whom she had drawn succour from the earliest days of their marriage, had dried up, leaving her with a thirst that would not be quenched in this earthly life. He had been like the cool water giving life to a plant, and she had been that plant. Without that sweet water, she was going to wither and die. She closed her eyes, screwing them tight, bracing against another onslaught of pain. It tore at her insides with sharp pointed teeth, picking her up and crashing her down. She welcomed the pain because it did not allow her time to think.

Her parched lips were wiped with a piece of dampened muslin. Kanta opened her eyes to an impenetrable look from jet–black eyes. They shifted, and *Boroma* dipped the cloth again in the bowl of ice water standing on a stool by the bed.

If only her mother were here, Kanta thought desperately – but that was not possible, she reminded herself. Her mother had the smallpox, a victim of yet another epidemic, in faraway Sarbogram. There had been a letter from her father and baskets of her favourite sweets and fruits, along with a red silk sari, and a gold necklace with matching earrings and bangles. In a separate velvet pouch, there were twenty *mohurs* for her lying-in. As tradition bade, she should have been in her father's house to deliver her first-born. But fate had ordained otherwise.

Kanta wished the pain would take her away to the other world, to be with her husband. Kunjan's letters, all three of them, were under her pillow. In one of the letters, he mentioned his one desire was to be with his wife when she gave birth to their child. But duty bound, he had to wait for a certain government official to ensure that the wells would be dug and drinking water provided to all residents in the villages he had been visiting.

Through the open window came the sound of honking borne on the wind as a gaggle of geese flew by, possibly searching for a place to rest. Kanta turned her face towards the sound. A strip of blue sky met her gaze. If only she could fly, she thought with longing. She would be out of this room in a moment. *Lucky birds.*

Now the pains came faster, without respite. She tasted blood, for she had bitten her lips and tongue. She would not scream. She only prayed for the nightmare to pass, for release. Wearily she focused her last remaining strength on the image of her husband, hoping it would give her the strength to birth their baby soon. The curve of Kunjan's lips when he smiled, the upward spring of dark hair showing the high forehead she loved to caress, the long-lashed eyes that would crinkle at the corners with teasing laughter.

She remembered the day she got married – Kunjan had seemed ancient. She had soon realized he had a generous heart that made it possible for him to show tremendous patience with his eleven-year-old bride. He was one in a million, and Kanta's love for him had grown in her so that she could not be without him for any length of time. If only she had been able to accompany him on that dreadful journey, her husband might very well be alive at this moment. His letters, ah yes, they were under the pillow.

She was thankful now for those days spent on the back verandah writing out the assignments her husband had set for her. But the person she really wanted to show off her writing to was gone forever.

The midwife, refreshed after her nap, wiped Kanta's brow. She urged her to start pushing. But it was no use. Kanta's strength was spent and she just could not sustain a push. The woman muttered that the baby's head was stuck and began to massage Kanta's belly with warm oil. However, there seemed to be no relief.

The exhausted Kanta had dozed off when a murmur of voices woke her, and she knew instinctively it had to do with Kunjan's journey through the villages. With eyes shut, she strained to listen.

Bina was talking. "Our Prince Kunjan was staying in the *saraikhana* in Beltala village...the villagers came daily with their tales and he listened. Of course, this was only the first...still another thirty-nine were left to visit. *Boroma's* order had to be obeyed." She muttered under her breath, too low for Kanta's ears.

"It was the wrong time to travel," said another voice. Must be the midwife, concluded Kanta. She bit her lip hard as another wave of pain invaded her body.

Bina clicked her tongue, annoyed at the interruption. "How could *Boroma* let this happen? She brought him up when his own mother died – he was only fourteen at that time. Anyway, that's all done now."

But the midwife wanted more. "Tell me, dear, what else your husband said, about the last day – he was with the master, wasn't he? Someone told me – I forget who – that all the villagers had died?"

"Yes, my husband is the manager of the estate," Bina said, unmistakable pride in her voice. "He remained with the young master who was still alive... but there were no bearers to carry the *palki* home; our master was too sick to travel on horseback, you understand. My husband was by our master's side all night, and when day broke, the owner of the *saraikhana* and my husband bore the *palki* on their own shoulders and brought the master home. Of course, by that time, he was with God."

Kanta let out a groan, the sound of raw pain hitting at the walls and ricocheting off, bringing the two women to her side in a flash.

Against all odds, a healthy baby boy was born to Kanta and the late Prince Kunjan, just after midnight.

Kanta lay still, her face bloodless. She had not opened her eyes, even when the baby announced its arrival. *Boroma* picked up the squalling little bundle of fury from the midwife's arms and carried him to his mother, but she appeared to have fallen asleep.

Only she wasn't. She simply did not have the strength to keep her eyes open. The last vestiges of strength had been used on strictly controlling a broken heart, and bearing the pain of childbirth, with the same self-control that she knew her own mother would have displayed under similar circumstances. Now she wanted to sleep, and if by keeping her eyes closed, she could somehow journey across to the other world and join her husband, she wanted to do just that.

Grief, however, must move to second place when there is duty to perform.

"Here *Bowma*, hold your son. Look how his arms and legs are thrashing around? He wants to go to his Ma."

The eyelids fluttered open. *Boroma* was holding out a bundle. Kanta took it – her son, a gift from her husband, a memento of the deep love they had shared. The outcome of that shared passion was this tiny human being. Her heart melted at the touch of his soft skin, and soon tears flowed. Between sobs, she covered the tiny face with kisses, saying brokenly, "Our son, I have so much to tell you about your father."

With her baby clutched to her bosom, she slept the sleep of exhaustion.

Next day dawned bright and clear. Life would continue for the living.

She was nursing her baby when she heard footsteps, soft yet recognizable to her ears. She stiffened. The involuntary action startled the baby, who began to whimper. Kanta settled him back at her breast and waited.

"Oh, you must not wake up so early." *Boroma* was holding a brass bowl, steam rising from it. She placed it gently by the side of the bed. A frown creased her brow. "Now, give him to me, you look like a ghost with no colour in your face." She held out her arms. "Bina will nurse him."

"I have decided to nurse and take care of my son."

Boroma straightened the bedclothes and smoothed Kanta's hair. She replied casually, as if the matter was of little consequence. "Whatever you wish, *Bowma*. But if you change your mind, just let me know." Pointing at the bowl, she said, "I brought you warm milk to help you sleep. Drink it up before Khokon wakes."

Kanta had a dislike of milk, but she was ready to set aside personal feelings if it meant that she could nurse her son. She brought the bowl to her mouth and took a sip, wrinkling her nose. She looked up to find *Boroma* watching closely.

"It tastes – I don't know – something's different."

Boroma cut her short, "Of course, it does. I added a drop of rose water and some sugar, knowing how much you dislike milk, and you will drink this every day."

Holding her breath, Kanta tried again, and this time she drank it all until the bowl was empty. *Boroma* picked up the empty bowl and left the room.

During the time that it took Kanta to recover from childbirth, *Boroma* had taken over caring for the baby. Mother and son slept in separate rooms. When she protested, she was told it was for her own good.

"My dear, you have no idea how to care for a baby – they can be so demanding. We want you to sleep and eat well, put some flesh on those skinny bones of yours, and then you'll have your son back." Her hands were busy with a comb and pins. Kanta had tensed, for she knew what was to follow. The long tresses were pulled tight until the veins around Kanta's forehead stood out. There was a slight pause, then the hair was rolled into a bun and a black hairpin pushed in with force.

The harangue continued to rain down on the unfortunate girl. "Now, don't fret, dear, Bina has more milk than she knows what to do with…and you, hardly anything, not your fault, maybe, it's how you were brought up." There she goes again, thought Kanta, always about her family and upbringing. The pins were biting into her scalp. She would let her hair down as soon as the old woman's back was turned.

She swallowed her tears, as she had been doing every day. Allowed to have her son for an hour each day, Kanta only lived for that one hour. She was planning to read out loud to her son the first letter she had received from her husband.

However, things did not go as planned.

Kanta's health began to deteriorate. She was plagued by headaches and even her vision was failing. Starting with the odd pricking sensation behind her eyes, it had gradually become constant, so that she now had trouble even focusing on objects. *Boroma* put it down to after-childbirth pains. More home-grown concoctions were made that Kanta had to swallow, almost by the hour, each day.

Notwithstanding her health problems, Kanta determined to go ahead with plans for her son's baptism. She expected opposition and was surprised when *Boroma* went so far as to suggest an elaborate lunch after the ceremony. Soon, however, the real reason behind her sudden goodwill became apparent. She unequivocally opposed Father Aloysius's involvement. The priest had taken charge of the school that Kunjan had established on the estate.

One day after lunch, when everyone had retired to their rooms, Kanta began to inch her way down the long corridor. She was headed for the room at the very end, the place where her son lived - eating, playing, growing by the minute, smiling and, also, like all babies, throwing tantrums. Sweet music to a mother's ear. Kanta was not a part of this daily routine. The walls offered support when her limbs gave way and her eyes would not co-operate.

When she reached her destination, she stood by the door quietly, taking in the scene before her. After a minute had elapsed, Kanta had had enough. She fought back angry tears and stepped forward. At the same time, *Boroma,* who was sitting on the floor with her back to the door, turned. From her lap, Khokon gurgled at the sight of his mother.

Kanta wanted to lash out, to hurt the old woman. The only way she knew how was to say, "Father Aloysius will perform the ceremony, so we'll have to send him word." She had had to give up Bible studies since the priest was no longer welcome at the house, not after Kunjan's death.

"We can do without the priest." Her black eyes flickered over Kanta's dishevelled figure. Then, popping a *paan* into her mouth, *Boroma* said, "He only comes here so he can get a free meal."

"That's not true, and we need him to perform the ceremony," Kanta said. When there was no response, she played her trump card. "You know Khokon's father would want it." With this, Kanta turned her back on the woman holding her baby and left. She was determined to win this fight. She looked around the hall, empty just like her own life had become, and tried to suppress a sob.

The ceremony took place in a hurried fashion. Father Aloysius had been given half an hour to work his magic, as *Boroma* described it, a smirk on her face. Lunch was not provided.

Kanta was learning to choose her battles, and she decided to let that one go.

One day, Kanta awoke to a dark world. She had slept badly. Her head hurt – again this was nothing new – and the warm milk which *Boroma* insisted she drink before retiring had made her vomit. She watched helplessly as Bina cleaned it up, and when the maid hesitated by the door, wondering if there was anything else, Kanta sent her away.

Now none of the objects in the room were visible. In a rising panic, she sat up and rubbed at her eyes furiously. When this did not help, Kanta stumbled to the bathroom to splash cold water on her eyes.

Soon after, her cry of pain, followed by a crash, brought the household running to the bathroom, where they found Kanta lying on the wet floor. Her white sari had splatters of blood, making a pattern of red dots. Clutched in her right hand was a mirror broken in half.

It appeared that she had picked up the mirror from where it always stood by the edge of the water reservoir. Mirror in one hand, she had stumbled against the bucket. The bathroom was dark, even during the day.

Boroma, calm and efficient, had said, "Don't just stand there staring, lift her – gently, mind you. And Bina, come here." The maid approached closer, a terrified expression on her face. "You will take care of your mistress. You know what to do."

That afternoon Kanta came down with a fever. Her body shook with violent shivers making even her teeth chatter. No number of covers seemed able to bring warmth to her cold limbs. *Boroma* sat by Kanta's bed, from time to time, trying to make her drink some milk and cool water. Then, at one point, she left the room.

Kanta turned her face towards Bina. She whispered, "Go, get the *baidyo*. I need the doctor...please." Her plea did not bring the desired result. It was decided by the old mistress that there was no place for a doctor when she knew how to take care of the sick.

The fever remained. On the third night, Kanta spoke again to the maid, who was helping to prepare her for bed. With the precious little remaining strength, she managed to say, "Get the priest."

Kanta lost count of days, hours, minutes. Drifting in and out of consciousness at one point, she became aware of another presence in the room and knew instinctively it was Father Aloysius. How did that happen? Something within her was telling her help had arrived. This priest had nursed her husband when he had been a boarder at St. Paul's, and had contracted typhoid. Kanta knew all about it. She had listened with fascination when her husband had told her the story.

Wanting to speak, she tried to open her mouth, but her jaw was clamped shut. Once again, Kanta fought desperately against these new sensations.

"So, what can you do that I haven't done already?" Kanta's heart fluttered, a great sigh escaped her lips, and she became motionless. No one had heard *Boroma* enter.

Standing at the door, Bina couldn't believe their bad luck. She had planned everything carefully, making sure of the exact time the old woman spent in the temple. Yet, they had all been fooled. And here she was, the reason for all of Kanta's misery. The maid huddled in her corner and waited for the storm to explode. Whether Father Aloysius sensed the fear in the room would never be known; he simply turned back to the bed and, folding the palms of his hands, began to pray. The moment of danger had passed.

The prayer ended after a few minutes. Kanta's hoarse whisper came as though from a distance, "Why did this happen to me? Why am I being punished? What wrong have I done? My husband did not even get a chance to see his son."

Choosing his words carefully, the priest answered, "Kantabali, I cannot explain the mysterious ways of God, but I can say that maybe when we think we have come to the end of our tether, we actually gain strength from our experiences, to move forward. You have been dealt a tragic and painful blow. Perhaps, the way to deal with this pain is to find out how you can use it to make you a stronger person to bring up your son."

Kanta's eyes opened and rested upon the priest's face. Her blind grey eyes held a world of sadness. Then from her mouth poured words and disjointed phrases, anguished appeals, angry remonstrations – she spoke rapidly, as if afraid time would run out.

At one point, Father Aloysius half turned towards the door where *Boroma* had been standing. It was empty. Bina stood in her place.

Kanta rushed on – allowed only a half hour with her own baby… he slept in the other room – far away, down the hall, how cruel… she was his mother, and must care for her own child, a legacy from her husband. She had finally run out of breath and lay on the bed heaving great sobs.

Boroma was supreme in the Rai household, especially after Kunjan's father died. Since their arrival at Bundhpur, the family temple dedicated to Lord Krishna and his consort Radha had been re-opened.

The priest hastened to assure her that since the baby had been baptized, Kanta had nothing to fear. "You need to take care of yourself, be strong so you can bring up your son in the Christian faith."

"But I do not feel strong," replied Kanta with trembling lips.

The priest knelt down beside the bed, his black cassock spreading out like the wings of a crow. He picked up one of Kanta's hands and began to speak, urgency lending depth to his already deep voice. "Do you remember how Kunjan used to play with you in the early days of your marriage? He told me that as you grew older, you learnt to stand up to *Boroma* and her unnecessary demands. So, there you see – you already have something that most of us need at some time or other. Courage. Kantabali, you have courage. Now, you have to call upon that hidden quality to see you through this very difficult period of your life. Do it for yourself and your son. Go forward in the memory of your husband."

Bina took a step forward; the priest was too close to Kanta, the way he held her hand did not look right. She felt she should intervene. Something stopped her though, and she remained where she was. Father Aloysius was gazing at Kanta with longing; there was tenderness in his blue eyes. The very air in the room had begun to tremble with a myriad of emotions, danger foremost, when Bina coughed. The sound broke the spell. Almost immediately, Father Aloysius stood up. The face he turned to the maid had a lopsided smile. Bina nodded slightly. This was the man who had rescued her from a horrible fate; sheltered and fed her, arranged for her to travel to the Rai estate in the company of Shanti Ram, who would later become her husband; all because he had loved and respected Prince Kunjan and wanted to help an innocent girl like herself. Besides her own husband, in Bina's opinion, if ever there was a man of integrity, then that was the priest.

Kanta's thoughts had flown like a homing bird to that part of the universe where her heart lay, beside her soulmate. She seemed not to notice the priest's proximity as she rose from the bed. With faltering steps, she proceeded to the verandah, their private sanctum, hers and Kunjan's, from the first day. She was heading for the chair in the far corner. Rain or shine, it stood in its place, as if waiting. Kunjan used to sit in this chair while Kanta, sitting cross-legged on the floor, did the lessons set by him.

The thin hand touched the chair, finger-tips gently brushing against the wickerwork. Then she lowered herself to the ground, and lay her head on the seat.

Kanta, why do you have to touch the puppy in front of Boroma? Now she'll make you take another bath. It was music, and poetry, in the voice, if that was possible, floating in the sudden wind, blowing its magic over Kanta. She closed her eyes, praying for it to stay; then, the wind veered and a swirl of dust blew through the branches of the nearby mango grove, only to disappear once again. The air became still.

Father Aloysius had followed her; he now stood hesitating by the steps leading to the backyard. Bina stood watching. Moments elapsed, after which he folded his palms together in leave-taking of the dreaming girl, then walked away.

Kanta sat alone, deep in thought, until her reverie was broken by the lusty wails of her young son. She left the chair in a rush, steps faltering in her weakened state. With a tremendous effort she managed to save herself by clutching at the door with one hand. Silently, she leaned against the warm wood, as if drawing strength. Kunjan used to lean against it while watching her play hopscotch.

She took a deep breath, tried to focus her eyes, and was barely able to make out the blurred image of the maid holding her baby. She began to walk forward. Bina placed the baby gently in her mistress's outstretched arms. She said, "*Bowma*, sit up on the bed and play with Khokon as long as you want. *Boroma* has returned to the temple."

ELEVEN

Chandni
Bundhpur – 1976

Chandni's eyes flew open. She was in a tiny hut, a fire pit at its centre with a small earthenware pot on the floor beside her, its bottom blackened, something a villager would use to cook. She blinked, then rubbed at her eyes, trying desperately to emerge from the fog that seemed to have her in its unshakeable grip. Where was she? Deeply puzzled, she looked around for clues, and she saw the sleeping form in the corner. With this discovery came relief. She was with *Dadaji*; they had travelled together through the jungle, eaten a meal and fallen asleep. Time to start for *Dadaji's* house. She rose from the cramped position where she had fallen asleep, walked to the prone figure by the firepit and tapped lightly on the shoulder. He awoke immediately.

"Should we start walking?" Chandni asked, although her feet screamed.

"Yes, *Beti*, let's do that. Soon it'll be dark."

They checked the pit, making sure the fire was out completely, then gathered up their belongings and walked through the door. Since wearing sandals was out of the question, Chandni had bound her feet with strips torn from her sari.

It seemed that she had run out of words, or was simply too tired to speak. She let him lead the way. Uppermost in her mind was finding shelter, and when she mentioned this, he assured her she could stay with his family. *Dadaji's* house was a mere mile away in the village of Bundhpur. She brightened at the good news; she would stop awhile at his house, clean up, maybe even spend a night. After the botched attempt to journey to Mauchak, she was in no mood to try it again, and was already planning to return to Masjidpur.

Chandni rubbed the nape of her neck. By now, TJ's parents must know about the train holdup. She kept her eyes on the ground, each step bringing them closer to safety, and refused to dwell on what had taken place. Time enough for that – she knew she could handle all the bother about getting a train ticket back. And, confronting her mother-in-law after the lies she had told? She'd sort it all out later.

The village heralded its proximity by the number of goats grazing in the bushes and a narrow path of stones and gravel that led to what appeared to be a meeting place under a banyan tree. Underneath it, and running the circumference of the broad trunk, was a bench of mud and stones closely packed together. On the bench sat a group of men.

Coming closer, Chandni saw they were smoking from a hookah, passing it around for each to take a puff. The setting sun cast shadows on the group, turning the whole into a semblance of a painting by a master painter. The day had darkened considerably; clouds hovering on the horizon promised rain.

With swift steps, *Dadaji* approached the group. Chandni hung back. She was starting to wonder if she had done the right thing in venturing to this village with a stranger for a guide. Perhaps she should have waited by the train, maybe even spoken to the people in the Jeep. What if *Dadaji's* friends did not like her? What if they turned out to be just as ruthless as those *dacoits*? Both belonged to this region – those *dacoits* and these villagers.

Dadaji had been kindness itself, and he had promised to take her to the one person who might be able to tell her about her grandparents. This, and this alone, stamped out the rising panic.

Just then, *Dadaji* turned and beckoned her over. After she had been introduced to the men, who were likely the *panchayat* of the village, it was agreed unanimously that she should be escorted to Bina, the woman who had been closely linked with the Rai family.

With mounting excitement, for now she was getting somewhere, she hurried after her companion, the cloth foot bindings coming loose due to the pace. But she wouldn't stop. Bloody blisters, tiredness and hunger were shoved to the corners of her consciousness.

Bina.

Repeating the name under her breath, the name which meant the stringed instrument played by the goddess Saraswati - goddess of music, wisdom, art and learning - she tried to gauge its nature. And, she felt sweetness.

She leaned forward, trying to see the ancient face beside her, half hidden under his turban. "Who is this woman? My mother never talked of her. And, most importantly, how did she get involved with the royal Rais?"

Dadaji said, "All we know is this woman served the Rais. She has been living in our community for a long time. I don't know anymore, *Beti*." He spread his hands palms up, head to one side. Chandni fell silent. Her mind whirled with questions, but she had to be satisfied with what she got. At least for now.

Bina's dwelling stood at some distance from the rest and exuded a certain air of prosperity. Built of mud and brick, it had a tiled roof, and in the light of the setting sun gave off a warm glow. Eager and nervous, Chandni let her gaze travel all over the cottage. A wooden gate opened into a tiny garden that appeared meticulously tended. Whoever looked after it must know what they were doing, for the vegetable patch sprouted beans, tomatoes and onions, along with herbs like coriander and mint. As if this wasn't enough, the gardener had thoughtfully planted a line of marigolds and another of hibiscus, to keep bugs at bay. The corner of Chandni's mouth quirked up; she was all too familiar with kitchen produce.

Her feet slowed and she hesitated. What would she find? Presumably information about her grandmother, she reminded herself.

Her hands clenched of their own accord. She discovered she had been holding her breath, which she now let out in a great sigh. Immediately, *Dadaji* was all concern. "Are you alright, *Beti*?"

Chandni nodded. She wasn't about to let on that she was afraid to enter the house.

"You have turned so pale," the old man said, indicating her face.

"How can you tell, *Dadaji*? The sun must have burnt my skin, after all that walking."

"*Beti*, you have the face of a *devi* with the pale skin to match. No amount of sun will take away that golden hue."

Taken aback, she pulled at the end of her *anchal*, covering her head. Any mention of her face, the close resemblance it bore to the goddess Durga, had always embarrassed her. On numerous occasions, her uncle had mentioned it, but never her mother. She was not one for extolling her daughter's beauty, which Chandni began to appreciate as she grew older.

Well, it was now or never.

She unhooked the latch and entered the garden. *"Here goes,"* she whispered to herself. In spite of the excitement and impatience she was feeling, she hesitated once again.

Dadaji, following close behind, saw her hesitation. He mounted the steps and called out, "*Mataji*, you have a guest."

There was a scurry of running feet and a girl of about five peeped out of the dark interior. She seemed to know the old man, for she dimpled at him, then ran back inside the cottage.

Chandni looked at *Dadaji*. He nodded at the open door. "That little girl is her great-granddaughter."

Soon there were shuffling footsteps accompanied by the tinkle of glass bangles. In the next instant, two figures emerged on the front stoop. Chandni's eyes widened. The one to the right, her tiny frame seemingly too frail to even hold up a head, had to be Bina. Silver strands of wayward hair were visible from under a black shawl. Thick glasses covered eyes that were looking intently at Chandni, who had the uncomfortable feeling that her innermost thoughts had just been uncovered. She was supported by another woman.

During the time of peril, escape being foremost on both their minds, formal introductions had seemed unnecessary. So, *Dadaji* did not know her name. Chandni stepped forward, and folding her palms together, said, "I am sorry for bothering you this way, but when *Dadaji*," she smiled at the old man standing beside her, "told me that you knew the Rai family, I had to see you."

The woman dropped her eyes. Chandni wondered if she had been too abrupt. Maybe she should have waited, but this was her chance – she couldn't wait any longer. She had to speak with this woman, find out what she knew.

Just when Chandni was about to ask *Dadaji* to intervene, Bina spoke. "Who are you, *Beti*?"

"My name is Chandni. I am the granddaughter of Prince Kunjan and his wife Kantabali."

The older woman murmured, adding something in a voice gravelly from disuse. She came closer, then placed the tip of a gnarled finger under Chandni's chin. The faded eyes scrutinized her face, seeming to take in every detail; she then touched Chandni's forehead as if in blessing.

At Bina's touch, a sensation of utter contentment flowed through her. Chandni smiled at her. She knew this person would be her ally, the one who held the key to the mystery she wanted to solve.

The wind rose and fell, creating a wave through the garden, and an air of hushed expectation pervaded the entire landscape.

Bina said, "You will spend the night with us. You seem tired and need to rest. We heard about the train holdup and we worried about him" – indicating *Dadaji* – "but I thank the gods that you remained untouched." To Chandni's immense surprise, Bina was speaking Bengali. But, of course. She *was* Bengali, although her clothes were typical of the local region.

"I accept your hospitality and thank you so much."

Before the old man took his leave, Chandni thanked him for bringing her to Bundhpur and Bina, promising to pay his family a visit. She then turned back to the cottage. This was going to be home for a couple of days.

That night, Chandni had a dream. In the dream, she saw a girl at the window of the hut where she had rested with *Dadaji*. When the girl beckoned, Chandni rose to follow, but the girl disappeared immediately. Not one to give up, Chandni, walking fast, was able to finally catch up with the girl. She wanted to see the face, but however much she tried, the girl's face remained in shadow. They passed the crumbling wall where Chandni had rested that morning. The day started to darken, with ominous clouds racing each other in the vast sky. Chandni shivered and tightened her *anchal* around her shoulder like a protective shield. Why was she following a stranger?

As if sensing her sudden doubts, the girl looked back. The face remained hidden, but Chandni knew it had a smile on it. It was a strange feeling, this smile that she could not see, but instinctively knew to be sweet and encouraging, and she was filled with renewed hope; all the tiredness and dreadful worries of the previous hours seemed to melt away, filling her instead with pure energy and a sense of infinite happiness.

They had now reached a thicket, which revealed the remains of an abandoned house. The girl opened the front door with a key hanging on a chain from her waist.

Chandni took a step forward, only to feel emptiness under her feet. Her body began to hurtle into a bottomless chasm.

"Wake up, *Didi*." Someone was shaking her shoulder. With great difficulty, Chandni opened eyes that seemed to be glued shut, and let her gaze roam around the room. She realized she had been dreaming. Like all dreams, this had appeared real, so much so that the image of the girl walking away remained in front of her.

But here was someone with a cup of tea, trying to wake her. Had she screamed? She asked the woman who had supported Bina in the doorway yesterday.

"No, no, *Didi,*" the woman assured her. "Drink this, then come out to the kitchen to have some food."

As the woman turned to leave, Chandni put out a hand to stop her and asked, "How are you related to Bina?"

The woman stopped and, looking steadily into Chandni's eyes, said, "*Didima*, that's what she is to me. And the little girl you saw yesterday, that's my daughter." She spoke freely, and yet Chandni felt that she was being teased. At the door, she added, "She's waiting for you."

She had said *Didima* – Bengali for maternal grandmother. In this region, where the dialect was as dry as the landscape, the sound of her own language filled her with warmth. Chandni began to feel more comfortable in her strange surroundings.

After washing up in the cold water that had been left for her use, Chandni searched out the kitchen, where she was served fresh roti and vegetables cooked in a simple gravy. She devoured the delicious meal then went in search of Bina.

Reflecting on the spate of events that had followed her marriage to TJ, she felt a twinge of guilt. Her husband of a few weeks had taken a back seat while she planned this trip. She'd make it up to him, she promised herself. Setting out from Masjidpur, she could not have foreseen what lay ahead, but she was glad she'd made the trip.

And, perversely, the train holdup now seemed to have been fated, bringing her to Bina.

She entered the courtyard. Here, draped in a black shawl, was the old woman of yesterday. She was seated on a woven cot under the shade of a *neem* tree and appeared to be lost in deep thought.

It was still early enough to retain some of the previous night's cooler air; a goat tethered to a post chewed contentedly while a few chickens scratched in the dirt. The smell of dung mingled in the morning air; it came from the single cow in her stall chewing her cud. This smell also had a comforting feel to it, just like the dung and mud Chandni had mixed to cover *Dadaji's* wound.

Had it been only yesterday?

She waited, unwilling to break into Bina's reverie, but her presence had been felt; without looking up, the old woman motioned for her to take a seat. Her hand tucked something away inside the folds of the shawl.

Perching herself in one corner of the cot, Chandni took out her notebook.

Bina smiled with such sweetness that all the fear, tiredness and self-doubt Chandni had been experiencing melted away, leaving in its wake senses sharpened as a honed knife. Despite the scratchiness, Bina's voice had a fluidity while the eyes behind the heavy lenses glowed.

"When I saw you for the first time, I thought Kantabali had come back to life."

Chandni's eyes widened. Had she heard right?

A sudden gust of wind caught at the end of the shawl, exposing the hand clutching at a piece of paper. After she had fixed her garment, Bina handed the paper to Chandni. It was a charcoal portrait of a young woman. As Chandni looked closely, the face began to take on an uncanny familiarity. She leaned closer, the drawing almost touching her nose. She was stunned. What she had in her hand was a replica of her own face.

Hand over mouth, she sat, her mind wrestling with question after question. Why hadn't her parents said anything? Didn't they know? Kanta had disappeared soon after her own father was born. There were no photographs of her at home. Her father had been brought up by his great-grandmother, *Boroma*. At the thought of *Boroma*, once again, Chandni was reminded of that momentous day. The broken picture frame, their neighbour maligning Kanta. All this so soon after her father's death.

She had been given a chance to get to the truth. Kanta's name had to be redeemed.

"You are excited?" Bina's simple question crashed against Chandni's ears, breaking up the turbulent thoughts. She had so many questions. After some thought, she decided to start with the photograph.

"How did you get this picture? Who was the artist?"

"I'll tell you, all in good time – you have to be patient."

"Did you know my grandfather, Prince Kunjan?"

Bina nodded, a faraway look coming across her features. "Yes, I knew him. If ever there was a courageous, loyal and loving soul, then that was Prince Kunjan." She stopped. Her eyes were hooded, staring into the distance, as if into another world.

Chandni decided to hold her peace, letting Bina's mind roam across those years, and for her patience was rewarded with a comforting smile.

"Daughter, I am tired with all this – you know I am ancient." Here she broke into delighted laughter and when Chandni responded likewise, she continued, "Let's eat and rest a while, and I promise you that you will hear a story the likes of which you have not heard before."

TWELVE

Bina speaks, Chandni listens
Bundhpur – 1976

I was sixteen when I first saw Kunjan. He must have been around the same age. I don't know. It happened like this. I was fond of singing and dancing, so when the *mela* came to our village, I went to see it, even when my father forbade me to. He wouldn't let me get married, turning down proposal after proposal. I knew how his mind worked. If I got married, who would look after him and my young brother? Of course, I resented it with all my heart. I had to watch my friends get married, one by one, and leave our village. I was young and hot-blooded. So, when the *mela* came, off I went to see it, drinking in the sights and sounds. Watching a dance, I never noticed how late it had become, not until the lamps had been lit and the road back home appeared a dark hole.

I was trying to decide which way to go, when all of a sudden, a man appeared, as if he had been waiting. His clothes were of the finest silk. On his fingers he wore gold rings and he smelled so good. What was a *bhodrolok* doing here? I never questioned, for I was smitten. Oh, he was handsome like Shiva and had a lovely smile. He offered to escort me home in his carriage. Stupid me, I agreed. Next thing I was lying flat on my face in the mud in the compound of a building and my head was bursting with pain. I tried to call out, "O Ma, where am I?" but no sound came from me. My mouth tasted horrible and my voice seemed to have disappeared.

I lay there, afraid to move. When someone came by, I pretended to be dead. It was just a sweeper woman. From her, I discovered that this was a brothel, you know, where men have fun with girls and women, in Kolkata's Golpara, that notorious place. I had been sold to the madame. I was lucky nothing had happened to me so far, just a few bruises, but soon I was supposed to be cleaned up before the madame put me to work.

Ram Ram, this was punishment for disobeying my father. But I had to get away. The question was, how? My body trembled with fright and I begged the sweeper woman to let me remain hidden under some rubbish, and she, bless her soul, agreed. She hated the madame. So, there I lay, hidden under a pile of garbage, when the door to the compound opened and in walked a tall white man. He was wearing a long garment of black cloth. I knew him to be a priest, for these people often came to our village to talk and play with the children. I had never taken any notice of them. But today it seemed one of these strange creatures would come to use. I needed only to remain hidden until such a time when I could tell him my story. My heart told me he was a kind man and would rescue me from this horrible place.

He was followed by a group of boys. They followed the priest to a room in the front of the building. This, I saw later, was the storeroom, with stacks of grain piled high. I called the sweeper woman and asked what was going on. She seemed to know everything. She said these were students from a Christian school the whites had built for boys of rich parents. They were here to teach by putting on a show. Why in a brothel? I asked. The woman said the priest and students came sometimes to do this kind of thing, and everyone loved them. At the mention of a show, or drama, my heart beat fast, and I thought, where's the harm in watching it, from afar that is, so no one sees me. She agreed. She seemed to have taken a liking to me almost as if I were her daughter. I crept up the stairs along with a bunch of children who belonged to the women of the brothel. I have always been small, so I could mingle easily with the children. I made sure to keep my face hidden under my hair. The boys set up a stage, and then a very strange drama began.

The small room was soon packed, some edging closer to the stage, among them a woman with a nursing baby. They were so close they could touch the actors had they wanted to.

The morning had turned stormy. O Ma, it felt like the gods were very upset. Lightning and thunder fighting to be in the front and us poor beings in the middle of this rage. Then came the rain. It drummed on the tin roof of the room like Lord Shiva's *damaru*. Children grew frightened, which kept the parents busy trying to calm them. Someone lit a lamp and placed it in the window, but the flame flickered in the wind, so it was moved to the floor, in front of the stage.

A young man, about my age, was standing to the side of the stage and reading from a book. It was in Bengali so we could all understand. I still remember the story – it was about two sons and their father. The younger demands his inheritance, gets it and leaves home. The older son stays to till the land and look after his father's property. One day, the younger son returns and is welcomed lovingly by his father.

Bina stopped in her narration and seemed lost in thought. Instinct told Chandni this was an important part, and she waited eagerly, but Bina did not display any inclination to carry on.

Minutes ticked by as Chandni waited. There was a lot more in Bina's story, she knew. And the end had to be heard today – for tomorrow she was heading back to Masjidpur.

At the expense of appearing rude, Chandni asked, her voice unnaturally loud in the stillness of the courtyard, "What happened next?"

Bina fixed her glasses firmly on her nose and sighed, a long quivering breath full of recollections. Once more she started to speak. This time her voice rose and fell as memories, like pictures, crowded in her mind.

The woman with the child got into trouble. She was watching the drama so closely that she failed to notice the flickering flame making its way up her sari, like a thief who scales the walls of a home, intent upon stealing. When she did notice, the tiny lick had spread and was about to reach the child. She began to scream, but her limbs wouldn't move. Some watched goggle-eyed, others joined in the screaming and yelling and useless advice, and fighting to get out, trampled upon each other, not bothering to help the ones that fell – I was one of those. I must have been very weak, for I hadn't eaten since the day before. But before I fell, I saw the white man come charging in and the one reading from the book joined him. I fainted.

Bina took a noisy sip from the brass tumbler, from which wisps of steam arose, only to dissipate in the air. There was tension in her body as if she were reliving, once again, that frightful day.

When I came to, I found the young man kneeling by my side and fanning my face. I was covered in a quilt. My clothes had been badly burnt and what remained of them were not enough to hide my shame. My hands and legs would not stop shivering. The madame was sure to look for me now.

He must have sensed my fear, for he said in the gentlest voice I have ever heard, "*Bon*, don't be afraid. I am Prince Kunjan Rai and want to help you, for I know, from the sweeper woman, that you have suffered grave injustice. We came to give the children a chance to watch a wonderful play. The story came from the Bible."

I listened to his soothing voice, mightily relieved that soon my troubles would be over. I felt safe in his presence. Soon the priest came along, and the two entered the house. I was in mortal fear. Would they help me escape? What if the madame did not give me up, for she had paid for me and would not want to lose out. My anxiety made me retch, but there was nothing to bring up. I continued to worry, my stomach in knots, and wondered if I should try to make a run for it. But where would I go? I did not know Kolkata at all. So, there I was, hot and cold by turn, huddled under the quilt and trying to make myself invisible to the curious stares.

What transpired in the house, I have no idea, but I believe they – the priest and the young man – forced the madame to hand me over. Who would have courage to stand against a high-born in the company of a *gora*?

Then the priest and Prince Kunjan had a discussion, and I knew it was about me, for the boys kept looking at me, not rudely, mind, but with curiosity and maybe a bit of wonder. They seemed to have reached an agreement. I was told that Prince Kunjan's estate manager would escort me home. And I found myself walking with Shanti Ram, manager of the Rai estate.

Cruel fate had other plans. When I reached home, my father slammed the door on my face. He said I was tainted, for I had been in the company of strange men.

Here, Bina's voice took on a husky note. It was Shanti Ram, a man of few words, and completely devoted to the royal Rai family, who had taken her heart.

A sixteen-year-old girl, who had been thrown out of her home, Bina's chances of survival were slim. And, yet, it was the Rais who came to her rescue, offering her employment when she was discarded by her own family.

Bina's story stayed with Chandni long after they had parted ways for the day. There was so much to absorb, and even more to write. The break seemed a good idea. She closed her eyes with a tired sigh. There was more, she was convinced. And the only way to hear all of it was to spend another day with Bina.

THIRTEEN

Bina speaks, Chandni listens
Bundhpur – 1976

With regret, Chandni had arrived at the decision to stay another day, knowing that spending an extra day here meant not going forward to Mauchak. But Bina's story had to be heard.

Chandni leaned back against the pillows, a small smile playing around her mouth. Bina's words, reminiscing about those long-ago days, had spilt out with the force of rushing water through a broken dam, free, unfettered – and there was more.

Having decided, Chandni felt a lightness of spirit and was about to rise when Bina's granddaughter appeared at the door. She had been summoned.

This time, Chandni came straight to the point. "Can you tell me about Kanta's marriage to Kunjan? And when did they move to Bundhpur? Also, tell me about Kunjan's *Boroma*, for I believe she came here with them."

Bina nodded, her mouth working vigorously in preparation to speak. Wrapped in her *anchal* was the same brass tumbler, brimming with hot tea. Chandni sat down and opened her notebook.

Kanta came to Golapdanga as Kunjan's bride. She was eleven. O Ma, was she ever naughty, forever getting into a scrape with *Boroma*! She was like the sun in monsoon, here one minute, gone the next.

I was installed as her personal maid, so I had to make sure she never ran around with her head uncovered, which happened so many times, or that she didn't play with the estate children. She wanted to. Of course, she wasn't allowed, for how could a bride of the mighty Rais do such a thing? So, she stuck to me, and we played with dolls that she had brought with her. Kunjan was teaching her to read and write in *Bangla* and the *gora bhasha* and later Kanta taught me some of it. That is why I can write my name and simple sentences in *Bangla*.

Kanta slept in *Boroma's* room; she hadn't bled yet and could not be a real wife to her husband. *Boroma* kept her on a leash, you know.

But Kanta, I discovered, didn't like rules; her parents had indulged her highly. She used to dip her hands in cold water, run to her husband's room and touch his face with wet hands – then laugh. Many times, I brought her back before anyone noticed. One day, I remember, she escaped from her room very early, and what do you think she did? I ran after her down the verandah. but she was hiding in Kunjan's bed, with him in it. I could do nothing then. Only stand guard. O Ma, in a few minutes Kunjan's personal servant arrived to wake his master. We both pretended not to notice the second pair of feet sticking out of the bedclothes.

I think Kanta was starting to fall in love with her husband and was impatient to be his wife. Even Kunjan's attitude had changed. Where in the beginning he would pinch her cheeks or pull her hair, now he never touched her except on the shoulder. Once I caught him gazing at Kanta with such longing in his eyes that I wondered how no one noticed. I felt it was high time *Boroma* allowed the two to live together. But who was I? My feelings were not important, lowly servant that I was. I could only watch and wait.

Just about this time, Kunjan decided to change his religion. You know, he became a Christian because of his teacher, the priest's influence. We found out that when the prince had typhoid, it was this priest who had looked after him and saved him from sure death. The two were great friends, and he even moved to Bundhpur when we came here.

Pen poised in mid-air, Chandni stopped writing to ask, "What was the fort like when you came here? And how old was Kanta then?"

Bina took a sip of tea and kneaded her knotted hands, one over the other, for the vessel was heavy. She called for her granddaughter, and when she arrived, Bina stretched out her legs. The younger woman began to massage them.

After a few minutes had elapsed, Bina sighed with contentment and, waving away her granddaughter, she continued her story.

Kanta was eleven-twelve, maybe? I'm not very sure. It was a few months after they were married. Kunjan's father, the raja, had booked a full train for us to journey to Bundhpur. Can you imagine how excited we were, Kanta and I? And it was so grand with beds, chairs, carpets, so many lights that my eyes remained dazzled, even our food was cooked in the special kitchen on the train. We travelled for two days and nights.

When we arrived at the station in Bundhpur, *palkis* were waiting, so we got in, the two of us in one, *Boroma* in another. Kunjan and the estate manager rode on horseback. The servants were on bullock carts to mind the luggage. And there was so much of everything. Runners had gone ahead to warn the servants at the fort. Rooms had to be readied. The family maintained a full staff in case the master, Kunjan's father, came to visit.

The carriers, four strong men, lifted our *palki* and we were off, swaying this way and that. They sang to keep time; it had a soothing effect on Kanta, for she soon dozed off. Poor thing, she was tired. I was too excited to close my eyes and stayed glued to the curtain, trying to take in as much as I could of the passing countryside. *Maa-go*, it was dry and dusty, so different from our beautiful Golapdanga. I didn't see a single *pukur* throughout.

Kanta woke when one of the carriers stumbled. She was thirsty, and I served her first before taking a drink, myself. We had left the dusty part and were travelling through a different kind of region. Now there was a jungle on either side, dark and treacherous.

We were nearing the fort, for its outline showed through the curtain. It was late afternoon. We stared at it with our mouths wide open. The Rai *rajbari* itself rose from the jungle to face us like Shiva's bull Nandi, powerful but kind, the stones shining in the sun. Oh, it was a wondrous sight. The high walls had been made out of rocks from the hills we had passed earlier.

Our procession slowed, for now we were climbing uphill. From houses on both sides, people came out to line up by the roadside. They must have known the Rais were coming, for they stood with heads bowed and did *pranam* to Kunjan and *Boroma*.

Now we came close to a wooden gate with a broad *chaukat*. It looked grand and menacing, for it was lined with pointed iron spikes, all staring down. I didn't like them. But the gate itself was a thing of beauty, all carved with chariots and horses and men in armour, also flowers, fruits and animals. A group of servants waited by this door.

Kanta took hold of the curtain and pulled it aside to get a better look. She gasped, pointing at the door. I guessed what was in her mind, but before I could say anything, she had jumped out. And, then what does she do? She hitched up her sari and ran towards the door, I guess to get a better look. Just then, *Boroma's palki* passed by. I caught the look she gave Kanta.

My blood ran cold. So much venom in that look. I was mortally afraid I would lose my job, for I was supposed to always keep an eye on the minx. But Prince Kunjan was already bending down from his horse and whispering to Kanta. She laughed and hurried back to our *palki*. I thanked Kunjan in my heart. He could make Kanta do anything.

Somehow, even with the age difference, they seemed to have a special bond.

I was still worried. What kind of punishment would *Boroma* mete out to us? I knew I would be punished, for I had failed to look after Kanta.

Well, nothing happened until the next morning. Kunjan had left early to meet the tenant farmers and would not be back until evening.

Sometime before, in Golapdanga, Kanta had rescued a stray. Well, now that I think about it, actually, it was me. We were caring for it and managed to smuggle him in to Bundhpur with one of the servants. Kunjan knew about it and was happy to help. Somehow, *Boroma* must have found out. She ordered me to escort Kanta to the inner verandah and stay behind the *chikh*. She said we needed to watch something, and learn.

We were standing behind the *chikh* when *Boroma* went down to the courtyard and spoke to a young man, one of the peasants.

Now we saw our pup in his arms.

In a clear voice *Boroma* ordered the pup to be drowned and gave him money to do it. I caught hold of Kanta before she could say anything – I knew her so well now – and dragged her into one of the rooms. Here I stayed with her, trying to reason while she trembled all over as though sick and swore to get even. I asked, "How? How will you get even with the old woman?" She raised tear-filled eyes and said, "You'll see. One day, I will." She grew quiet after that and I was relieved.

I tell you, that *budhia* was evil. Always so loving in front of Kunjan, but the minute his back was turned. she would do things, little ones but very hurtful, to Kanta. We, the servants, knew she had no love for Kunjan's bride. Maybe that is why she was keeping them apart.

Chandni's hand gripped the pen, knuckles showing white against its black tube. She would never know what had gone on in the young Kanta's mind at this kind of treatment.

"Did she, Kanta, ever show her feelings to you, since you were with her most of the time? Did you see her cry?"

Bina shook her head. "No, I never saw her cry, but I did see her sitting quietly sometimes, and this was difficult since she was always very active, talking to her dolls or playing. I once overheard her saying to her doll not to be sad, that they would visit their parents soon. I drew closer to hear more. Kanta made up a story of sprouting wings and flying away, away from the cave where they were held prisoner by a witch, but they had to wait for the prince. For they couldn't leave him behind."

Bina stopped speaking, took off her spectacles and closed her eyes. With a guilty start, Chandni realized she had kept the woman talking far too long. She began to apologize.

Bina patted Chandni's arm and said, "This old body of mine has no respect for guests. It demands rest even when I don't want to."

"Oh, of course, I am so sorry – I should have noticed."

"Never mind, we can talk again tomorrow. Now you go and rest also."

Chandni walked over to the small garden. Even in the heat, surprisingly, it seemed to have a good yield. Choosing a spot beside a row of potatoes, she sat down, lifted a clump of earth to bring it close to her nose and inhaled its earthiness. This act helped to calm her nerves. But the picture of Kanta – alone, helpless, the only person remotely sympathetic being the maid, taking refuge in imaginary conversations with dolls – would not leave.

It was getting late. The shadows brought on by the setting sun seemed to speak in the language of melancholy. Chandni stood up, heavy of heart. She felt as ancient as Bina.

She had many more questions to ask, which meant spending yet another day with Bina.

FOURTEEN

Bina speaks, Chandni listens
Bundhpur – 1976

Chandni had worked late once again, going through her notes and putting them in order. She wished she had a recorder. That would have made her task easier. There was so much yet to be done. She was afraid that she was tiring the old woman and said so to Bina, who simply told her it had to come out. She had been holding it all for so long and finally could release it all to Chandni, to a member of the Rai family.

Chandni agreed and settled down in her usual spot in a corner of the cot. "Today, can you tell me about the priest?"

Bina gave her a long, speculative look. Then, she cleared her throat, and taking a sip from the perpetual tumbler in her hand, she began to speak. To Chandni's ears, the words rising and falling were nothing short of magic.

He had come to the family before Kunjan went to that school. The priest convinced Kunjan's father, the raja, that was the best school for his son. He used to visit often, playing cricket with Kunjan and the children of the estate. I think he was about twenty-five, but I could be wrong – these *goras* look older than their age. He had red hair – we had never seen anything like it – and blue eyes that were almost transparent. I had the shivers whenever I saw him. He frightened me. He was tall like a grown tree. But, his voice, O Ma, it was like a soft song, you know, almost like an angel, so when he spoke, you felt he had always known you and cared about you.

I think he had a good heart, for the raja liked him and later so did Kunjan. *Boroma* hated him. She threatened her son with all kinds of bad things if he did not stop this friendship with that Christian, and a *gora* man. But it was no use. I heard it all, hidden behind doors. You smile, but how else could I get information? For my own safety, I needed to know whatever I could about the family I served.

Well, anyway, where was I? Oh, yes, the priest. Well, he followed us to Bundhpur the year after we came here. Wanted to open a school for the villagers, he said. Of course, Kunjan was very excited and offered to get it built. That's the reason the priest came to Bundhpur, so he could get money and also to convert people to his religion. I understand that now. *Boroma* protested every time he came to our place, but Kunjan wouldn't listen. He was just like his father, quiet but firm, and if his mind were made up, there was no one on earth who could shake it.

Kanta started taking lessons from the priest, and I was ordered to be in the room at that time. Cheeh, cheeh, how terrible. Even the Rai *bodhu* was learning to be a Christian, for it was from their book that the priest taught. They made sure *Boroma* was not around those days, when classes took place from the priest's book. Kunjan seemed to know a lot and held discussions. Kanta joined in these discussions; she wasn't shy at all. She asked a lot of questions, and if she wasn't satisfied with the answers, she insisted they go back to the book. Sometimes I envied her, for I would have liked to have spoken. I already knew how to read and write through Kanta's kindness. But I kept quiet and listened.

"There are so many things I didn't know about my own family. Do you know anything about the time Kanta's son was born?" Chandni asked, without raising her eyes from the page she was writing on. This part was tricky territory, as it was about her own father, Kanta and Kunjan's son.

When Bina did not answer immediately, she raised her eyes to find the other's filled with doubt. The silent gaze unnerved Chandni, and she dropped her eyes. But she also understood the struggle taking place in the other woman. If she were holding secrets that had happened so long ago, she would be very hesitant to share them with a stranger now.

She didn't want Bina to stop speaking, not now. From the little she knew, it was at about this time that the major troubles began in Kanta's life. Her own father's aloof manner towards his children came to Chandni's mind. She needed to be patient and allow the older woman to gather her thoughts.

A smile, uncertain, tremulous, hovered around her mouth as Chandni raised her eyes once more towards Bina. She was relieved to find the doubt that had been in the old eyes had been replaced with something else.

"Come closer, my child," Bina said, and when Chandni did as asked, she ran her dry fingers with extreme care around the contours of Chandni's face. Nodding with satisfaction, she said, "Just like her, the same bones, and ah – the smile. Full of sweetness with that hint of mischief. No wonder Kunjan was *pagol*, mad with love."

Chandni sat still, letting Bina's hand travel all over her face and hair. She knew she had won her trust.

It was the day of the picnic, an important day, for we were going to *Jhuri Pahar*. None of us had been there, and Kanta and I couldn't wait. She was fourteen years of age then, growing to be a beautiful young woman, with the face of a *debi*, just like yours. The high spirits had calmed as she grew older, and she seemed to spend a lot of time thinking.

Kunjan was away a lot, tending to his duties. He also taught at the school. Kanta wanted to open a similar school for girls, but couldn't, for that would be unthinkable. Girls didn't have to learn to read and write. But Kanta thought this was wrong; she spoke to me often about it, as I was her constant companion. At first, I thought this was a madcap idea.

"You can read and write now," she reminded me one day, when Kunjan had been away for some time and *Boroma* was especially unkind.

Yes, I had to admit. I understood then what she was trying to do: bring some freedom into girls' lives. If they could even sign their name, maybe they would not be cheated.

She began to teach the daughters of the estate workers, seating them on the verandah with me in attendance. At first, *Boroma* was angry, very angry. Then all of a sudden, she gave in. Kanta couldn't believe her luck. To say I wasn't surprised would be wrong but, somehow, I knew there was more to this. Of course, the old woman had given me a job after my father had disowned me. There must have been some good in her. She did not like Kanta, I can swear. Did not want Kunjan to love his wife. She had a crooked mind. I think she felt if Kanta were kept busy, she would not follow Kunjan around. The priest was still coming regularly to our house.

Here Bina had to stop as a paroxysm of coughing overcame her. Chandni reached over quickly to rub her back, which seemed to help, for soon Bina resumed her story.

As I was saying, we went on a picnic. Kanta and Kunjan had gone on their own to the jungle to find the waterfall. Something happened between the two, for there was a change in their behaviour when they returned. And it was from that night, Kanta was allowed to sleep with her husband. I was very happy.

It was about time, I thought.

After two years, we had a famine, a terrible time it was. People in villages were dying, though not ours, because people here were looked after by the *rajbari*. But in other places, farther away, people were dying of the famine. *Boroma* wanted Kunjan to visit the tenant farmers, take care of the dying and distribute grain. At this time, Kanta was pregnant. Kunjan had a violent argument with *Boroma*, for he did not want to leave his wife. Who could blame him? But *Boroma* refused to listen. She said the people needed to know the Rais cared for their tenants.

And what about the poor little mother-to-be? Did she not need her husband? Of course, I kept my mouth shut and ears open.

I overheard a conversation between Kunjan and Kanta one evening when she was packing his clothes. Kanta said she was afraid of *Boroma.* This must have been the first time she said it, for Kunjan was shocked and wanted to know what she meant. I wanted to shout exactly what she meant, for I knew Kanta would not. The only thing Kanta said was she would pray for his return before the baby arrived. That was it. Kunjan let it be. That was a mistake.

He left the next morning.

Two weeks later the whole world fell apart. They brought Kunjan's body home. He had died in one of the villages he was visiting – it was cholera. That very day their son was born.

Chandni gasped. The baby, born after Kunjan died, was her father. How tragic. He never got to know his own father. She had been aware of this fact, but now she could put it in context – his reluctance to discuss his family, the way he spent long hours in quiet contemplation. It was all starting to make sense. Waves of remorse swept through Chandni. Why hadn't she tried to spend more time with her father? He would have welcomed it, she was sure, but no, she was too busy with her own life at that time.

His aloof demeanour, which had kept her and Kunal from their father, could have been just a cover, a protective armour against opening up his heart to love.

Although she was burning to know more, Chandni felt a need to collect her thoughts and suggested they take a break. Bina agreed to meet again after lunch "and a nap," she added with a mischievous grin. At this glimpse of humour in Bina's character, some of the gloom that had pervaded Chandni's spirits lifted, and she returned to her room with a lighter step.

A little after the mid-day meal, Chandni headed out of her room towards the courtyard. She was meeting her storyteller.

Earlier I mentioned the famine. How could we have known that it would bring such evil into the Rai family? Kunjan's body returned and was laid out in the front room.

Boroma had me guarding Kanta, for who knew what she might do, she said. I found this odd. Wasn't Kanta the wife, and shouldn't she be told about Kunjan? But I was just the servant, ordered to do as bid.

I need not have worried.

Kanta knew. When the pains increased and her water broke, I was not in the room. The midwife had dozed off, the stupid cow. I returned, and finding the room empty except for the snoring midwife – I could have slapped her but did not – I ran out to the front. I had a feeling Kanta would be there.

I was right.

There was a crazed look in her eyes, like a goat at the slaughter, and she was mumbling something like: "Why will you not open your eyes? Look at me. It is your Kanta. Our child is about to come and we need you."

I stood listening to the words tumbling out of Kanta's mouth, my heart a huge big hole. I worried how I was going to get her back before *Boroma* found out.

Just then, *Boroma* appeared. She had not shed a tear – too busy taking care of cremation arrangements, I supposed. Where I had not succeeded, *Boroma*, with firmness, took hold of Kanta by the elbow and almost dragged her back to her room.

Once inside, she pulled my hair with such force my head snapped back. "You stupid girl, why did you let her get away?" she whispered, each word hitting me with the force of her anger. Then, without waiting for an answer, she slapped the midwife (served her right, I thought), and said to me, "Don't just stare out of those big useless eyes. Help me put her in bed."

We managed to haul, drag, and shove Kanta in bed – she had become a dead weight, not helping at all. *Boroma* sat beside her, sponging her forehead, while I sat on the ground. What was there to do but wait?

"We must get Father Aloysius." Kanta's voice came from the bed. It sounded strong, not at all like a voice coming from a person in pain; even *Boroma* was surprised. She tried to hide it and said, in her usual forceful manner, that it was not necessary.

But Kanta seemed bent on getting her own way. Her body might have been wracked with pain and her lips bloodied, but she would not back down. She wanted her husband to be buried according to the Christian religion.

When *Boroma* tried to argue, Kanta held up a hand and spoke quietly, "My husband was Christian, and should be buried according to Christian rites, or his soul will not find peace."

I saw the old woman's eyes glitter. She looked like she was about to say something, then kept quiet. She began to re-arrange the bedclothes and I jumped up to help. That is when I saw her hands tremble and for a moment, I felt pity. After all, Kunjan had been her favourite grandson. He died far from home, and here she was planning for the last rites. No grandmother should have to do this for their grandson. She did not have a stone for a heart. She just did not have the time for tears.

Next instant, I felt a stinging slap on the cheek that brought tears to my eyes. I was dragged to the door and told in a hoarse whisper, from which poison dripped like raindrops from trees during monsoon, that I would be thrown out if I didn't keep a closer watch on Kanta. I was ordered not to move from the door unless told. Then she hurried away.

The priest arrived and Kunjan was buried. I suppose *Boroma* had to cancel cremation, for she was afraid to hurt Kunjan's spirit. It seemed everything in this house was buried with Kunjan, such was the air around us at sundown – until we heard the cries of a baby.

Kanta's son had arrived. But she couldn't even rejoice, for when she would have put him to her breast, *Boroma* snatched him up. She ordered me to suckle him. I had just lost my first-born. You see, *Boroma* had already planned this. My milk still flowed. Oh, I will never forget the look on Kanta's face as she begged *Boroma* to let her feed her son, but that woman would not listen. Of course, she made out as if it were for Kanta's good, but I sensed the truth.

Boroma was already planning her next step. How to alienate babe from mother.

I was proven right, for the baby was sleeping in *Boroma's* room with only an hour given to Kanta to hold and play with him. Around this time, I began to notice a change in Kanta's appearance, which at first, I put down to childbirth. She had difficulty with her eyes, saying they hurt and she couldn't see properly. *Boroma* dosed her with her own herbal medicines, but the condition worsened and I was frightened – what if Kanta lost her sight completely?

At this time, there was another drama unfolding. Kanta wanted her son to have a ceremony in the Christian way; she said it was to name him. I didn't understand all that, but felt sorry for her. Of course, the old woman tried her best to put a stop to it all. But somehow Kanta managed to do exactly what she wanted and her son had the naming done by the priest.

I was the closest my mistress had for a friend. The poor girl was in enough pain already, both physically and mentally.

I swear *Boroma* was envious, for she put me on kitchen duty while she herself took to tending Kanta's needs. I came upon her one day, combing Kanta's hair with such force that the veins on the girl's forehead stood out and her eyes were shut tight so as not to let the tears fall. Cheeh, cheeh, for shame, how could a grown woman be that cruel?

One day, my mistress fell in the bathing room. She could see very little by then. When she fell and her cheek was cut, there was so much blood all over the floor. I had gone to the kitchen to get something, I don't remember what, but *Boroma* had sent me. So, there I was in the kitchen when there was a mad rush by everyone, running here and there.

I think, in my mind, I knew something bad had happened. I was right. I ran to Kanta's room. It was empty. Then I heard voices from the bathing room; so, I rushed there. There was *Boroma* bent over Kanta, who was on the wet floor with a bloody face. She was in great pain, I could see.

Boroma ordered everyone to get out. Then she said to me, "Go, get the manager." My husband, she meant. I wanted to help my mistress but couldn't, for I had to do the old woman's bidding. My husband was in the estate office, which was on the other side of the estate – a long way, but I was running and sweating and talking to the wind, for I was so shocked at what had happened.

When my husband and I returned, *Boroma* told him to pick up Kanta and take her to the bed in her room. She told me to clean up the bathing room, for there were bits of glass from a broken mirror scattered all over. I wanted to take care of my mistress, for her sari was wet and I knew she shouldn't be left like that – but it was the old woman again, whose orders I had to obey.

When I had cleaned the floor and picked up all the glass, I turned to leave – then I caught sight of something. I bent down for a better look. It was my mistress's soap on the floor. I held it up, puzzled, for it always stayed in its box high up on the ledge. Only I was supposed to use it on my mistress. What was it doing on the floor?

Kanta started a fever that night. We thought it would go by the next day. We were wrong.

Her skin burnt for three days, and when it went higher, I asked *Boroma* if the *baidyo* should be called.

She said, "Oh no, no, I will take care of our little Kanta," and spooned some more of the herbal drink into Kanta's mouth. The poor girl vomited it all. I was beginning to notice a pattern. Drinking that stupid thing made my mistress even more sick. Now I was so worried that I wanted the priest to come and say his prayers. I didn't care that his was a *gora* religion. Kunjan had conformed to that religion, and what good had it done him? But, still, I believed the priest could do some good.

To hell with that old woman, I said to my husband, go get the priest. Let him say his prayers. Maybe that will help my mistress to get well. My husband did not want me to create problems. We were living very well, good food, nice quarters, clothes and bonus at festivals. Why risk these, he asked and would have stopped me if he could. I knew I could twist him round my little finger: I was attractive, a lot younger than him and could still bear children.

So, the very next day, when the old woman had gone to the temple, we arranged for the priest to arrive. He was praying by the bed when the old witch appeared. No one had heard her footsteps; like a snake, she had slithered into the room. She asked the priest, "What can you do that I haven't done already?"

The priest was surprised but not afraid. He continued praying. That man was something, I tell you. I was frightened – I could lose my job and my husband too. When *Boroma* saw the priest wasn't afraid, she went away.

Then Kanta began to say all kinds of things – she had gone crazy with grief and disappointment. Of course, what she was saying was the truth, but you don't say such things to strangers. It was as if she had given up all hope and didn't care what happened to her from here on.

All this time, I had been standing just by the door; now I came in, thinking maybe she needed a drink of water. O Ma, that's when I saw the look on his face. Such longing and also love. I turned to stone. This *gora* was in love with my mistress.

Here was a problem about to explode. I was happy in a way, for at least this man would have Kanta's best interests at heart, but I could not see a happy ending.

Bina stopped speaking, her eyes behind their thick lenses surprisingly moist. She was gazing into the distance, perhaps reliving her time with the Rais.

Chandni had visited the fort the previous day. When *Dadaji* had come to enquire after her, which was so touching, she had prevailed upon him to escort her to Bundhpur Fort. They had walked companionably, chatting with the easy familiarity of two people who had gone through a lot together.

When they reached the fort, a line of tourists waited by its massive gate. Chandni and *Dadaji* joined them. She felt ridiculous – she was not a tourist, not here; nevertheless, a desire to see the rooms, especially the one used by Kanta and Kunjan, drove her on, and she fell in behind their guide, a young student from the nearby college.

This time, however, it felt different for Chandni. Some of the mystery was lost amidst the constant chatter. Following the guide, they walked through the outer courtyard, the same where she had sat and had her first glimpse of Kunjan and Kanta. That scene would be forever etched in her mind.

Do the dead come back? Yes, Chandni answered herself without a doubt in her mind, they are troubled, and I must write about them; only then can their souls be set free. The world must know of their love.

For the hundredth time, Chandni wished that Bina could have accompanied her, but that was asking too much. The woman was old, ninety if a day, and when Chandni mentioned her proposed visit to the fort, she met a wall of silence. Eventually, the reason was revealed – something about bad luck. Bina had tried to dissuade Chandni from making this trip. But Chandni had reasoned – gently, for she had not wanted to offend – that it was too good an opportunity to pass up, and she had set out with *Dadaji.*

The group, like obedient sheep behind their leader, had climbed a flight of stairs, surprisingly intact when compared to the rest of the place. These led to a terrace, which encompassed the length and breadth of the area around which the fortress had been built. Chandni walked over to the parapet to put some distance between herself and the rest. Leaning against the warm stone, she let her eyes drink in the panoramic view. She tried to people the place with those who had lived within these walls.

If stones and mortar could speak, they would fill in the gaps in Bina's story.

Chandni's throat constricted, and she had a sudden desire to order the people out. This was sacred ground, built by her ancestors, not to be gawked at by strangers who came because it was free and who had no real interest in its background.

She touched *Dadaji's* sleeve and said, "I shouldn't have come, not with strangers walking all over the place. So sorry to have wasted your time, *Dadaji*." He nodded as if he had expected it and looked away, but not before Chandni had caught a glimpse of pity in the piercing depth of his wise eyes. This man of few words had felt her sadness, the turmoil that had beset her heart. They walked away from the fort in silence.

As she listened to Bina, Chandni had the distinct feeling she was about to witness something of grave importance. And for this, she needed to be calm. She should not succumb to the sense of foreboding spreading slowly within her.

She rubbed her hands together to wipe away the sweat that dampened her palms. Even in the heat, a sudden shiver travelled through her entire body.

The old woman was sitting hunched under the shawl, as if cold, the planes of her face stark against the late morning sun.

Chandni swallowed a few times, then leaned forward and touched Bina's hand. "Tell me more about the priest, and also, why was Kanta growing weak?"

Yes, Kanta grew weaker. *Boroma* continued to dose her with her own herbal medicines. The other servants gossiped among themselves, but I stayed away. Poor Kanta could hardly see anything, and I had to help her even with very personal tasks.

Khokababu, the baby, still slept in *Boroma's* room, and it broke my heart to be a witness to Kanta's pain.

One day I decided to take matters into my hands. As soon as *Boroma* left for the temple early in the morning, I brought *Khokababu* to Kanta. You see, she was only allowed one hour with her son, but I outwitted that evil crone. Every day I did this and loved watching the baby playing on his mother's lap. My husband was also helping. He would give us the signal that *Boroma* was returning, and I would take *Khokababu* back to *Boroma's* room. That one never found out. We had managed to outwit her, the old witch.

But, in the end, we could not help Kanta get her health back. She was withering away; a skeleton she looked, sunken cheeks where once the roses bloomed, arms and legs like sticks, and her hair, which used to get her in trouble because it was so thick and curly, was growing grey and falling.

The priest returned once. *Boroma* ordered him out. After that, he never came back. I guessed that he must have said something about Kanta and the baby. A few days later, we discovered he had locked up the school and returned to Kolkata.

It was the month of December, three years later, and a very cold winter we had that year. I had just given birth to my second daughter when *Boroma* sent word for me to get back to my duties. So back I came. Kanta had stopped speaking, as if struck dumb, but I tried to get her to play with *Khokababu* to make her smile, at least. It was no use. She had taken herself to another place where she lived and spoke to voices that only she heard. I have never witnessed such a sorry state.

The cold nights made us all get in bed earlier than usual. I always made sure a brazier was left burning in Kanta's room, for she suffered from the cold, being so thin and all.

Anyway, one morning she disappeared. Just like that – poof, gone.

When the rest were looking for her, I entered her room – I don't know why, perhaps hoping she had returned. I decided to make the bed and clean the floor, although this was not my duty – cleaning floors. I wanted the room to look nice for Kanta when she returned. After everything was done, I bent to get the brazier for it would need fresh charcoal, but it wasn't there. I clearly remembered leaving it there the night before.

Where would it go? No one had come to that room.

I left with a troubled heart and told my husband. I dared not say anything to *Boroma*, for, actually, I wasn't supposed to have brought it to Kanta's room. The old woman would have driven me out by my hair had she known that I was trying to be kind to the girl, trying to bring warmth during those cold nights.

The men searched everywhere, but Kanta couldn't be found. When night arrived, *Boroma* called off the search. *Khokababu* was crying and going on something terrible. Some even said maybe Kanta had gone for a walk and got lost in the jungle and maybe wild animals had attacked her. I shut my ears – I couldn't bear that image.

We waited for her to show up the next day, and the next, but there was no Kanta. Life went on in this fashion, waiting and watching. A month had gone by when *Boroma* announced she was leaving with *Khokababu.*

We were dismissed, just like that; after all those years of faithful service, we were thrown out.

The heartless witch!

She said they were going to settle in a village in the east, somewhere in Bengal. I didn't care – I had had enough of this family's goings-on. It's the rich who are so heartless, and we were relieved to be done with them. But my husband and I would talk about Kanta and Kunjan often, and I got in the habit of looking at every strange woman with searching eyes. What if she showed up? How wonderful that would be!

You see, I had developed a fondness for that girl, who had gone through hell before she disappeared.

Bina stopped speaking. The granddaughter who had been hovering in the background, ostensibly to keep an eye on her *Didima* that she didn't overtire, came forward. With a smile directed at Chandni, she sat close to her grandmother. Bina stretched her hand to run her fingers through her hair. Looking on, Chandni could feel the depth of affection running through those ancient fingers, images of her own mother filling her mind and bringing on a wave of homesickness.

It was almost lunchtime. That day, Chandni had an overwhelming desire to eat with this loving family and asked if she could join them and not be treated as a guest. She had been eating in her own room up to then, Bina having laid down the rule since Chandni was one of the masters. The meal was eaten sitting outdoors on the cot. Rice, *dal*, a vegetable dish of spinach and potato, pickle on the side and a cup of yogourt.

After the dishes had been taken away, Bina lay down and was soon snoring. Bees droned in the air, for they had found a few late flowers. Chandni left her to rest. She had a mind to write for a good hour and so walked to her room. She had some specific questions. This would be her last chance. She had left instructions with the granddaughter to let her know as soon as Bina awoke from her nap, so she was prepared when the knock came.

Bina had heard Chandni's footsteps and looked up. There was a wary look in her eyes, and she seemed to have shrunk even more, although the smile remained welcoming. She smoothed the cover, indicating her guest should sit down. Then she began retelling the story – the one Chandni had wanted to hear. Midway, Chandni's pen remained poised in air, her hands refusing to write what she heard, a protective screen around her horrified sensibilities like a curtain on stage hiding the actors. Tears streaming down her cheeks went unchecked.

This, then, was the end of the story for which Chandni had waited.

One day a shepherd boy, while tending his animals, found a brazier made of handwrought iron. He brought it home, but his neighbours saw it and told him he should sell the thing for it would fetch a good price.

So off he went to the market. Instead of trying to sell it, he went to the ironmonger's shed and asked him to set its value. The ironmonger recognized it as one he had made for the Rai family, and he caught the shepherd and hauled him over to the elders of the village, who heard the shepherd's story.

When my husband heard about it, he immediately set out a search party. I tried to stop him. Don't ask why – I just had a bad feeling. Kanta had been gone so long; if she hadn't returned even now, what was there to do? But my husband was a very determined man; he didn't say much, but what he believed, he did.

They, my husband and the shepherd, found her. But not the way we had imagined.

When my husband sent for me, I refused to go. But then something told me I should forget my own feelings and do what I should.

I was escorted to the spot in the overgrown jungle. When I saw there was something on the ground, dug up looked like, I cried out loud and hid my face in my sari. My husband ordered me to uncover my face in a voice I had never heard before.

So, I looked, this way and that, then let my eyes return to the bundle, and I recognized the border of the sari.

The body was burnt so badly you couldn't tell anything, but the feet were not. Kanta's feet were unique, very slim, the toes long and curved at the end. She used to laugh at them, and even Kunjan used to join in.

My mistress, the sweet naughty girl, the one who used to run around like a wild thing and then grew quieter as she grew up. My mistress who was adored by her husband. She was brought to the school where Kunjan had been buried.

Lord, lord, where is justice?

In the school, there was a small pavilion with a statue of the mother of Jesu, and here it was that the priest used to pray. My husband told me. The priest had long gone.

Now there was another priest, and he took care of things. At least, now Kanta could lie beside her husband.

When we returned home, I insisted that my husband write to the Rai family, but he said that should not be done. I was furious, and asked why not. He said there could be police involved. Anyone in the household could be implicated in this death – family or retainer. Did I want that? I didn't. But later, I realized we had a duty to Kunjan and Kanta, so really *Boroma* should be told about what had been found. When my husband knew I would not shut up, he agreed to send a note to *Boroma.* We knew by now where she had moved. It was to Mauchak, in Bengal.

Bina had fallen silent. Chandni wiped her eyes absently. She was remembering the day *Boroma's* picture had broken, the note she had found behind the frame. That had started a whole chain of events in her own life – first, the conviction to clear Kanta's name, then taking that fateful train journey, travelling with *Dadaji*, to eventually reach Bundhpur and Bina.

Was *Boroma* implicated in Kanta's death? If yes, then how? These were questions to which she knew answers would remain unknown.

By the evening, Chandni had lost all desire for food and company. Her wishes were respected, the family leaving her alone.

She had to confront her own thoughts, fight her demons in her own way. For the hundredth time, she traversed the well-worn path through the vegetable garden; back and forth she walked, her footsteps beating time with the turbulence in her mind. At one point, her feet stopped of their own accord. Chandni gazed up at the sky, streaked orange and red by the setting sun, colours of untold beauty and a strange ferocity. The air was still, waiting. She spoke softly in the night air, "*Baba*, now I understand to a certain degree all those times you sat alone immersed in your own thoughts. How lonely you must have felt, not knowing your own parents. Did you ever find out what happened to your mother?"

She shook her head to rid herself of the sense of gloom that weighed down her spirits, slowing her steps, until she came to a halt. Her mind was made up. This she had to do as much for her ancestors' sake as for herself.

It seemed so final. At least, all these years, there had been this story in her mind, an ongoing story without end, and she had clung to it.

There now remained yet another journey, one she would have to undertake to get a modicum of peace for herself and her family.

Always a light sleeper, that night Chandni found it even more difficult to fall asleep, until she gave up in frustration.

Drawing a chair to the window, she decided to wait out the night. The darkness of night was lifting gradually. It was that moment between night and dawn when everything seems to take on a life of its own. She must have dozed off at one point when of a sudden she jolted awake. She had the distinct sensation of being watched. In the dark, the faint outline of a face became visible. Chandni tried to rise and felt herself falling. She struck at the arm of the chair, thus waking herself.

Eyes wide open, thoroughly awake now, she looked around the small room. She wasn't sure whether the vision had been real. However, she felt her spirits rise from the immense gloom into which they had fallen and from which there had seemed no exit. A positive energy filled her limbs.

Chandni lifted her hand to fix her hair and winced at the pain where she had hit it against the chair.

That day, she would leave Bundhpur. She was heading back to Masjidpur.

But before she set out on her homeward journey, there was something she had to do.

She bathed in the cold water drawn from Bina's well, and without breaking her fast, set off for the fort. It was easy to find the school, the one built by Kunjan and Father Aloysius. The early morning air carried with it the strains of a song in the sweet treble of children's voices. It was situated just below the walls of the fortress – a one-room affair with a verandah running the length of the building, the whole under a tiled roof. She didn't stop there.

Her feet took her to the back where she found the grotto, exactly as Bina had described. Opening the small gate of wrought iron, she stepped in. In this overgrown garden, lying disused from years of neglect and where the grass grew in some places almost as tall as the bougainvillea draped around the grotto walls, the Madonna and Child looked on serenely. It seemed, as if she was expected, a feeling so natural that Chandni's hands folded automatically, and she knelt.

Chandni said a prayer of thanksgiving and asked for blessings from the Mother of Christ; then she rose from her knees and walked to the side of the grotto.

Here was a small gate, clumsily put together, its wooden slats falling apart. Possibly the person who had built it did not know much of carpentry or was in a rush to complete the job. The yard, however, appeared well-tended, with trellises of bougainvillea piercing the harsh surroundings with their colour and bringing a semblance of gaiety, of youthfulness, to the place.

Chandni stopped in front of two mounds. They had been created with rocks from the nearby hills. A wooden crucifix had been mounted on each, plain yet beautiful in its simplicity. The same hand seemed to have written an inscription between the mounds. She knelt on the ground to read better.

Kunjan Rai with wife Kantabali.

Just that. No dates. No epitaph.

Finding the last resting place of her grandparents had brought some peace, yet she had still not solved the mystery about Kanta's death. Chandni continued to sit on the dry earth, futility sapping her energy.

She didn't know how long she sat there; gradually, however, she became aware of a light breeze that whispered in her ears, laying gentle fingers through her tresses. She began to relax. Her face brightened as if Kanta had spoken. A sudden wave of love had flown over her. She felt deeply the pure energy of forgiveness. It seemed Kanta had forgiven *Boroma* from the beyond. Even if Chandni could not excuse the torture that *Boroma* had inflicted on her grandmother, she knew that she would have to let go of the bitterness. Ancestors needed to be forgiven. If not, it was their descendants who would continue to suffer. She needed to lay this story down. She did not want her children to live with what had come between her and her own father.

In a few hours, she would be leaving Bundhpur. But she wanted to honour Kanta and Kunjan in a ritual they would have chosen. She recited the Lord's Prayer, made the sign of the cross and laid a branch of the brilliant blossoms between the two mounds, saluting those whose hearts had beat as one. Despite all the pain and suffering, these two brave souls had found each other again. She hoped that in their heaven, they would be together forever.

In place of the breeze, a silence more powerful than words had fallen, surrounding Chandni and filling her with a unique energy. She felt unburdened. She rose, her eyes falling on the two mounds, and she sensed their presence gazing back at her in benediction.

Chandni's hand caressed the weather-beaten wood of the gate. The maker of the gate had been a good person, she decided. Her grandparents had been brought together. Dates were not necessary.

FIFTEEN

Chandni
Masjidpur – 1976

Chandni was back on the train to Masjidpur. The series of incidents that had taken place since she embarked on that fateful journey to see her mother had left her with an urgency to join TJ in Manchester.

She sat with eyes fixed ahead. From time to time, she let out a deep breath. She wondered if she should tell her mother about Kanta's story. She gripped her hands together as another thought followed on the heels of the first.

Ma and *Baba* must have suspected. What was the word? She screwed her eyes shut and leaned back, trying to think of the right word. Unnatural – ah, that's it. Her parents must have known about Kanta's disappearance. Or had they? *Boroma* could have said that Kanta had died soon after her own father's birth. Oh, this was too much. Chandni put up a hand to press against her temple.

Then they started again, doubts and questions, and a sense of loss. Did she have any right to dig up the murky past? Bina wasn't sure what had really happened to Kanta, how she had died. Unanswered questions led to a time of shame for the Rai family. What good would it do to bring it up now? At least the two, Kanta and Kunjan, lay together in death, accomplished through the faithful service of their old retainers – Bina and her husband Shanti Ram. Chandni's new-found maturity approved her decision.

She would, of course, tell TJ's mother about the train holdup, she owed her that, but not all the details, and hopefully there would not be too many questions. Later, she would explain all in a letter to her mother – her experiences of the afternoon when she and *Dadaji* made it to Bundhpur Fort, the hazy figures, the horses, the faint outline of a face through the curtain of the *palanquin*. The dreamy, mystical, otherworldly experience.

She began to make a mental list so that her letter to her mother would have all the important details of Kanta's life – how the child bride grew up to be a beautiful, talented and graceful woman, the early days when she lived and loved the prince, the birth of their son. Kanta's story.

Her thoughts swerved again towards the doubt that lay on her breast with the weight of a huge stone. Not even to herself would she admit the possible, and perhaps ugly, truth behind Kanta's death. Unable to shut it out of her mind, she fell to contemplating the view rushing past the window. It proved of no use, however, for questions hammered at her head. She tried to focus on her imminent departure from India and the excitement of being with TJ. She wondered if there was a letter waiting for her.

And, then it began, once again, questions to which there were no answers. She begged them to go away, but they shouted in anger – why would Kanta leave her baby? To die in the wilderness? Why?

She had to take hold of herself, trample the doubts, smash them underfoot. Never let them show, for that would be disloyal to the family. She would think of something totally different.

This was Chandni's slow development and entry into the adult world.

Pretense became a mantle drawn in protection against the invasion of questions and doubts.

She determined not to divulge her experience at the fort to TJ. What she had heard and seen, the supernatural experience, had left her with a deep emotional craving – something hard to fathom, but there it was, occupying every minute of her time.

The train hissed its way into Masjidpur station in the early evening. Coolies clad in red uniforms hung on to the windows, shouting for customers, while hawkers plying their trade jumped into the moving train.

Chandni picked up her light case and clambered down the steps, fending off coolies. She made her way down the platform to the gate leading out, a whirl of thoughts crowding her mind pondering on the best way to approach TJ's parents. She had not been able to contact Manisha – there were no phones in Bina's village. Chandni prayed that her friend had kept her mouth shut, which must have been hard to do, for she must have been sick with worry when Chandni's train failed to show up at Calcutta station at its appointed time.

Different scenarios played in her mind as she considered the best approach – should she brazen it out and tell all, or should she make up a few white lies? Certainly, the newspapers must have reported the train robbery. Then there was no need to go into details when just the gist would do. She nodded her head, pleased with her decision.

The night was moonless. Scudding clouds promised rain. Chandni's steps faltered as she approached the rickshaw stand. The three-wheeled vehicles looked like ghosts; their drivers huddled under thin shawls. Giving them a quick once-over, she continued to walk until her customary sense of caution prevailed, and she hailed a rickshaw. It was a short distance to the house, but she didn't bother to bargain.

Chandni had started a letter to her mother on the return journey to Masjidpur. Trying to explain without giving too much information, she had glossed over the train robbery, but then had to stop. It was simply impossible to describe on paper what she had gone through. She didn't finish the letter.

"*Didi*, here we are." The rickshaw driver's voice broke into her thoughts. They had reached the Ramsay house. Chandni dismounted, and after paying the man, started forward, the suitcase clutched tight in her hand.

Her home, by virtue of marriage.

She reached for the bell, paused for a second, wondering how to ring it quietly, then realized the ludicrousness of her thought. A bell can't be rung quietly. Mrs. Ramsay had not given her a key. Without warning, Chandni's eyes filled up. She swallowed the tears of frustration and anger. She should have been in Mauchak with Ma, being pampered and cosseted, the only daughter of her parents, not standing cowering at the doorstep of a house where she was uncertain of the reception. Biting her lip, she jabbed at the doorbell and waited. Despite the care they had received at

Bina's, the blisters on Chandni's feet hurt terribly. She couldn't stand still, moving constantly.

If Mrs. Ramsay refused to give her daughter-in-law a key, then she better be prepared to open the door, late as it was. For hadn't she asked for a set? And hadn't Mrs. Ramsay made some faint excuse about not wanting to provide one for fear of Chandni misplacing or losing it? Utter rubbish. Her lip stuck out in defiance.

After a minute or two, the door opened and TJ's mother stood at the threshold. She must have checked through the peephole.

"Why, it's you, Chandni! You are back so soon. We weren't expecting you tonight," she stated the obvious.

"I know," Chandni responded, trying to keep the note of impatience out of her voice. Mrs. Ramsay stepped aside and Chandni walked in, already regretting her earlier rudeness. She should apologize. Her sudden appearance would have unsettled her mother-in-law.

Setting the case by the door, she turned towards the older woman. What she saw was enough to erase all feelings of irritation. A woman, perhaps her mother's age, stood in the hallway, her frail body covered in a shabby nightgown, a look of doubt, and also a touch of fear, in the peering eyes. Chandni regretted her abrupt behaviour, so she quickly put an arm around Rebecca Ramsay, to be rewarded with a warm embrace.

They stood thus for some time, then disengaging herself, Chandni steered her mother-in-law towards the sitting area. "Why don't you sit here while I quickly wash up, and then we can talk."

Once again, Chandni found herself taking the lead. She found this awkward, for she had been brought up to follow her elders. To be seen and not heard.

Her world was turning upside down.

On the coffee table lay an inland letter, blue in colour, with the customary three flaps folded and glued on all sides. Mrs. Ramsay picked it up and handed it to Chandni, "This is for you, from your mother. It arrived the very day you left here and that made me sad. I said to myself, why did it have to come today, and, not when she was here? But then, your mother must have mentioned it when you saw her." She paused for a moment, her brows knit in puzzlement. "Oh, no, I suppose you didn't go there, then. I am a little confused, my dear. Our postal service…" She rambled on, but Chandni had stopped listening. She was looking at her mother's letter lying in her hand, the address written in her familiar writing.

She picked it up, letting her fingers smooth the square of paper and was about to tear it open when she changed her mind and set it aside. She would read it later, in the privacy of her room.

Chandni gave a filtered summary of the train robbery. The newspapers had reported it, said Rebecca Ramsay, and she expressed concern that Chandni had to go through such a harrowing experience. Chandni flashed a smile at her mother-in-law and assured her no harm had been done to herself. The local authorities had been kind, issuing new tickets to all the passengers so that they could carry on to their destinations. Adding, in order to forestall more questions from her mother-in-law, that she had joined a group of women and children at a nearby hotel.

"It is rather late for you. We can talk tomorrow." The lies she told exhausted Chandni. She wanted to escape to her room before further questions should come.

Mrs. Ramsay agreed, "Yes, it is late, and I have not been well. I am so glad you decided to come back to Masjidpur after the horrible experience." Noticing Chandni's slight flinch, she hastened to add, "Don't think of that anymore, just change, make sure you eat something; there are sandwiches in the fridge, leftovers, you know, from lunch." With that injunction, she left the room.

Sitting cross-legged on the bed, a plate of sandwiches by her side, Chandni gazed at her mother's letter in her hand. She laid it aside and took a bite from a sandwich. She wasn't hungry. She pushed a finger under the flap of one side of the inland letter and continued in this manner on to the two other sides until the letter fell open to reveal the beautiful Bengali script. Hunched over the piece of paper, Chandni began to read, her lips moving soundlessly with each word.

Dear Chandni,

I pray that you are well and adjusting to your new life in your new home. By the time this letter reaches you, TJ will have left for Manchester and although you will miss him, his absence might make it easier for you to get to know his parents. I trust you are taking care of the household and allowing Mrs. Ramsay to rest easy, for her husband does not enjoy good health. Just having a young person in the house makes for a happier feeling, which I am sure Mrs. Ramsay will agree with, so make sure you chat with your in-laws. Though, I know, as your mother, some days you will want to be by yourself.

Has your passport arrived? I only wish I could see you one more time before you leave for Manchester.

(Chandni gave a great sob and hid her face in her hands. Then she blew her nose, picked up the letter, and continued reading).

Daughter, I am afraid I have some sad news to impart. Your Pima passed away three days ago of a massive heart attack. It was sudden. He never regained consciousness once he was moved to the hospital. I remained by his side until the end. He was a good man. When he lost his wife, he became close to your father. Yet, it was his wife who was related to your father, being his second cousin. Your Pima had donned the mantle of a parent to you and Kunal ever since the passing of your father. But you were always his favourite. He doted on you, Chandni, bless him, and always wanted the best for you.

I wish you could be here, but that's selfish of me for you must leave to join your husband as soon as your passport arrives, whenever that will be. Before I end, I must remind you of the promise you have given me – that is, not to mention your inheritance from Pima to anyone. I repeat – not to anyone. Somehow, I don't feel easy about the whole thing. When he struck his own son off, we were shocked, but Pima was a man set in his ways. According to him, his son had gone against tradition by marrying a German woman. So, I was rather surprised when he named you in his will as the sole owner of his estate. When I asked him, does he not mind that TJ is Anglo-Indian? he smiled and kept quiet. And, it was then that I discovered that you, and only you, will inherit Pima's property; none of it will ever go to your husband. He was smart. I am only thankful that none of this will take place for a few years. You will be a rich woman one day. Opportunists are lurking at every corner, ready to pounce upon unsuspecting individuals. Dear child, I don't mean to alarm you, it's just the feeling of protection a mother feels towards her children and that is what I am going through.

Take care of yourself, stay out of the rain and remember to change into dry clothes if you should get wet. You need to keep well until your departure.

May God bless you.

Ma

Chandni continued to sit in the same position long after the letter was read. Her fingers curled around the paper as she gazed into space with unseeing eyes. What would she not give to attempt, one more time, the aborted journey to Mauchak? Her mother seemed lonely, although she would never acknowledge it, certainly not to her daughter.

She leaned back, trying to find a more comfortable position. The tensions of the last few days culminated in a throbbing pain around her temples that just did not want her to relax. During the journey and what took place after, she had discovered an inner strength she hadn't known she possessed. This strength helped her to keep a degree of calm through the series of events that pulled her out of her comfortable and predictable life into a world she had not known could exist – the train holdup and the tragedies she had to witness, the fearsome journey through a forest whose dark interior hid wild animals and even wilder humans, the scorching sun producing constant thirst, acute physical pain and, finally, her arrival at Bundhpur Fort, then on to Bina's village.

She was back now and should be able to relax.

However, her mind refused to let up, to ease the tension. She had come so close, but fate had had other plans. She now believed that she was unable to see her mother because it was not meant to be. Instead, she had been taken to Bundhpur village to hear Kanta's story. And, that *was* meant to be.

When had she turned fatalistic? She who had scoffed at fate and the supernatural, maintaining they were so old school?

Chandni had been back for just over a week. When, even at the end of the second week, there was no call for an interview at the passport office, she began to feel the first stirrings of anxiety. What if her application had been lost in the mail? The postal system was not to be trusted. She should have personally handed it in.

But the journey to Bundhpur had borne fruit.

She picked up the phone and dialled the passport office. After the fifth ring, a voice came through, listened to Chandni's query, then put her on hold. She glanced at her watch – fifteen minutes had elapsed. Her feet beat a tattoo on the floor; just when she was about to hang up, a different voice came on the line. She was asked to provide all of the information, once again. Trying to hide the growing irritation from her voice, she complied. The man put her on hold. After another fifteen minutes, the same person returned to tell Chandni they were looking for her file, which seemed to have been misplaced.

"What do you mean, misplaced?" Her voice rose a notch.

"Madam, we will call you as soon as the file has been located." That's all they would say.

The urge to bang the phone down was great, but she resisted. Instead, she thanked the man and, after placing the receiver carefully back in its cradle, returned to her room. What was she supposed to do now? Call TJ? Arrrgh – it was all his fault. She eyed her bed, neatly made with the sheet tucked in precisely, the pillows stacked one on top of the other. Just like her life used to be. Simple, well-ordered.

She flung out an arm towards the lamp and it tottered, about to crash to the ground. She caught it deftly and returned the object in its rightful place, feeling ridiculous.

It was TJ's fault for leaving so soon. He should have stayed and looked after her – that's what husbands are for, aren't they? Looking after their wives.

Chandni was nothing if not absolutely honest about herself. She was thinking about the last few days, how she had taken care of things and come out safe. Gradually, the black mood started to lift, and, in its place began to emerge a sense of achievement. She didn't have to depend on others. She was perfectly capable of looking after herself. What a team she and *Dadaji* had made.

That night, Chandni sat down to finish the letter to her mother. After several attempts, she decided to come right out and tell her about meeting Bina and the story she had heard: the love shared by Kunjan and Kanta, *Boroma's* antagonism cleverly hidden, how even the maid's loyalty could not ultimately protect Kanta.

Chandni wrote late into the night, and when she had finished, she continued to sit, reliving that momentous day when she had seen the face behind the curtains of the *palanquin*. The tightness in her chest grew in acknowledgement of grief; she had found the last resting place of her grandparents, and yet, was no closer to solving the mystery of Kanta's death.

SIXTEEN

Chandni
Manchester, England – 1976

Chandni reached Manchester on a damp and windy day in the month of October.

The plane thudded and bumped along the tarmac to finally skid to a halt. She couldn't wait to get out of the confined space, breathe in real air. Her first plane ride had been at age five, to London to attend a cousin's wedding. Kunal, who was writing exams at that time, had stayed behind, and she remembered the excitement of having her parents to herself, even sharing their bed. Her keen eyes had noted the difference in their attitude, the open affection displayed towards each other.

She looked out of the small window. A dark pall hung over the tarmac, the darkness brought on by rain-filled black clouds chasing across the sky. Local time was eleven in the morning. Chandni shivered. She should have listened to TJ and brought along a sweater.

Passengers stretched aching limbs, eager to get off the plane. Some even began to haul down belongings from overhead bins and under the seats. Chandni did the same. The little dog-eared notebook tucked away in the cloth bag of Rajasthani mirror-work, a going-away gift from Manisha, was filled with hurried notes she had jotted down between flights. She patted the bag with affection. The notes would have to be transferred to the leather-bound diary, a gift from Pima, who had teasingly remarked that she was now too old for the cheaper ones she used.

Thinking of her uncle, Chandni's lips lifted in a fond smile. Pima had tried hard to be a surrogate father to his wife's niece and nephew. With him gone, it felt to her that some of the old world she was used to was slipping out of reach. First her father, now Pima.

She joined the line of weary travellers snaking their way in single file between the narrow aisles of the aircraft. Happening to glance down at her pants, she wrinkled her nose. A hot bath, that's what was needed. And then, wear the pretty cotton robe her mother had stitched for her. They had gone to the bazaar together to Uncle Sharma's fabric store, and Chandni had picked the blue-flowered material. Afterwards, her mother had chosen a length of matching satin ribbon to go with it. Before heading home, they had stopped at Gauribabu's hotel for cups of steaming hot tea and a plate of his famous *nimki.*

Finally, she would be with TJ.

A waiting bus loaded the passengers, and a short drive later stopped at the entrance of the airport. There was a surge towards the open doors as people rushed to get out. Someone pushed Chandni, and she grabbed the bar running the length of the bus, her fingers contacting another hand. She apologized. The hand belonged to a woman who smiled kindly, indicating no harm was done.

Chandni smiled in return. Her heart sang – soon she would be with TJ; his eyes would crinkle in that funny way and he would talk nonsense, and here was this nice woman. A perfect way to embark on a new life. Later, while standing in line at immigration, once again it was TJ's face in her mind. Handsome TJ with broad shoulders and the tiniest waist she had ever seen on a man. Well, that wasn't true, for where had she ever seen a man up close like TJ? And the way he kissed. She grew warm, experiencing the familiar tingle between her thighs.

"Next." The immigration officer was looking at her.

Clutching her passport, Chandni took a deep breath and walked quickly to the counter where the officer inspected her documents. She was requested to follow him to a small room. There were two such rooms along the hall, one of which was already occupied. Chandni followed the man into the second room and slid into a straight-backed chair, letting her eyes flit quickly around the room. Its lack of furniture and the dull fluorescent light added to its cold appearance. She crossed her feet at the ankles and held her hands together in her lap.

Reading through the paperwork, he asked her once more, "When did you leave India?"

Chandni's eyes shifted to the customs and immigration form held in the man's hand. "Second of October," she replied. She had filled the form so carefully, so why would he ask her this question? Was something wrong?

But he seemed satisfied with her answers, stamped the passport, then escorted her to the luggage carousel where she would have to retrieve her cases. She thanked him, then turned to get a cart, and picked a vacant spot with a good view of the ramp.

Suitcases, boxes, large duffel bags and packages of all sizes and descriptions continued to hurtle down the ramp, but the two brown suitcases holding her belongings did not appear. Where could they be? Chandni's eyes darted to the mouth of the carousel, willing it to disgorge just two more. It remained empty and silent.

An hour had gone by, and still no luggage. She was the only one waiting. Chandni had had enough. She was debating her next step when, happening to turn around, her eyes fell on a heap of luggage beside the next carousel, and there they were, her missing suitcases. They had been there all this time while she had her back to them. How stupid.

Wheels screeched as she turned the cart forcefully; a couple of workers glanced up at the sound. Chandni pulled, gritting her teeth, and the heavy cases were heaved up and loaded - only to be unloaded - again, opened, and checked at customs.

Repacking with great difficulty, she bent the keys when trying to lock the cases. "Oh, damn," Chandni muttered under her breath, now really angry at herself. Tugging at the key made it worse, so she had to leave them as they were. Her co-passengers had been swallowed up by welcoming relatives. TJ should have been behind those doors. She made for a bench right beside the entrance. From this vantage point, finding each other would definitely be easier.

About half an hour later, a female voice asked for the time. It came from somewhere very close to where she was sitting. It was the woman from the bus, a cart piled high with luggage in front and a man close behind. She looked to be about fifty years, stout of girth and short of stature with bright inquisitive eyes that seemed to take in everything wherever they fell.

"Almost four," Chandni said in Hindi. She had been at the airport roughly three hours.

The woman smiled her thanks and asked in Gujarati, "Are you waiting for your folks?"

"I am sorry. I don't understand," Chandni apologized with a smile.

"Don't worry," the woman replied in Hindi, "we can still hold a decent conversation in our national language, can't we?" and with that, she settled herself comfortably beside Chandni. Her blue silk sari whispered expensive. The man, her husband, took the opposite seat, the newspaper under his arm came up with a flourish, and he disappeared behind it.

The couple, Chandni learnt, lived with their son in the city. He was delayed due to car trouble, so they would have to wait for their ride, just like herself. Their surname was Jamshedji. They were Parsi. Of course, she understood now, the name itself was typical and they spoke Gujarati. Chandni introduced herself, barely paying any attention to Mrs. Jamshedji's delighted exclamation about meeting a Bengali.

Where was TJ? Chandni's eyes darted restlessly, seeking out empty spaces, behind columns. Hands on lap, fingers twisting the wedding band round and round, she looked far and near, willing the familiar figure to materialize – out of thin air if possible. She regretted now not having his phone number. When she had asked, TJ had laughingly accused her of distrusting him. She knew he would arrive. Only she didn't know when.

At that moment, Mrs. Jamshedji chimed in. "Why don't you phone your husband?" She jerked her head towards a phone booth.

"I don't have the phone number." Chandni's voice sounded small, lonely, and lost. She was a bundle of nerves, and Mrs. Jamshedji's question had pointed out her stupidity.

"Oh, you don't? That's the one thing you should have with you – coming to a foreign country and not knowing anyone here except your husband is like stepping in the dark."

Chandni couldn't take it anymore. Arms crossed on chest, she spoke, enunciating each word precisely. "I know what you say is true, but I also know he will come; it must be a delay of some sort, not his fault."

"But of course, your husband will be here in no time, you'll see. These things happen, so not to worry, dear," Mrs. Jamshedji was quick to add. Chandni nodded mutely; there was nothing to say. She was wishing she had planned on taking a taxi to TJ's place, but the little amount of money she possessed would hardly go far.

Mrs. Jamshedji fished out a crumpled packet from her handbag and offered it to Chandni. "Have some biscuits while you are waiting. You look like you could do with some food."

Chandni accepted the peace offering with a brilliant smile. She *was* hungry. The sugared biscuit tasted delicious as she licked her lips of the last crumbs.

Another hour passed.

During a lull in their desultory conversation, Chandni looked at her watch, and at that precise moment, a young man approached the bench.

A loud laugh erupted from the depths of Mrs. Jamshedji. Her husband's face appeared from behind the newspaper, eyes blinking rapidly, and she fell upon the man saying incoherently, "Arshu, finally!" Then remembering her husband, she announced loudly, "Your father and I have been so worried. Are you all right? Is the car okay?" The three hugged and kissed, all talking at the same time. Remembering her manners, Mrs. Jamshedji turned around and introduced Chandni to her son.

They gathered their belongings and were ready to leave when Mrs. Jamshedji said, "I know your husband will come soon to pick you up but keep our phone number just in case, all right?" Chandni nodded in assent, accepted the piece of paper and tucked it in her purse where it lay amidst passport, papers, notebook and airline ticket, along with five British pounds and twenty Indian rupees. Her sole funds.

The Jamshedjis left. Chandni gazed with longing at the departing figures. At least they had provided company, although at the beginning she had wished to be left alone. But Mrs. Jamshedji had insisted on carrying on a conversation, drawing her out gradually, until Chandni had started to talk about her own wedding, describing it in great detail, the shyness disappearing under the older woman's warmth. Ma, Manisha and Pima, all part of the life she had left behind. And when she spoke of TJ, a depth of such longing in her voice that it took the cadence of prayer.

The older woman had patted her arm in understanding, and when Chandni would have spoken Mrs. Jamshedji had said, "Soon the two of you will be together, and even the homesickness you feel now will vanish." Mrs. Jamshedji had cocked an eyebrow and hunched her shoulders, smiling widely at Chandni's look of surprise. "Chandni, I am a mother."

The minutes stretched inexorably; a slow pain began to grip her belly. Images of TJ, blood-splattered and broken, appeared before her eyes. An uncertainty, born of anxiety, began to set in. What if he had forgotten the date? But he sent me the ticket, she reminded herself, he should know I arrive today. No, she would not give in to these ridiculous thoughts – so gritting her teeth, she willed herself to think of other things.

Another hour passed, and still no sign of TJ. She needed to use the toilet but was afraid to leave in case he showed up. The long and arduous flight, then the long wait, finally took its toll, forcing Chandni to shut her eyes. Only for a moment, she promised herself, resting her forehead on the cool metal handle of the luggage cart.

She was floating high above the ground, weightless, wrapped in bits of gossamer resembling clouds to become one with the sky. She looked down from her lofty perch, saw herself slumped in deep slumber.

A slight tap on the shoulder and Chandni's eyes flew open.

She gazed with wonder at the figure standing before her.

"What, not even a smile, for me?" The unmistakable voice rose from the depths of her consciousness to caress her ears with the softness of summer rain in Mauchak.

This was the moment she had been waiting for, ever since the long plane journey from India, across the ocean and through many countries. Here, at last, was her husband, her TJ, who had come to take her home.

She stood up in a rush, bumping her shin against the cart, but the pain did not register.

TJ gathered Chandni into his arms with a force that knocked the wind out of her. She gasped, then rising on her toes, linked her arms around his neck. A shuddering sob ran through her entire body.

"What's the matter, darling?" TJ was holding her face in his hands, a question darkening his eyes.

Chandni took a deep breath, swallowed, and said, a quiver in her voice, "I was afraid you'd forgotten me." She hid her face on his chest, not wanting to show how upset she'd been.

There was a barely perceptible pause, during which Chandni moved out of TJ's arms, not about to let him off the hook quite so easily.

TJ said, "How can you even think that…?" He drew her back into his arms. "You know, it was raining, and of course, there had to be a meeting." When Chandni would have spoken, he rushed on, "And my manager was away. So, who gets to chair this bloody meeting? And I missed the train." He glared to make his point.

Chandni smiled up at the handsome face. How could she ever be upset with this man? She loved him with all her heart.

"You are so nice to everyone. You can never say no, can you?"

TJ buried his face in Chandni's neck, inhaling deeply. He had missed her adoration, the innocent charm. As for Chandni, all her tiredness seemed to have disappeared, leaving her fresh and eager to head home. No more was said about TJ's lateness.

Chatting easily, they left the airport building. When TJ hailed a taxi, Chandni, looking on, was impressed. He made it look so easy, she thought. Within thirty minutes, they were at the door of Mrs. Douglas, a widow and retired postal worker from whom TJ was renting a room.

It was a small house with a small yard in front, small windows on either side of a very small door. Just like a child's drawing. As the taxi pulled in, Chandni noticed a shadow behind a curtained window.

TJ gave a soft whistle. "This is a special welcome for you, my dear," he said, jerking his chin at the window, "I am not allowed to enter through the front door." Chandni lifted her eyebrows at this revelation. TJ continued, "There's a side entrance – it opens into my room."

"You mean we have to use a side door? Like the fruit and vegetable seller and the fishmonger back home? But why? We aren't selling anything."

"Things are different here, love. You'll learn soon."

Detecting a note of defence in his voice, Chandni crept closer to TJ and said, "It's okay, don't worry."

The woman was holding the door open. A slight rain had started. Chandni shivered. She was wondering if she'd ever be warm again.

Mrs. Douglas was saying, "Well, don't just stand there, come in, and mind you wipe your feet first." They stepped inside.

"You can take the luggage to your room, then join us for a spot of tea. I am going to take your wife inside – she looks tired, the poor dear, ready to drop." Chandni frowned at the tone and hesitated. TJ had disappeared into the night. A well of love swelled in her breast in which was also pity; he was probably just as tired as she was, for didn't he say he had to stay back for a meeting, and missed the train because of it? Without warning, her eyes filled up. She blinked hard.

Oblivious of the silence, Mrs. D was asking, "What is your name, dearie?" and, without waiting for an answer, carried on in the same breath, "Take off your shoes and come into the kitchen."

Chandni did as instructed. As she was about to enter the kitchen, an enormous black shape shot up from a chair. She sprang back with a smothered scream, the shape streaked past her to disappear into the hall.

She couldn't bear cats, had always shooed them away if any ever strayed into the courtyard in Mauchak.

"Oh, don't mind Freddie." Mrs. D, who hadn't cracked a smile all this time, laughed in great amusement at Chandni's discomfiture. "He's harmless. Now you sit here." Indicating a hard-back chair, she took a cushioned armchair herself.

As Chandni eased into the seat, she was suddenly reminded of the rascally dog Tommy –tail wagging, tongue hanging, eyes pleading, all those times when she had protected him after another one of his escapades. Chandni wondered what he would be doing now that she was gone. How she missed him and wished this woman had a dog instead of a cat.

"Milk and sugar are on the table if you need any, and here's bread and butter." Mrs. D's booming voice broke through Chandni's train of thought. She looked up to be confronted by a pair of incredibly blue eyes behind pink butterfly frames. She was being assessed.

Soon there was a soft rap followed by a creak, and TJ entered the kitchen. Without a word, he pulled up a chair, then lit a cigarette. Chandni flashed him a bright smile, but he didn't seem to notice. Her eyes dropped and she brought the cup to her lips, feeling awkward.

Meanwhile, Mrs. D kept up a steady stream of conversation, flinging questions to the air, never waiting for a response. Chandni found this disconcerting, although TJ seemed not to notice as he continued to puff away. He still hadn't spoken.

Just when Chandni was starting to wonder when it would be polite to leave, TJ roused himself from his silence and said, "It's late. We should be going."

Mrs. D turned from the sink where she was wringing a dishcloth in her wide capable hands. She said, "Right you are…it's late, run along now, you two. Mind that you get a good night's sleep. Are you going to work tomorrow, TJ?"

"Yes, I have to." Here, his landlady gave him a long look which wasn't lost on Chandni. "Saturdays are always busy." This last was said in a rush. Mrs. D nodded. Chandni heard this exchange with a growing sense of disappointment.

They weren't going to spend their first day together.

She was hurt and bewildered by his behaviour. This was a different person, not the TJ she knew.

At the door, Chandni turned to thank Mrs. D for the tea. Their landlady waved her off, as if dusting off cobwebs. She said to TJ, "Your wife, now, why can't I remember her name? Anyway, we will give her another name." Her red lips stretched, which Chandni presumed was a smile, although it failed to reach the woman's eyes. "I'll show her the market tomorrow; she must learn her way around." The door closed and the light in the hall went out.

They had reached their room, their home. TJ turned the key and stepped aside for Chandni to enter. She hesitated at the threshold, her eyes roaming all over; there wasn't much, a bed beside which stood a small table. There was another table, slightly bigger, and a chair laden high with clothes of every sort. On the table there were piles of newspaper and magazines, an overflowing ashtray and a collection of cereal boxes.

TJ had disappeared into the bathroom. Having their own bathroom had been a point she had worried about throughout the journey. Finding out they didn't have to share with their landlady brought such relief that she was ready to overlook her bad behaviour.

The toilet flushed, followed by the sound of running water. Chandni, fidgeting by the door, ducked in as soon as the door opened, saying over her shoulder, "Got to go."

"Do you have to work tomorrow?" A slight tremor punctuated the question. Chandni looked around for a place to sit. Her eyes lingered on the single chair in the room, which seemed to be the depository for TJ's clothes. She determined to do something about it. But not now.

"Rent's got to be paid," TJ said, sounding defensive.

"I know." Chandni's conciliatory tone had the effect of wiping the frown from TJ's face, "Only that I was so looking forward to being with you on my first day." She came closer, and putting her arms around his waist, continued, "You are newly married. I'm sure your boss will understand."

"Don't be silly. The boss doesn't care about that, and you should know food and rent are not exactly cheap." He removed her arms, walked to the table, and shuffled through the mess until he found what he was looking for. A cigarette dangled from his mouth when he turned back. "Come to bed." Not exactly an order, although in Chandni's tired state, it sounded like one. She stiffened.

"TJ, it's horribly cold. I think I'll have a hot bath. I must freshen up before bed."

"Oh, plenty of time for that tomorrow. Tonight, we celebrate." He pulled her with such force that she landed on his lap. "I'll warm you." His voice thickened, one hand encircling her waist. With the other, he fumbled at the zipper of her pants. In vain, she tried to free herself.

"TJ, please, not like this…"

But he was beyond caring. All he wanted was to undress her. She was his wife, she belonged to him, and she had wifely duties to perform. Chandni's struggles excited him even more, and this she understood. She lay quiet under his weight, eyes closed, head to one side, wanting to be made love to but not like this.

They needed to talk, she decided, for this was a different TJ, not the happy-go-lucky charmer of their college days.

The room fell silent until a loud groan erupted from TJ as he released himself into her, then moved aside to fall asleep immediately.

Chandni awoke to pitch-black nothingness. Where was she? This was not her room, for there was no comforting beam of moonlight filtering in through the window. *Where was the window?*

She lay still. A few moments later, the fog of confusion had started to lift. Turning her head slightly, she contemplated the sleeping form of TJ. An urgency to touch, to make sure that they were really together again, made her lift a hand, then just as quickly, it was withdrawn. Last night's memory, with its accompanying shame, returned. Was love supposed to hurt like this? Their wedding night had been equally painful. TJ had promised that things would get better with time. Her knowledge of the male species being sparse, Chandni knew she had to depend on her husband's direction. At least, that's what all well-born Indian girls did.

She couldn't wait to tell him about her journey here. But, in a few hours, he was going to work. She shifted slightly, moving away from TJ, and gradually drifted into sleep.

When next she awoke, TJ had left. Chandni looked around the alien room, loneliness of such magnitude overcoming her that a soft moan escaped her lips. They should have been together today. The minutes ticked by. There must be a clock somewhere in the mess on the table. She must swallow her hurt and start cleaning the room, try to get rid of the smell pervading throughout.

Throwing back the covers, she swung her legs to the floor – only to scramble back to bed. Cupping her cold toes in the palms of her hands, she threw a speculative look at the floor. It should be covered with a rug or something, just like their landlady's hall and kitchen. How could TJ live here? But of course, she reminded herself, he was at work most of the time, from what she had seen so far.

She determined to tackle their room immediately – after breakfast. With images of a plate of buttered toast, and a mug of hot, sweet tea, swimming before her eyes, Chandni dressed quickly and left the room.

She crossed the wet flagstones with brisk steps, and turning the corner, came upon their landlady sitting on her haunches, gardening shears in hand. A heap of dead branches lay on the ground. This was the front lawn, scraggly grass and patches where the grass had died, a bush that looked like a rose plant, and that was it.

Relieved that she need not ring the doorbell, Chandni forced a smile and said, "Good morning, Mrs. Douglas."

Mrs. D looked up. "Oh, you are up, dearie. I was about to come to wake you, seeing as how late it is. Almost time for lunch."

Chandni apologized for sleeping in and asked if she could have some breakfast. Mrs. D's pencilled eyebrows went up a notch, and she said, "Breakfast is always served at seven. Didn't TJ tell you? If we don't have it on time, then lunch will be late, which won't do. So, you either wait another hour and have lunch with me, or have some cereal that TJ should have in his room – your room, now." She laughed at her own joke, the laughter ending in a rasping cough.

Did she hear right? How could she be accused of getting up late? Had she not travelled thousands of miles from a different country? Chandni remained speechless, wondering what to do next. It was obvious there would be no breakfast, for Mrs. D had turned back to the task on hand.

Chandni's face darkened. Her fists clenched as tears of anger gathered in her eyes. She swallowed them in a hurry.

How dare this woman treat her so?

A sudden vision of the *dacoit* bending over her swam before her eyes. Well, if she had outsmarted a dangerous criminal, Mrs. D should be putty in her hands. With this encouraging thought, Chandni turned on her heel and marched back the way she had come.

She determined to have it out with TJ later. If they were paying for meals, breakfast had better be included or she would make it in their own room. Rules be damned.

When she entered their room, the boxes of cereal seemed to mock her. With one sweep of her hand, she sent them flying off the table to land on the floor, spilling their contents.

Hunger, fatigue, loneliness threatened to take over. She had just about had enough. But the floor had to be swept clean. Now there was an urgency to clear all clutter. She set about making the bed, then gathered all litter, including empty beer bottles from under the bed, into a plastic bag, stowed dirty clothes into the tiny cupboard. In this cupboard were a broom and pan. Envisioning TJ with these in his hands, she burst into laughter. It helped lift the gloom into which her spirits had plummeted. TJ was a darling, a funny one, to be sure, but she loved him so much. It should be easy enough to talk to him about their landlady's peculiar rules, bend them to their convenience.

An hour later, Chandni surveyed her handiwork with pride. Except for the occasional whiff of a mouldy smell, their room now had a nice lived-in appearance almost bordering on the cozy. She couldn't wait to put up the family pictures packed so carefully in the suitcase. But they will have to wait until frames had been bought.

Humming under her breath, she entered the bathroom for the much-needed shower.

Lunch turned out to be soup of an indeterminate colour with shreds of cabbage floating atop, and pieces of undercooked chicken.

A bowl of this sorry mess had been served up and was waiting for Chandni. Surveying it from the kitchen door, she had a wild desire to flee, away from everything, especially this house and Mrs. D's stupid chatter.

Why did TJ have to work today?

She pulled out a chair and sat down, years of discipline taught by her parents taking over. One spoonful at a time, she swallowed, trying not to breathe in the smell. When the bowl was half empty, Mrs. D slid a plate across the table on which rested a slice of bread. Gratefully Chandni picked it up – it was still warm from the oven – and bit into it. Heavenly.

"Thank you."

"That's nothing." Mrs. D waved her hand as though swatting a fly, then said, as an afterthought, "TJ loves my bread." Chandni smiled, her mouth full.

"We'll have to put some meat on your bones – you are so skinny. Hope you are not sick or anything." Mrs. D's eyes raked over Chandni's tiny frame. She poured apple juice into a small glass and set it on the table.

Chandni choked, coughed and quickly took a sip from the glass.

"I look fine as I am, thank you…I certainly don't wish to put on extra pounds." She fought down an urge to say that she would lose even more weight here. Her eyes wandered around the room – the cracked tiles behind the rusted stove, the dripping tap, ragged matting on the floor – until they focused back on Mrs. D.

Mrs. D asked, voice smooth as butter, "Have you taken a honeymoon yet?" Once again, she had managed to impress that Chandni's opinion was of no account.

"No," came the grudging response from Chandni. She was already regretting her earlier rudeness. What would Ma say?

Feigning interest, she asked, "Can you tell me a little about Manchester and its surrounding parts, places to see?"

Mrs. D brightened visibly. She sat down, ample arms resting on the tiny kitchen table, and began, "Let's see now… the Lake District is close, about thirty-five miles or so from here, and is the most romantic spot on earth." She looked at Chandni doubtfully, "Have you heard of it?"

"Of course," Chandni responded, a smile lurking in her eyes. This was her territory. She'd show this bossy woman. "Wordsworth, one of my favourite poets, was from the Lake District." She continued eagerly, "I am sure you are familiar with the poem about daffodils." Seeing Mrs. D's doubtful look, she explained, "This poem is taught in every school and in ours we were made to recite it from memory, so you see these are things most Indian children would know." She couldn't help relishing that she had upped Mrs. D, who couldn't or wouldn't remember Chandni's name.

All the time she was speaking, Mrs. D's eyes had been inspecting her own long pointed nails, polished bright red. She now asked as if Chandni hadn't spoken, "You should stay in bed and breakfasts."

Chandni had never heard of such a thing. "What is a bed and breakfast?"

"Oh, they are cheaper places to stay and provide a really lovely breakfast, all included in the price." This from the one who scrimped on breakfast. Hilarious. Chandni swallowed her mirth with difficulty and asked for addresses, for she had decided they deserved a honeymoon. She left soon after; she had a lot to do and exploring the neighbourhood was first on her agenda.

Mrs. D should not see her leave. Chandni did not want her company; she wanted to be alone, to think things through. She had concluded their landlady could not be trusted: she was inquisitive, rude, and ignorant, and just the sort to snoop around their room. And then there was the curious familiarity she displayed around TJ; Chandni's jaw hardened. The woman needed to be put in her place. TJ should be more assertive.

She was still angry about the food. How shocked would the woman be if she made herself a cup of tea, thought Chandni, imagining Mrs. D's blue eyes popping out of their butterfly frames.

She left when the front yard proved empty. Her mood improved considerably as she walked swiftly until the house grew smaller. A great sense of freedom filled her and with it came happiness, at last; she slowed her steps and exhaled.

TJ's day at the store had gone from bad to worse. The other clerk had not shown up, leaving him to muddle through the cash register, an occupation he disliked. Then a customer had banged into a piano, hurting his hand. TJ found himself comforting the man when all he really wanted to do was wring his neck. What fool would walk around a tiny music store holding two big bags of groceries? The man had finally left, complaining loudly of the narrow aisles in the store.

TJ was tired and grumpy. Even the thought of Chandni waiting for him did nothing to lift his spirits. In fact, he felt worse. He wasn't used to explaining himself to anyone, passing the days just as he pleased. However, he now had an extra mouth to feed. He hoped that she would get a job soon. Being educated and knowing the language should make it easy. He decided to ask Mrs. D for ideas.

He had just lit up, thinking to take a quick break, when the front door of the store chimed, indicating the arrival of a customer. Cursing under his breath, TJ stubbed the cigarette.

It was Amy.

TJ smiled.

"Hi, handsome," Amy said, leaning over the counter to plant a kiss on his mouth. Her small bosom, no larger than a young boy's, peeped tantalizingly above a gauzy blouse.

"I am a married man now, so you have to behave yourself." TJ smacked her on the arm playfully. He shifted slightly to hide the bulge under his pants.

"Ouch, that hurt! Now you have to make it better." Pouting, Amy leaned even further to press her face to TJ's chest; with tongue and teeth she worked on the shirt buttons in an attempt to undress him.

TJ grew alarmed. "Hey, don't. Customers might walk in." He moved out of her reach to the other side of the counter and busied himself clearing up clutter, keeping a wary eye on the girl. She heaved herself up on the counter, a flash of alabaster flesh under the short skirt; TJ's nostrils flared and a glaze spread across his eyes. He tried to appear busy with a cloth and can of glass cleaner. He must not succumb to temptation.

Amy smiled. She had seen the struggle, the fruitless shuffling of items on the counter.

"TJ, are you coming to my show?"

"Bugger – I can't, only one here today – and have to go home."

The girl let out a shrill laugh. "Wife waiting at home, I guess." Then she became serious. "If Auntie hadn't told me you were married, I wouldn't have known. That wasn't fair, TJ. We are friends, but you kept your wedding a secret. What are you afraid of, anyway?" She jumped down to the other side and grabbed TJ's shirt, pulling him forcefully against her.

TJ's arms went around her; with a groan of desperation, he nuzzled Amy's neck. He knew his weakness and whispered, "Don't be angry, love. It wasn't done on purpose. You had disappeared, remember, and I had to leave for India."

"Oh, I was just teasing, you stupid man." Amy rubbed her palm against the bulge in TJ's pants. "Just a sample – more, later!"

At the door, she stopped for a second. As an afterthought, she flung over her shoulder, "Be there!" And was gone.

SEVENTEEN

Chandni
Manchester, England – 1976-77

Chandni had been walking for some time. So deep was she in thought that without quite realizing it, she was now facing an intersection. Her attention was riveted to the street leading to a park; the profusion of flowers laid in neat rows, a willow tree leaning gracefully towards a small pond, brought a delighted smile to her face. Across the street stood a brown building. The constant movement of people entering and leaving piqued her interest. They carried bulging bags, even children. Possibly a library, she surmised.

A gust of wind rose; and in its wake, came cold, hard rain. She quickly snapped open the umbrella she had remembered to bring. Should she turn back? The umbrella didn't stand a chance, but she was determined to find out about that building – and she was reluctant to return to Mrs. D's damp quarters.

She had reached the gate when she became aware of the figure, a little ahead, hurrying with long strides. Something about his gait seemed familiar. She walked faster, her shoes squishing in the rain-sodden grass until she was almost behind the figure.

She had guessed right. "TJ!" she called out.

The figure spun around, rainwater dripping from the face. For a fleeting second, Chandni fancied seeing a frown. The next instant, TJ had lifted her off the ground.

"Put me down, TJ. People are staring."

The umbrella rolled away, picked up by the wind, and disappeared into a bush.

"Fancy meeting you here," TJ said.

Chandni opened her mouth to answer, but the hard press of TJ's lips was on hers, hungry and demanding. She forgot everything – the discomforts, Mrs. D's inquisitiveness and unpalatable meals, the cold rain – nothing mattered anymore.

TJ was murmuring nonsense into her ears. Chandni stiffened. Quite perversely, she who had never tasted, seen or smelled alcohol, had recognized it in TJ's breath. "Do you drink at work?" she asked, narrowing her eyes.

A faint shadow crossed his features. It was gone in an instant. He put her down, keeping his arms around her.

"Hey, why are you wandering alone? You could get lost – lucky I found you."

She pressed against him, savouring the warmth, and tilting her head, said with a laugh, "Don't be silly. How can I get lost when I'm only a few minutes from the house?" She had quite forgotten her original question. Then with pride in her voice, Chandni continued, "I have memorized landmarks, you know."

The corners of his eyes crinkled. "Aren't you smart! Anyway, in case you're wondering I was coming home early to surprise you, but it looks like I am the one who's been given a surprise." He lowered a hand to squeeze her bottom, at the same time keeping his distance.

She gently removed his hand and, linking it to her own, began to walk, pulling him along. "TJ, I am so happy right now that I feel I could fly. I can't believe that we are finally together and no one can part us, ever."

He looked down at Chandni's upturned face, and he was momentarily silent. It was this quality in Chandni that had first attracted him. Then he shook himself, like a dog shaking his coat, scattering rainwater, making her laugh.

TJ began to sing, Chandni joined in. He used to hum this song every time he walked past her in college, which used to be several times a day.

TJ's loud guffaw resounded through the empty park, but stopped abruptly when he felt the sting of sharp nails on his arm. He shook a finger at Chandni. "Ow, that's not fair."

"Good. If you make fun of me again, I'll never forgive you." She knew, oh how well she knew, that even if her life depended on it, she wouldn't be able to carry a tune. It was a sore point. TJ, and her brother Kunal could sing. They both had an ear for music. TJ apologized, and pulling Chandni close, promising to behave.

Linking arms again, they walked, homeward bound. At one point, she slowed to look back. She must return soon, to visit the library.

That evening Chandni's voice, laced with laughter, filled the small room. She recounted how he had approached her the first time in the college library, the stolen meetings after that, then their wedding, the long and exhausting plane ride. TJ listened, silent for a change, a cigarette dangling from a corner of his mouth.

There was one subject, however, she did not mention; her journey to Bundhpur. That vision, of Kantabali and Kunjan through swirls of red dust, carried a deeper meaning, she was now convinced. She tucked it away, like filing an important file, to be taken out and reviewed at a later date.

Breakfast was now provided until eight, a feat Chandni had accomplished after threatening to make it herself in their room. A feather in her cap.

In their room, there was one tiny window. Years of dirt had gathered around the glass and frame. Grimy, as it was, one day Chandni began to see it in a new light. She would clean and dress it up.

Positioning herself in the centre of the room, she ran a critical eye over the window. It was high and she needed a ladder. Mrs. D might have one, but she'd rather die than ask her. So Chandni did what anyone in her position would have done.

It had to be the table. She dragged the bed to one side, then pushed the table until it stood directly under the window. Armed with a broom, she climbed up to first clean cobwebs, then tied the dampened towel she had had the foresight to bring to the broom. This she used to clean the glass, inside and out. Thankfully, the window was small, so it didn't take long.

Grinning from ear to ear, Chandni gazed upon her handiwork when a flash of colour caught her eye. It disappeared within an instant. She supposed that whoever it was had mistakenly approached their door instead of Mrs. D's. Although, that was rather puzzling; how could a person miss the front door? The incident made her realize the window needed a curtain. Also, she would hang a sign at their door. Mr. and Mrs. TJ Ramsay.

She washed her hands in the clean sink and smiled at her reflection in the sparkling mirror. She wished she could walk right through into Mrs. D's kitchen, and if the woman was eating something other than what was served to her tenants, she would whack her on the head, then disappear. She stuck out her tongue and laughed at her nonsense, then turned back to the room.

There was work to be done.

She pulled out the larger of the two suitcases from the corner by the door and opened it to choose a sari. It was a simple matter of cutting it up, running a hem through, and there was a curtain. TJ would have to hang it up; the mere idea of asking Mrs. D for hammer and nail filled Chandni with distaste.

The next day, she would look for the post office, wherever it was, buy stamps and write to her mother, and of course to Manisha. A sudden wave of homesickness spread through her. She wondered what they were doing. Then, all of a sudden, Kunal's name came to mind. She was still hurt that he hadn't responded to the note their mother had sent him, telling him about Chandni's marriage. Chandni and her mother had begged the priests of the school to let them have Kunal's address in Australia. The priests had refused at first, then taken pity and promised to forward the letter. However, the family still had no idea which seminary Kunal belonged to.

She had just closed the suitcase when her sharp ears picked up the sound of footsteps on the gravel. Chandni ran to the door and flung it open. TJ was home.

Chandni had not been feeling well for some time. Her face had lost its healthy glow, and even TJ, to whom his wife always looked beautiful, noticed the change.

He asked, "Hey, you okay?"

"I need a kitchen," Chandni announced, the tone of her voice implying she would brook no argument.

TJ, who was getting dressed for work, gave a bark of laughter. "Why? You are not cooking or anything." When Chandni would have interrupted, he walked to the bed where she lay listlessly turning the pages of a magazine, and picked up her hand, "Look at these pretty hands. Don't spoil them on kitchen work."

"TJ, I cannot stand that woman – and her food. You call that food? Makes me want to vomit when I see the mess she serves up. Why can't we move?" She knew this was a delicate subject. They had already gone over it again and again. TJ said his salary just wasn't enough. Chandni was determined to do something about it. She should get a job.

"Well, I'm off," TJ said, blowing her a kiss from the door. He had not answered her question. She waved at him, trying to put a smile on her face, but it was difficult. She was just too tired; even to get up for breakfast seemed a waste of energy and she had little to spare.

She dozed awhile; however, by afternoon Chandni felt the first pangs of hunger, and they were strong enough for her to contemplate going in search of food. She picked up a shirt, threw it on, and turning to the bathroom mirror, ran a comb through her hair. Through half-open eyes, she took in the drooping shoulders of the garment. All the clothes she possessed seemed large these days. Why was she losing weight? Even to her tired mind, the answer was obvious – it had to do with Mrs. D's unpalatable food.

Chandni's listlessness refused to leave, and she continued to lose weight at an alarming rate. One Saturday morning in mid-November, a month and half from the first day of her arrival in Manchester, she fainted. TJ was home, a rare occurrence, and he bundled her in a taxi. Panic-stricken, he yelled at the driver, demanding he speed to the clinic. Chandni protested the whole way that there was nothing the matter with her.

"Mrs. Ramsay, when did you last have your period?" the doctor asked. He had checked her and was busy writing.

She looked up from buttoning her shirt, "About two months ago, I think." He stopped writing, pen in mid-air, and she quickly added, "I have never been regular."

"Let's call your husband, shall we?" he said, smiling, and left the room. Chandni sat on the high bed, dazed. A few minutes elapsed, and then the doctor was back, with TJ following close behind. Chandni extended a hand to TJ. She wanted him beside her; she had understood what the doctor was going to tell them.

"Well, Mr. and Mrs. Ramsay," the doctor's eyes twinkled behind gold-rimmed glasses, "get ready for some good news. You are going to become parents. Congratulations."

Chandni felt TJ's hand clench. She stole a look at him – he was frowning, which he quickly replaced with a smile when he caught her eyes on him. "Thanks, doc. This is a surprise." He stood up.

"I am glad she came in; I'll write a prescription for iron pills, essential during pregnancy. You'll need to eat well. Get plenty of fresh air and rest often." He wrote the prescription, handed it to Chandni, and left the room.

That night, Chandni ventured once more to give voice to her hope. "I wish we could have our own place," she said, and waited for TJ to speak. When he didn't, she raised herself on one elbow to look at him. He remained silent, a cigarette cupped in his hand. He took a long drag, then stubbed it on the ashtray that was sitting on his chest. Still, he didn't speak.

"There's hardly any sunlight in this room, and I know a baby needs it to be healthy. Why don't we look for an apartment, a regular kind, in one of those tall buildings out there?" She pointed in the general direction of the street across from Mrs. D's house. "Maybe we could even get something closer to your work."

TJ picked up the ashtray. Aware of Chandni's scrutiny, he turned his back to her, ostensibly to place the ashtray on the floor. A small frown was gathering between her eyes. She hated his habit of smoking in bed. She hoped he would stop when the baby came. When he hadn't spoken, Chandni became impatient and nudged at him.

TJ stirred finally. With restless hands, he fixed the bedclothes, then gave his pillow a good whack. All this while, he was aware of Chandni's eyes fixed on him.

He spoke finally. "It'll be expensive; Lot more than this sunless room, as you call it…got to stay here, at least for some time."

Not to be dismissed summarily, she said, "Not even a one-bedroom? And kitchen? To have my own kitchen…" Her voice trailed off, losing itself in the darkness. Within the short time they had been married, she had learnt not to goad TJ – it only got his back up. She would have to use a different approach. She was learning fast.

"I could look for a job," she announced suddenly. There, that should help move things along, her education ought to be worth something.

"Should have done that as soon as you arrived," TJ said, sounding irritated.

Hot tears, brought on by a rising anger, gathered behind Chandni's eyelids. She blinked hard.

But TJ hadn't finished. "You are pregnant, and women in your condition grow big with time." With a finger, he touched her flat belly.

"You make it sound like a disease!" She moved away as though scalded.

"Can't you take a joke?" TJ lit up again, then continued, a serious note lending gruffness to his voice. "Chandni, we're okay as we are. Why complicate matters?"

She knew what he said made sense, but he could have been gentler. She couldn't call this place – this tiny airless room – home, nor continue to eat that disgusting food in someone else's kitchen. TJ should do something about it. And they needed a bigger bed.

Sitting on the edge of the bed, TJ glanced at her out of the corner of his eye. Chandni was sitting perfectly still. He leaned over and gripped her tiny hands in his. "It'll be better, love, I promise you…"

Chandni started. She had been far away, imagining having her baby in her father's house in Mauchak. She swallowed and putting on a brilliant smile, said, "I know, TJ. Don't worry about me. Everything will be okay."

Just then, the phone rang.

TJ reached across and picked up the receiver. Whoever it was on the other end spoke at length, and during all that time, he listened, gripping the receiver, a dark frown settling across his face. Chandni moved uncomfortably. TJ's arm on her stomach was growing heavy. She wished he would hurry and end the conversation. He really should tell the person, whoever it was, that he was busy. Half an hour later, when Chandni was about to shove him off her, he hung up, and without a word, walked across to the bathroom.

"So, who was it?" Chandni was dying to find out. She wanted everything to go back as before, the lovable TJ to return and hold her in his arms murmuring silly things in her ear. He was no longer the same man.

TJ ran nervous fingers through his curly hair, "Oh, just my boss. He wants me to come in for a while."

At this time? She knew it was crazy. Chandni pressed her lips together. She had decided not to say a word. TJ stood by her side of the bed, then lifting her chin with a finger, forced her to meet his eyes. "Look, so sorry and all – must do what the boss asks. Maybe we can move shortly," he offered, like throwing a carrot to a horse. He leaned over, but Chandni had moved away.

"You don't have to explain anything to me. You must do what you think is right." She managed to sound calm, then all of a sudden, her lips began to tremble and she turned her face away. TJ had already walked to the door, and here he stood, for a moment, as if undecided. Then, without a backward glance, he left the room.

She slept fitfully until the creaking of the door broke through her slumber, her body tensing as she watched TJ creep in soft-footed. Without undressing, he slid under the covers. Then the sound of even breathing filled the room. It was nearly dawn.

Chandni had begun to miss meals, frequenting the corner store and picking up candy, the only inexpensive item on display, although her eyes strayed to the chocolates.

One day, a craving for *dal* and rice grew so great that she marched to Mrs. D's, entering the kitchen through the open front door. She had to have that most common of all foods – in India a poor man's food. Mrs. D turned from the sink where she had been washing up and stared at her as if

Chandni had grown two horns. In a voice made louder, for she had started to lose confidence, and she was summoning her last ounce, Chandni said, "Could I borrow your stove for a bit? I want to cook rice and *dal*."

"Now, why would you bother with a mess like that, dearie?" Mrs. D asked, raising a pencilled eyebrow, mouth screwed into a button. She seemed to know what *dal* was.

An immense urge to do something drastic coursed through Chandni and her eyes flew to the bubbling pot. Her thin arms clenched, then with a great effort she dragged her eyes away from the stove, turned on her heel and left.

That was that.

TJ was no help either, coming home late most nights, tired and out of sorts, only to flop into bed almost the moment he entered their room.

Chandni found herself visiting the library almost every day, arriving early, and walking in their garden until the doors opened. The staff grew fond of her. They recommended books to borrow and encouraged her writing when they noticed her diligence in filling the pages of her notebook.

From her position by one of the many library windows, Chandni had an unrestricted view of a crèche next door. She was taking a new interest in the toddlers engaged in their daily routine. Soon she would have one of those, like the babies she saw daily in the park, to hold and spoil. She would have preferred to have had her first baby in her childhood home, but she put the idea out of her head, concentrating instead on starting the story of her ancestors. It helped her forget her homesickness, the drab room and lack of food.

Early one morning, on a particularly cold April day, Chandni's pains arrived like avenging angels.

"TJ, wake up."

"What – what?" TJ finally spoke, his voice sounding rough, fumes of alcohol rampant on his morning breath. It had been another late night.

"Sorry to wake you, but you need to take me to the hospital." Chandni was trying to raise herself, but after a few attempts gave up, the pains were too intense.

"Get a taxi," she gasped, clutching at her belly.

TJ finally scrambled out of bed and groaned aloud, holding his head. He managed to pull on some clothes and was out the door.

"No, no – don't go, call a taxi."

But TJ had disappeared.

Chandni tried to lie still, as if by ordering her limbs to stop their agitated movements, she could make the pain fade. It gripped her back with steel-like claws and spread across her belly. She doubled up in agony, a guttural moan escaping her lips as yet another spasm hit her body. Oh God, take this pain away, I can't bear it, Chandni prayed. Where was He when needed?

Minutes ticked by. Between the spasms, Chandni kept an eye on the clock. There was still no sign of TJ. She couldn't stay here by herself any longer. She would have to look for him. Her heart beat with a frightening intensity making it hard to breathe. Even through the pain and feeling of helplessness, Chandni refused to give in to fear. Repeatedly she told herself how she had escaped the *dacoits*, with cunning and courage, then the long walk through the frightful forest with a complete stranger as a guide.

She gripped the bedclothes and tried to rise, but fell back when another spasm seized her middle. It was deathly cold in the room the walls were closing in on her; she was alone. A voice within her lashed out, "Now, look, what you've done, you've driven TJ away. Are you satisfied?"

When TJ returned, she was on the floor, knees drawn to her distended belly, shivering uncontrollably.

"I thought you'd never come. I was trying to get to the door…" Chandni stopped. The stout form of Mrs. D loomed behind her husband.

They managed to bundle Chandni in the bedclothes. Then TJ carried her to the waiting taxi.

EIGHTEEN

Chandni
Manchester, England - 1977

The homely sound of boiling water filled Mrs. D's kitchen. Swirls of steam rose from a large stainless-steel pot set on the stove, only to dissolve and disappear into the rusty vent above. The cat had been banished to the hall. Ignoring his hiss of disapproval, Chandni had shut the door with a determined snap.

She was sterilizing feeding bottles, humming softly and glancing from time to time at the bassinet on the floor, placed at a safe distance, but near enough for her to keep an eye on the sleeping baby. Her face glowed, and she couldn't help but steal glances at him. She reminded herself that the job had to be completed before the return of the dragon lady. Mrs. D was getting her hair done, a weekly ritual, and soon, baby would wake for his feed.

Each bottle was picked from the steaming pot with a pair of tongs and laid in a neat row on a snow-white towel on the counter. Her mind kept pace with her busy hands, going over the latest argument with TJ.

Shedding all restraint this time, she had come right out and asked him about his salary. This was so contrary to Chandni's nature that at first TJ hadn't known how to reply.

"Oh, you don't have to bother about such things," he finally said with a shrug of his shoulders. This time, Chandni wasn't going to give up. She was determined to show her husband that she was no longer the shy girl he had married.

"TJ, I am your wife. Don't you think we should share everything? Like, the bank account?" She had dropped this piece as an afterthought, fully expecting her husband to come up with a charming response, extolling her looks, how busy she was with the baby and other chores, and then leave.

She must have taken him by surprise, as he did not speak. She produced the piece of paper she had found in his pants pocket at the laundromat. It was an account of their monthly rent of seventy-five pounds written in TJ's hand, and a further payment of fifty pounds each month to Mrs. Douglas.

He scanned through the scrap, stuffed it in his pocket and without another word, stomped out of the room.

That night, TJ took Chandni with such force that she was afraid she'd be torn in two. Eyes shut tight and head to one side, she lay inert under his weight, refusing to cry out. Something told her she was being punished. Afterwards, Chandni ran to the bathroom and washed herself over and over again. TJ had fallen asleep.

Two more bottles to sterilize. Chandni massaged her aching back, casting a quick look at Sonny. As if on cue, the baby stirred. She checked her watch; it had been almost an hour. Mrs. D would be back within thirty minutes.

At the thought of the landlady, Chandni's mind went back to the day when they had brought their baby home, the feeling of utter desolation when she stepped into their messy room with Sonny in her arms, TJ and Mrs. D bringing up the rear. When her steps had faltered, she had taken a deep breath, straightened her back, and stepped in the door, only to stumble on some empty cans. Casting a furious look at TJ, she walked straight to the bassinet. At least this looked clean, exactly the way she had left it. With care, she laid down the bundle and escaped to the bathroom, choking on the sobs that had overcome every shred of self-control she possessed. Locking the door behind her, Chandni ran the tap in the sink, letting the water gush noisily.

When she left her refuge, Mrs. D was cooing at Sonny. TJ stood nearby, a cigarette dangling from his mouth.

With barely suppressed anger, she said firmly, "Don't smoke here." She pointed at the door. "If you must, do it outside."

Mrs. D stared at Chandni, speculation rife in the blue eyes. Chandni stared back until the other woman dropped her eyes, but she tapped TJ on the shoulder with a long nail and said, as she walked to the door, "If you need anything, I'll be in the kitchen." He nodded, eyes down, a slow flush rising from neck to face. Chandni knew he'd torment her for calling him out in front of Mrs. D.

All twelve bottles were now sterilized. Chandni started to pack them carefully in a deep plastic box. She wondered if TJ would be back for dinner. If they had their own kitchen, perhaps he would spend time with his family.

On those rare evenings when TJ was home, Mrs. D would barge in, asking for help. The sink was leaking again, the cat had disappeared and would be run over by some drunk if they didn't find it, the toilet wouldn't flush. Chandni, helpless and angry, would watch TJ leave immediately to do as he was bid.

When Chandni wanted the room painted, TJ said their landlady wouldn't like it. "But have you asked?" She eyed with distaste the peeling paint where moisture and mildew showed through. Instead of replying, TJ said he was tired. She was starting to wonder about that, too.

Had it been that girl Amy who had peeked through their window and vanished? When she mentioned this to TJ, he explained that he and Amy were friends. She was also Mrs. D's niece. So then why the secrecy? Amy didn't seem to want Chandni to know about her. TJ had simply shrugged it off.

She tried to convince herself there was no reason to be suspicious, but then one day she heard TJ and Mrs. D talking about Amy. They stopped when Chandni appeared. Later, thinking about their sudden silence, she felt uneasy; the feeling kept growing, like a mosquito bite grew with continuous scratching.

As the nights grew shorter, bringing with them a promise of warmer days, Chandni began to venture out of the house, pushing a second-hand pram in which Sonny lay cocooned in layers of blankets. They usually ended up at the library, where Chandni was greeted with great affection, and the baby was held up to be admired and cooed over.

One day, as she was settling into her favourite armchair by the window, and Sonny slept in the pram, she happened to look up, and her eyes lit on a familiar figure at the far end of the room.

The way she wore her sari, Parsi style, so that it draped across the front of her right shoulder was unmistakable. It was the woman from the airport – Mrs. Jamshedji.

How wonderful to see her again! Chandni wanted to rush over, eager to renew their acquaintance. Mrs. Jamshedji spotted her at the same time.

"Fancy meeting you here, Chandni," she exclaimed, folding the younger woman to her ample bosom. "You are wondering how I remember your name?" she asked at Chandni's look of surprise. "I used to wonder what happened to you." At this, Chandni's eyes lowered, but they lifted again, for Mrs. Jamshedji hadn't stopped speaking. "Often when I see the moon, I remembered you'd told me your father named you Chandni, although you were born on a moonless night."

"I have thought of you often as well, Mrs. Jamshedji," Chandni said, warmth creeping into her voice, "especially when our son was born. I wanted to let you know, but I had misplaced your phone number."

Mrs. Jamshedji bent to peer at the sleeping baby, then straightened and beamed at Chandni. "Exact copy of you, my dear. How old is he now?"

"Two months."

"And you are feeling well and all? Did you have an easy delivery? Did your mother come over to stay with you?"

Uncomfortable, and unsure how to answer the barrage of questions, Chandni began tentatively, "My mother couldn't come, and anyway, we had help from our landlady, so we were all right. He came a bit early but the hospital was wonderful…they helped a lot." She finished in a rush, painfully aware how unconvincing she sounded.

"Oh, I see. So where do you live?" the older woman continued, settling comfortably in the opposite chair.

After a pause, Chandni replied, "It's a one-bedroom flat in the back of a house." She fiddled with a button on her cardigan.

The slight hesitation did not go unnoticed. Mrs. Jamshedji pursed her lips. "My dear, if you don't mind my asking, and I am old enough to be your mother, I get the feeling that you are not happy with your place."

"It's not the flat," began Chandni, then stopped abruptly. How could she tell this nice woman, stranger nevertheless, about their dragon landlady, TJ's strange reluctance to confront her, the many times she was made to feel like an outsider. She could not gossip about her own husband. That would be disloyal. After all, TJ had said they would move to a better place when it was financially safe to do so.

The silence stretched, each busy with their own thoughts; the weight of unspoken questions lay between them. Chandni bent down, pretending to tuck in the blankets around the sleeping form in the pram.

Mrs. Jamshedji straightened her sari and leaned forward. "Chandni, I am going to ask you something that might sound rude, but you are like my own daughter, so I won't stand on ceremony."

Chandni looked up. She didn't speak. She didn't have to. There was consternation on Mrs. Jamshedji's face. She brought her chair closer, and dropping her voice to a whisper, asked, "Chandni, you are not very comfortable at this place, am I right?" A worried frown drew a line between her piercing dark eyes, eyes that seemed to miss nothing.

Chandni sat up straight, tension lodged in every angle of her body. She had been expecting questions, but wasn't ready to discuss her marital problems with anyone, not even Mrs. Jamshedji. She gave herself a mental shake. Of course, Mrs. Jamshedji wasn't asking about her married life. Mrs. Jamshedji merely wanted to know how she was getting along. That was easy to answer.

"I can't say that I am completely unhappy with our place." She almost choked at this untruth. "It's Mrs. Douglas, the landlady. She is the problem. We have no privacy; she comes and goes whenever the mood hits, never calling in advance. And her meals are almost inedible."

"Don't you cook your own meals?" Mrs. Jamshedji asked, a puzzled frown on her face.

"We don't have a kitchen, and Mrs. Douglas does not want us to smell up her place." Chandni paused, letting her eyes fix on the open window and to the garden beyond. She blinked at the sudden pricking behind her eyes, and quickly bent down again to fix the blankets around the sleeping Sonny.

Feeling a light touch on the shoulder, Chandni looked up into a sea of warmth. Taking a deep breath, she decided to take the final plunge. "Our meals," she began, "are included in the rent, but Auntie, they smell terrible, there's never enough to eat, and I have not been able to get a hot breakfast so far." It felt good to vent. This caring woman had sat with her through those agonizing hours at the airport and she had given her phone number.

This was no stranger, but a friend.

"I am so sorry to hear that and only wish we had met earlier – I could have helped you. This landlady, she seems to have no feelings. I am sure you never got to eat the food you craved while carrying little Sonny. Am I correct?" When Chandni would have spoken, Mrs. Jamshedji continued, "I have a feeling you didn't. What needs to be done is to get you out and into a place that will be good for all of you."

Chandni felt compelled to speak, "I am not sure if we can afford to move."

Mrs. Jamshedji held up a hand, "Now, hear me out, my dear. I am going to set my husband to look for a reasonably priced flat. You would be surprised," she nodded at Chandni's wondering look. "Yes, there are ways to find out. My son is also in real estate, did I tell you?"

For the first time in months, Chandni felt a swell of hope.

"Now, my husband has nothing to do all day, just reads the papers." Mrs. Jamshedji lifted a hand in a dismissive gesture. She arranged herself more comfortably in the chair and continued, "He can work with our son. It will get him out of the house and out of my hair." This was said with a chuckle, so infectious that Chandni responded automatically. "And I promise you that we will get something within the week. We will meet next Monday here," she jabbed at the air in front, "and I can guarantee I'll have good news. You can depend on me," she finished, rubbing her hands together.

Chandni found herself confiding in her new friend, at first with hesitation, then with growing confidence, about TJ's reluctance to move. She had no idea if the rent they were currently paying was on par with other places. Then there was the food or lack of, and her growing weakness; she had had to stop nursing Sonny because of it. She was desperate to find a job, but who would look after the baby?

So many questions, each outlined with doubt and fear, and her own all-encompassing sense of aloneness in this foreign land.

At one point, she stopped, suddenly crushed with the weight of guilt and doubt. Should she really divulge so much of her private life to Mrs. Jamshedji, who, however kind, was still an outsider? But, the longing to unburden was great; she desperately needed to talk to someone, to have an older person to lean on.

While Chandni was speaking, Mrs. Jamshedji listened, at times with furrowed brow giving way to wide-eyed comprehension, but she did not interrupt the flow of words. She only pulled a small packet of savouries out of her purse and handed it insistently to Chandni, who discreetly nibbled the deep-fried lentils.

The two continued to chat easily well into the afternoon, the difference in their ages slipping away, and the bond of friendship grew. As the hours passed, Mrs. Jamshedji continued to produce snacks from her seemingly bottomless purse. Dried mango in a small baggie closed with a twist tie. A chocolate-covered granola bar. A packet of the same type of sugar-coated biscuits she had eaten hungrily at the airport. Chandni enjoyed being spoilt as she knew she would have been at home as a new mother.

When Mrs. Jamshedji hugged her at parting, Chandni reciprocated with warmth. Then with a wave of her hand, Mrs. Jamshedji sailed out of the library and into the late afternoon sunshine.

Chandni had not mentioned the nights of pain and humiliation, a direct result of TJ's increasingly violent demands. She felt ashamed, dirty. Often, after one of these assaults, her mind would wander to the fun-filled college days and the romantic courting of the boy who had won her heart. Discussing marital problems was something they did not do in her family. Even had she wanted to confront TJ, she wouldn't have known how. How could she ask why her husband preferred abuse to gentle lovemaking? She had married him and must carry on.

The blankets stirred - Sonny was waking up. The tiny mouth worked worriedly, looking to latch and not finding what it wanted, sent up a loud wail. Chandni picked him up and brought him close to her face, planting a kiss on his fat cheek. He gurgled in delight. Something fell on her lap. It was a twenty-pound bill. In India, a new baby was lavished with monetary gifts. A rush of tenderness for Mrs. Jamshedji filled her.

Mrs. Jamshedji kept her promise. Soon, they were able to move to a small one-bedroom flat in a four-floor apartment building. Her happiness knew no bounds when she saw that the building was also close to the library. Much to Chandni's surprise, TJ had consented to move. She put it down to her having confronted him about opening a joint bank account. She resolved not to think of anything that would ruin their relationship.

Chandni found a job at the library sorting books, and although the hours were few, only three per day, the vast number of precious books, the quiet space, friendly staff and easy distance from home all seemed to work together. She was even allowed to bring Sonny with her. He had turned into a mascot of sorts for the library staff and even some of the patrons.

She had also started to take in sewing. When the other tenants found out she could sew and darn, they began to ask for help, and then wanted to pay her. Chandni decided to swallow her pride and accepted payment, and as if by instinct, keeping it a secret from TJ. He left early and returned late. It was better that way, Chandni admitted to herself. She enjoyed the quiet of the apartment when she and Sonny were on their own.

One spring day, Chandni decided to take four-year old Sonny to the park. Impatient to be off, he squirmed when she tried to put his arm through the sleeve. The stitching at the armhole where the lining met the warm material had come loose, and the arm went through the hole to lose itself inside the lining.

With infinite patience, she untangled the small arm from the hole and, holding her son close to her body, managed to get it through the sleeve. She increasingly struggled with failing vision, constant weakness and headaches. It had started soon after Sonny's birth. When she mentioned it to TJ, he suggested it could be due to her late-night reading; she'd sacrificed her reading, but it did not help. The doctor at the family clinic prescribed painkillers for the headaches. They were just migraines, he had said, somewhat dismissively. Women had them after childbirth. Chandni had tried to be satisfied with this. Then with the help of a magnifying lens bought from the corner store, she had solved the immediate problem of her failing vision.

Sonny was tugging at her arm. "Mummy, let's go." She gave the signal and he ran to fetch the cane from its place on the wall. TJ had asked why she insisted on using a cane when there was nothing wrong with her legs. Chandni tried to explain to him the sudden feelings of weakness that sometimes overcame her. Using the cane, she could cross roads and climb stairs with confidence. TJ had let it go.

They crossed the street to the other side, and then through the small gate that led into the park. This is where they went every day, rain or shine, in an attempt to shed the thoughts that denied her sleep.

At the park, she could let her mind wander, to recall happier times, the quiet serenity of her hometown Mauchak and her mother's warm presence.

"Mummy, push," commanded Sonny.

With a laugh, Chandni gave a gentle push to the swing to be rewarded with his shriek of excitement.

She missed Mrs. Jamshedji, who had returned to India. They had kept in touch through long letters for a while, a poor substitute to their regular chats. Then the letters had stopped coming. Chandni was so unwell, she had put off phoning Mrs. Jamshedji's son. A year passed, and yet another. She decided then to leave it at that, knowing she had received much more than she could ever give in return. When one day, they met in the aisle of the grocery store, Chandni left her shopping cart and flew to her friend. Even then, Chandni would not talk about herself, asking, instead, questions about India and what brought her friend back to Manchester. They were visiting their son.

The park was starting to fill. Children ran around, their high-pitched voices reverberating in the air. The older kids hung from monkey bars, daring each other to let go their hands; one child's scream of pain as he fell off a swing was quickly hushed by a parent.

Chandni peered at the round face of the watch on her wrist and was just able to make out the number four on the dial.

"Sonny, time to go home." She stopped the swing with both her hands and braced herself for the usual pleadings.

"Mummy, no – we just got here," the boy protested, refusing to move.

She was ready for this. Gathering him in her arms, she whispered in his ear, "Darling, Mummy will tell you two, no, three stories, tonight. You would like that, wouldn't you?" Sonny appeared torn between his desire to carry on swinging and to have his mother tell him three stories instead of his usual quota of one.

"Okay," he conceded, adding quickly, "Is Daddy home?"

"Maybe," Chandni said, helping him down. "You know he's a very busy man." She prayed TJ was home to help with dinner. Visions of the full laundry basket, dishes in the sink, the un-swept floor, changed the nagging pain behind her eyes into an inferno. For a moment, she squeezed shut her eyelids, trying to will the pain to go away. Then she took Sonny's soft hand in hers and started for home.

There was no sign of TJ when they returned. A letter lay on the floor by the door – the postman must have been late on his rounds. Chandni picked it up, examining the stamps closely – they looked quite foreign.

It would have to wait. Sonny needed his dinner, and she was in dire need of a cup of tea.

The phone rang, and instead of picking it up immediately, she let it ring until it stopped. She washed Sonny's hands at the kitchen sink, then he clambered into his chair. Turning to get the pot of soup from the stove, her eyes fell on the letter, which she had left on the counter. No, she didn't have time for it just yet.

There was a sudden clang. Sonny giggled, hugely entertained at the noise he had made with a metal spoon. Sparks of mischief lit his dark-lashed grey eyes.

"Sonny, don't. Mummy's head hurts."

Clang.

Chandni grabbed the spoon and fixed a stern eye on her son, "I said, don't do that." She ignored his trembling lips. It had been foolish, damn that ego of hers, not to get plastic dinnerware for Sonny. Safer and quieter.

But plastic looked cheap. Stoneware it had to be. Cheaper than china, heavier also, but at least not plastic.

The phone rang, again.

This time, she picked it up and heard TJ's voice at the other end. "You will never guess what happened today." His voice, it seemed, was coming from a great distance. "I was all ready to leave when who should walk in? The big boss. He wanted me to join them for drinks. Now, I couldn't say no, could I? You understand, don't you, love?" his tone became wheedling.

He had not given Chandni a chance to say a word. She stood with the receiver in her hand, a helpless rage enveloping her entire being.

TJ was still speaking. "I'll be home as soon as I can get away… tell Sonny to be a good boy." And he hung up.

Just like that.

Not a word about how she had spent her day, or even how she was feeling.

Her eyes narrowed, and she returned the receiver to its cradle. He was a liar. Did he take her for a fool? And, what about Sonny? Surely their son deserved better?

She went to the window and threw it open. The wind hit her face, cold and hard, with a trace of winter lingering in its wake. Mouth open, she took long draughts, like an animal slaking its thirst at a pool of water. Crying was for the helpless. She was her parent's daughter, a warrior. She knew now what she had not noticed during the heady days of their romance. She had mistaken TJ's immaturity for charm. Did she love him? She couldn't tell anymore…

And the nights, what about them?

A sudden cry from Sonny brought her back to the present. He had dropped the bowl, thick lentil soup amidst shattered pieces on the floor.

Like her life.

Soon he began to cry. She felt like joining him.

With great caution she stepped around the mess, and picked up her son. Sonny's arms wrapped around her neck. She stood for a few moments, just pressing her son to her bosom, letting the moment take away some of the pain from her heart.

"Mummy," Sonny struggled – she had been holding him too hard and let him go with a kiss on his forehead – "I want more soup."

"Yes, sweetheart." She scraped the bottom of the pot, pouring all its contents into another bowl for Sonny. She could go without dinner.

After he had hung up, TJ let his eyes take in the store with a practised glance. Everything was in order, dusted and cleaned, ready for the next day. The last customer had left fifteen minutes before. He lit a cigarette, puffing quickly, trying to rid himself of the tension.

It happened every time he spoke to Chandni. Self-doubt combined with a niggling sense of guilt, as if he were on the stand. It had been no different this time.

He gazed into the distance, blowing rings in the air. Never one to dwell on things, pleasant or not, he still realized he was undergoing a change. Slight, but still irritating enough to give him pause for thought. He loved Chandni. But she had changed ever since Sonny arrived. Part of Chandni's problems – the headaches and blurred vision – could have been fixed earlier, TJ reflected. When she wouldn't listen to reasoning, he had made an appointment with an optometrist. That was something, he told himself. Why hadn't the glasses helped? She couldn't even keep the flat tidy, for God's sake. He dragged hard on the stub.

The laundry was never done on time; he had to find his own clothes. His mother had always done the work around the house; his father had brought in a paycheque. That's what he was doing. She did bring in some money. His mouth twisted. A few pounds, anyway. He flung the stub to the floor and ground it with his foot.

Then his mind veered to the complaint that was always present at the back of his mind. Why the hell did she get pregnant? She should have taken care of that. He had suggested it, but no, she wanted a baby right away. At the thought of his son, he felt his muscles soften. He loved Sonny. He wanted to buy him toys, sweets, clothes, but there was never enough money.

Every penny of his salary went to rent and food, and the other thing.

He hadn't forgotten the day, four years ago, when Chandni demanded to know about the piece of paper from his pocket. He was pretty sure that he had fobbed her off. She had no right to meddle in his affairs. As a man, he had every right to it.

Thank God for Amy! An image of her dancing on stage sprang in his mind and he felt the heat of anticipation of the evening.

Sonny had been put to bed in the corner of the kitchen they'd partitioned off for him. Chandni made herself comfortable on the bed, a steaming cup of tea on the bedside table. With a sigh, she rested her back on some pillows. The letter lay on her lap. For a reason she could not fathom, she was strangely reluctant to open it.

She took a sip of tea, then another, savouring its sweetness. The quiet flat seemed to hum in its silence. Maybe she should check on Sonny – he sometimes wanted a drink. No, she was only trying to put off reading the letter.

She blew on her glasses, polished them, then put them back on. Now she was ready. She picked up the envelope. It had come from Australia originally, been sent to their old address at Mrs. Douglas's, then re-directed to the apartment. There was no return address, and yet Chandni recognized the hand that had written her original address. With an accelerated heartbeat, she tore it open, laid the one sheet of paper flat on her lap and held it down.

The letter was from Kunal.

Her brother had never been able to write a good script, and his handwriting hadn't changed. His letter was short, asking her about herself and about Manchester. He appeared not to know she had a son.

The final sentence leapt off the page, striking Chandni with the force of a cyclone, the ones that used to come to Mauchak in the fall, ravaging all that stood in their way.

> *...Brace yourself, sister, for I have sad news. Our mother passed away. I do not know the exact circumstances but this I know: she didn't survive the stroke. May her soul rest in heavenly peace.*

He continued on to say that he was trying to get a flight out to India, but didn't go into any details. Chandni skimmed through the rest with dull, unseeing eyes, her lips stiff and dry.

Kunal had to be wrong. How would he know? He'd run away, leaving them to fend for themselves?

Ma couldn't just leave.

Just when she had been secretly planning a visit to India. Just one word would have sent her to beg or borrow money to buy airline tickets. The staff at the library, friends now, would surely have helped. The long silence when her mother's letters stopped arriving…she should have delved deeper, should have made inquiries.

She had been too busy with her own health, constant anxiety about TJ's whereabouts and behaviour. Taking care of Sonny.

But these were excuses. She should have been with her mother. She should never have left India. What did she get out of being in England, anyway? An empty marriage to someone who was hardly ever home, who only used her to slake his lust.

Now was not the time to think of her own situation, she decided, pushing her hair off her face. That would take careful planning, to map out her next steps.

She tried to marshal her thoughts, going back to the last letter her mother had written. No, there had been no indication of bad health anywhere. Why didn't Ma tell her she was sick? Or was she? What happened at the end?

She was filled with recriminations and guilt, the two worst enemies of the human mind.

Chandni sat dry-eyed, her limbs still, as though the mere act of stillness would bring back her mother. She wanted… what did she want? TJ? Yes, she wanted a husband to console her. She wanted someone to tell her it would be all right. She shook her head.

The clock in the bedroom announced the inexorable passage of time. Chandni's mind had shut down. She continued to sit in her cramped position, knees drawn to chin, staring straight ahead, Kunal's letter in hand.

A key turned, finally breaking the silence. The muffled sound registered in Chandni's mind. She stirred, letting her eyes go to the clock. It was five in the morning. Sonny would be up soon. Faint light filtered through the drawn curtain, heralding the arrival of a new day.

Unlocking her knees, she climbed down from the bed and walked towards the door, but turned around when half-way, only to walk back again. Like a sleepwalker, she moved towards the flickering light of the television, where TJ was sitting with eyes half closed, a cigarette dangling from slack lips.

TJ had intended to call it a night after the last dance, but Amy had pouted. She had such luscious lips. She insisted on one more drink and offered to share a taxi with him. Then one thing led to another, and he found himself in Amy's flat. It wasn't like his wife at home would love him the way Amy did.

Many drinks later, they fell into bed. But here, too, TJ's desire remained unfulfilled. Amy was too tired and only wanted to sleep. He wanted to hit her. But the look in her eyes –challenging, calculating – stopped him, and he had brought his fist down.

All his thwarted energies now focused on his wife, the cold woman who was supposed to love him unconditionally, bending to his will. She did, most of the time, he admitted, walking quickly, the soles of his shoes beating a staccato on the empty street. But she was frigid! He had discovered this truth after the birth of Sonny.

It was all her fault for pushing him into another woman's arms. Chandni was always too busy with the boy; she had forgotten her wifely duties. A vein popped out in his neck.

The memory of Amy turning on her back, saying she needed to sleep, burnt in his memory.

He swore viciously. He had been taken for granted by the little tramp. Crooking a finger whenever she wanted to be serviced. Obviously, he meant nothing to her; all those evenings sitting through her shows had been a waste of time. His jaw hardened, sharpening the angles of his face. He took a long drag at the cigarette, but it didn't help and he flung it away in disgust. Then he lit another.

Chandni stood silent, watching her husband. All of a sudden, his head lifted. "Why are you up?" TJ's voice rang through the flat rife with suppressed anger, and she started as though waking from a trance.

After a few minutes of glaring at the still figure, TJ's eyes riveted back to the screen. He seemed to have forgotten her presence.

After a while, he turned off the television and announced he was going to bed. He started towards the bedroom. When he turned around, Chandni hadn't moved or spoken.

"Come to bed, love," TJ said. He wanted her. He had to have her.

When Chandni did not respond, he tugged at her arm.

She knew what was to follow. Every time he returned home at an unearthly hour, she had to submit to his attentions. She had found out, entirely by chance, that TJ loved to watch strippers and visited them after work. It was those nights she feared the most. And she hated herself for giving in to his demands to maintain peace, so as not to wake Sonny.

Once again, she felt the pressure of TJ's hand on her arm. Please, God, not today. Her plea for help was spoken without sound – then taking a deep breath, she addressed her husband, keeping her voice low for fear of waking their son. "I have to tell you something."

"It has to wait," he said, coming closer, and now she smelled his breath. She stepped back involuntarily, but he was having none of that. He pulled her into his arms, and forcing open her mouth with a probing tongue, kissed her violently.

Chandni dared not move; it would only serve to inflame his senses. TJ picked her up with ease and headed to the bedroom.

Shutting the door, he ordered her to take off her clothes.

"No, I won't," she breathed, at the same time trying to wrench the door open.

TJ came at her then, his face suffused with rage, and lifted her. Chandni tried to pry his fingers open, thinking if she could get to the door, she might yet get away from him. But his hands were like steel. TJ simply laughed at her weak attempt, and with a grunt of satisfaction, threw her on the bed. Suddenly, all the fight went out of her. She, who had faced the *dacoit* must now lie helpless. He was breathing hard; with one thrust of his knee, he spread her legs with such force she cried out. He forced his way into her. Spent, he turned on his back and fell fast asleep.

Carefully, so as not to wake him, Chandni eased herself out of bed and with soft feet, entered the bathroom, where she threw up into the toilet. In a frenzy now, she tore at her clothes until, completely naked, she stared into the mirror. Grey eyes, the distended iris standing out like orbs, stared back in horror; her mouth bruised and open showed the outline of teeth. Her breath came in great gasps.

If she had felt unclean before, now she felt completely debased.

NINETEEN

Chandni
Mauchak – 1983

Chandni lifted her head to take in the early December morning splendour. She wanted to be out there, in the garden, to feel the sun on her face, allow the soft breeze to run through her hair. But the sheaf of papers in front waited. She picked up her pen and resumed writing. The pen scratched busily for a few minutes. When a pigeon cooed, her concentration broke a second time.

Flexing her cramped fingers, she rose, then clutched the table for support. The momentary dizziness passed.

She looked at her reflection in the mirror that hung from a hook on the wall directly above the writing desk. Running a slim finger along the length of the scar on the right cheek, she gazed at herself for a long moment. The scar was growing faint with the passage of time, but was still visible. Enough to keep alive the memory of the events that determined her actions that day, two years before. The physical pain associated with the scar was long gone; however, her memory of the incident that had given birth to the scar would remain. Creams and lotions were not for her. She wanted to see this reminder, from time to time, her flag of freedom flown with pride.

She inhaled deeply, then squaring her shoulders, let it out slowly as if to dispel all thoughts of her life in Manchester, with the man she had thought worthy of love.

"Mummy, where are you going?"

A smile lit up her face at the sound of her son's voice.

"Just heading to the garden. He's waiting for me." She nodded towards the open door of the garden, where the stooped figure of the gardener going through a bag of seedlings was just visible. The earth was newly turned and lay in neat symmetrical furrows.

Chandni was proud of how Sonny had adapted to their lives in India. She chucked him under the chin. "What are you up to? You have been very quiet, not cooking up mischief, I hope."

"Remember, test tomorrow?" He tugged free from his mother and ran off. Chandni chuckled. He was planning her birthday celebration; she was certain. She would be twenty-six the next day.

The opening of the front gate reached her ears. She peered at her wrist-watch. Guessing it was the postman, she made her way to the front room, opened the door that led to the verandah, and stepped out. The man was about to ring the bell when he saw Chandni. She took the envelope from his hand. The unmistakably cramped script of her brother Kunal seemed to leap up; she uttered a surprised gasp, then tore open the envelope. The thin sheet of paper held just a few lines.

Dear Chandni,

You are wondering how I know that you are in India. Well, it's a long story, but this much I'll tell you: that I had been wanting to contact you for some time but pride got in the way. Pride and also a feeling of hurt. Why couldn't you have told me what you were going through? All you had to do was get in touch with the school. They would have forwarded your letter. Well, enough of that – what I want to tell you is that I am returning to India, soon, as soon as I can get my things in order here. I am being transferred to Mauchak. More later.

Love,
Dada

Chandni looked up from the sheet and drew in her breath. Kunal was coming home. Waves of happiness surged through her.

They had so much to talk about – she decided there should be no more secrets. She would tell Kunal everything. That included TJ's duplicity and her own abuse at his hands. She would tell him about her journey to Bundhpur and Kantabali's story. Her brother, who she had not stopped loving, was coming home. She would have another pair of hands to take some of the load she had been carrying.

Her mind raced with plans for the future. She had already resolved to give up this house to her brother. She and Sonny could live in Pima's house; that way, they would be closer to the school, whose construction was in full swing. Kantabali School for Girls. Wait till Kunal saw it. Her eyes sparkled with something of the old mischief.

Two years before, she had left England with her four-year-old son. Sometimes, she wondered where she had found the strength to make the long journey back, broken, empty of all feelings except an all-consuming desire for the familiar air of Mauchak. If she had looked deep inside, Chandni would have recognized that the gradual change in her character had started from the day she defied the *dacoit* during the terrifying train holdup.

The day after Kunal's letter arrived with the dreadful news of their mother's death, and after the assault by her husband, Chandni had waited by the door of their flat in the early hours for TJ to wake up. Her mind had blanked off all shame. She had determined what her next step would be.

She would leave; escape was the word. But not like a thief who comes in the middle of the night. She would confront the man who had brought her pain and humiliation, broken faith, not lived up to their sacred marriage vows. She wanted restitution.

Chandni waited for dawn to arrive.

In its own time, there appeared a gradual lightening behind the window curtain, and soon her ears picked up the sound of footsteps. TJ entered the bathroom, minutes elapsed, and then he was standing before Chandni.

"What's the matter? Why are you up so early?" The words came out slurred. He cleared his throat, at the same time running his tongue over dry lips. Her expression hardened.

"I am leaving you and taking Sonny with me." The words came out clear and precise. For a fleeting second, she let her eyes sweep across his face, taking in the blood-shot eyes, the slack mouth and her lips curled.

"What the hell? Are you crazy or what?" He ran a shaking hand through his tousled hair. "Look, we'll talk tonight. I'll be late for work if you don't get out of the way."

Chandni did not budge. "It's only six. Stores don't open for another three hours. Why do you leave so early every day?"

"None of your business, woman. Get back to bed. Get some beauty sleep before the boy wakes up." A vein throbbed in his temple. He tried to shove past Chandni.

"You really don't remember what you did to me last night?" She flung the question at him and tasted the bile of shame and injustice, and a deep anger.

His eyes widened for one second, then with a close-lipped smile, he said, "Oh, that? You know how much I love you, and just wanted to show it."

"You are despicable." Chandni was breathing hard. "I am leaving with Sonny – probably take the evening Air India to Delhi – and you will give me money to buy the ticket." Clenching her fists to stop the trembling that threatened to overcome her, she threw at him, "Or have you given your last paycheque to that terrible woman and her niece?"

It happened then. So fast that Chandni had no way of escaping. She was only aware of a stinging pain in the flesh around her cheek. Stars floated in front of her eyes and she felt herself falling.

Fast as lightning TJ strode out of the flat, the worn carpet in the corridor absorbing all sound. Reaching the main door of the building, he hesitated, just for an instant, then with a muttered oath, pulled it open. The early morning damp greeted him with open arms, and he gulped it in greedily, willing it to erase the memory of his wife lying on the ground as he pushed past her. He had wanted to stop to help her up. Why hadn't he?

He gripped the door handle and laid his throbbing head on the cold glass. Chandni's face – cold, implacable, accusing – floated behind his lids and he cursed again. She shouldn't have spoken that way about his money. It was his to do with whatever he wanted. She had no right to it, anyway.

TJ lit a cigarette, took a few deep puffs, and started walking. He knew how to fix things. He'd buy her some flowers and come home early. No strip club tonight.

A whimper, soft as the sound of a newborn kitten, broke through the silence to finally penetrate her brain. Her eyes fluttered open, coming to rest on the white face of her son. Frightened grey eyes met her own. She had no idea how long she had lain there, slumped against the wall. The door to the flat was half open. She tried to stretch her legs; they must have folded under her in this awkward position when she fell. At the slight movement, pain shot through her. She bit her lip.

Sonny was sobbing. Chandni snapped to the present. She opened her arms and he scrambled into her lap, clutching his blankie. He must have climbed down from his bed in the kitchen. How long had he been up?

The sudden realization that their four-year-old son might have seen his father hit her filled her with such rage that she had to take a few deep breaths to calm down. Oh, the shame, but most of all anger at the man who had done it. In that moment was born a resolve. Never to bow down, not to a husband or to society.

A slight shake of the head to clear her thoughts set it spinning. She had an urge to vomit, which she swallowed and, instead, held her son close. She could hear his heart beat against her own.

"Let's get breakfast, Sonny. What will it be?"

Sonny looked up and placed a soft hand against his mother's cheek.

Her son's action brought pain, this time of the heart, a swelling of maternal love for this child she and TJ had brought to the world. All her instincts screamed at her to get up, dust herself off, and plan the next move. The Rais were born to fight, not wallow in self-pity. She could almost hear Kantabali's voice, urgent, insistent: *Remember Chandni, I could not save myself. You have to. Leave.*

Sonny was speaking. "I want egg, toast, chocolate milk, and I don't want to change."

"You can have that, but you do have to change, darling." She lay a gentle finger against his mouth, for Sonny was about to protest, and continued,

"Right after breakfast, we'll go out, okay?" He nodded vigorously and ran off to the toy box, where he started to pull out his toys.

Breakfast was done and the dishes cleared. The moment had arrived. Only for a second, her fingers faltered, then feverishly she dialled the number, the one she had memorized but never imagined would need, not for something like this. If she thought too much, she knew that she would never do what she was about to do. Mentally switching her mind off, she waited. When the familiar voice sounded at the other end, she nearly broke down, but with a huge effort controlled herself and asked Mrs. Jamshedji for a ride to TJ's store.

A blue Fiat pulled up just as Chandni and Sonny appeared at the entrance of the brown brick building, the boy holding his mother's hand and measuring his steps to match her faltering ones. She had forgotten the cane.

"Good morning, dear," Mrs. Jamshedji's greeting, full of warmth and cheer, brought reassurance to Chandni in her shattered world. Here, at least, was one she could turn to. It was panacea to her wounded soul.

Mrs. Jamshedji was holding the door open. Chandni looked up to offer thanks, and that is when the other woman saw the swollen cheek, an angry red circle with purple streaks that were specks of dried blood. She gasped.

She shut the engine and placed her warm hands gently over the tiny cold ones.

Chandni put a finger to her lips, nodding at Sonny seated on her lap. She spoke in Hindi, "Auntie, it seems you have always been there for me, helping without fail…and me…me? Never giving anything in return…" her voice broke. She turned her face to the window.

"Chandni, stop it right now, I say. You are the daughter I never had, but God sent you to me." Mrs. Jamshedji paused, fumbled in her purse to look for a handkerchief, wiped her eyes. One hand went out to touch Chandni's shoulder who remained in the same position, head turned away.

"Mothers don't do favours for daughters. They help them because daughters are precious. You don't know how much I admire and love you. What strength you have shown coming out to a foreign land without knowing anyone, except, of course, your husband. And he has harmed you. You need help. I can provide it." She blew her nose. "I thank God I returned from India."

"Thank you, Auntie." Chandni's shoulders relaxed visibly. She placed a swift kiss on the top of Sonny's curly head and tried to smile, but grimaced with pain instead.

"Let me take you to my house and look after that wound." But Chandni shook her head. Her mind was made up. It was time she took charge of her own destiny.

The car slid to a halt as close as possible to the entrance of the music store. Douglas Music Store. The name danced before her eyes. Stamping out her shame with a ruthlessness that had surprised even herself, Chandni had phoned Mrs. D for TJ's work address. She had discovered the store was owned by Mrs. D's late husband's cousin. Why hadn't TJ said anything?

She took a tentative step, tested the ground, then turned to give a reassuring wave to the occupants of the car. Mrs. Jamshedji looked on anxiously. Even Sonny had become quiet, with the ancient wisdom of a child who has witnessed trauma. He knew he had to be good for his mother's sake.

She entered the store, the action setting up an immediate jangle and bringing TJ rushing out from the back of the store. Expecting a customer, but finding his wife instead, the words of welcome died and he fell silent. Chandni's face throbbed, the pain intense as heat from a fire. It ran through her veins like an extra flow of blood, supplying energy, strength of purpose and courage. She waited calmly, running her eyes over the man who stood before her, her husband, the father of her son. When she wouldn't look away, TJ dropped his eyes, turned and took up position behind the counter.

"As I said before, I am leaving you and taking Sonny with me," she said, lightly touching her cheek. There was no trace of anger or fear or any other emotion on her face. "You will bring me enough money to cover the cost of an airline ticket." She had his full attention now.

"You can't just walk out! You are my wife, and Sonny is my son, also."

"Try me." The two words rang out like a pistol shot in the quiet of the store.

"Sweetheart," TJ began, "let's not get carried away. I am sorry and promise never to repeat it." He started to walk towards her. "Don't I get a say?" he demanded, almost stuttering with anger underlined by fear at the morning's incident.

Chandni looked at him for a long moment through her one good eye, the other having puffed to such an extent it remained closed. Each word measured into exact syllables, she said, "If you don't bring me the money, and quickly, I will report you to the police."

"You can't take my son," he said, his face flushing. When she refused to be drawn, he shouted at her, "I'll see you in court if that's the last thing I do!"

Chandni turned her back on him and walked out. But she hadn't gone a few steps when a voice sounded close by.

"We have never met, but I know who you are." Amy blocked Chandni from walking any further.

"Somehow, I expected to see you here," Chandni responded, a deadly calm in her voice. She continued, "I happen to be married to that man in the store and over there," she pointed at the car, "sits our son." Amy was staring at her face. Chandni touched her cheek. "Yes, he did it."

"Well, you brought it on yourself, I'm sure." Amy flicked a stray hair out of her face with a polished nail. "TJ has always loved me and had promised to marry me, even before he married you."

It was starting to make sense to Chandni now, TJ's initial reluctance to make a commitment – but she would never know why he actually returned to get married. What had he wanted from Chandni? Well, it was all over. She was leaving him. He wouldn't dare stand in her way.

She had to muster the last bit of strength to walk past Amy. Mrs. Jamshedji started the engine. Only then did Chandni let herself relax, letting her head lean back against the seat.

"Auntie, would you mind dropping us home?" There was a faint tremble in the voice, hardly discernable except to the sharp ears of her companion. Chandni bit her lip to gain control.

"Chandni, come with me. Let me at least dress the wound," Mrs. Jamshedji begged her.

In halting words, her voice barely above a whisper, she told Mrs. Jamshedji her ultimatum to TJ and his response.

"My dear, if you don't mind my saying so, your husband is just bluffing. He won't want to let this out, not after how he's treated you."

"I know – that's why I didn't bother answering."

"You are a brave young woman – an example to us all." Mrs. Jamshedji paused, then she continued. "Listen, dear, if you are thinking TJ will bring in the money, then you have to wake up, Chandni. I don't want to appear harsh, but your husband will never let you go, and this is his excuse. For your son's sake and for yourself, you have to let me help you."

Chandni tried to smile. Mrs. Jamshedji then pleaded for her not to return to the flat, to instead stay in her house until, at least, she had recovered from the wound. She also offered to buy the plane tickets.

"Thank you, Auntie. I wish…oh, how I wish I could leave right now with Sonny."

"That's easy," said Mrs. Jamshedji, peering at the traffic light ahead. "We are going to your flat, pick up your luggage and drive to my place. After that, we are heading for the airport."

Chandni turned to look at the figure hunched over the wheel and her throat filled up. She fell silent. She and Sonny were in good hands.

TJ stood staring at the departing figure. All his instincts were telling him to run after her, to plead for forgiveness and try to renew what they'd had.

He had made a terrible mess – hard to admit but true. And now, she wanted to leave him. He hit the counter with a clenched fist, sending the bottle of cleaning liquid skittering along its length. Cursing loudly, he managed to grab the bottle before it hit the ground.

A vein throbbed in his neck. How the hell did she get this idea? She was too simple. She knew nothing about life. He admitted he had spent more than he should at the club. That's when it had all started, with Mrs. D lending him money.

At this point in his self-recriminations, the door jangled a second time, and in walked Amy. One look at her face and TJ knew he was in trouble here, as well. He decided to brazen it out. "Hi, love. I am very busy now, as you can see. Got to clean up before customers start coming in."

"Stop babbling," Amy commanded and grabbed hold of his hands. "I just met your woman and I saw what you did to her. You better not think of doing anything like that to me. Ever. Do you understand?"

She let go of his hands, and opening her purse, took out a lipstick. She turned this way and that as she applied it on her full lips, to see better in the small mirror in her other hand. After she had finished, she snapped her purse closed and began to walk around the store, like a panther on stilettos stalking its prey. TJ watched, mesmerized. For once, he couldn't wait for Amy to leave. He planned on going home early.

Just then, in walked a group of customers – mum, dad and a teenage daughter who was saying loudly that she did not need piano lessons. Amy smiled sweetly at TJ, "Thanks so much. I have changed my mind and won't need that record. Ta." She breezed out, leaving a whiff of perfume, one he had smelled on her skin many times.

Chandni hurried up, with Mrs. Jamshedji and Sonny bringing up the rear. Into the two brown suitcases, she threw in Sonny's clothes plus some toys she'd been able to buy and some presented by the women at the library. For herself, she decided to take only the ones brought four years ago. A couple of sweaters bought in Manchester would remain in the cupboard. She wanted no reminders of the place. She had made do with the clothes she'd brought from India, even preferring the long cool drape of a sari during her pregnancy. These went in, followed by the cosmetics from her wedding trousseau given by her mother.

She surveyed the contents, meagre but all her own, and snapped shut the lids. Sonny wanted to carry the monkey without the tail and his teddy. She let him.

Mr. Jamshedji took the suitcases from her hand and headed towards the lift. Chandni locked the flat, slid the key through the slot, and taking Sonny by the arm, hurried to the waiting lift.

Around five, TJ left work and rushed to the flat.

When he arrived home to find it empty, he rushed out again, and not bothering to wait for the lift, ran down the four flights of stairs. Crossing the road, he hailed a taxi. "Heathrow – fast," he barked at the driver and instructed him to drop him at Air India's departure gate.

"Mummy, peepee…" Chandni hugged him and whispered for him to hold on. She prayed he wouldn't have an accident, then focused her attention on the clerk at the check-in counter. Finally, with her passport stamped, boarding pass in hand and the two suitcases checked, she turned around and took deep breaths. People glanced at her face. She was getting used to it. She touched the bruised eye lightly.

Mrs. Jamshedji was waving at her. Chandni hurried over, "Auntie, I can't thank you enough! I'll pay you back, every penny, as soon as I get home."

"Shush, Chandni, don't even think of it. Just get home safe and sound, and let me know, send me a telegram or something – okay?" She wiped her eyes. Her husband was trying to smile, but he was also teary-eyed. He pinched Sonny's cheek.

Sonny tugged at his mother's hand. "Yes, dear, I'll take you to the toilet." She took turns hugging both Mr. and Mrs. Jamshedji. Her throat hurt from trying to hold back tears.

She had just wiped Sonny's sticky mouth with a damp towel when she heard her name announced on the PA. Her heart gave a sudden lurch; she held the sink for support, and in so doing, noticed the time. She was being paged because she was late. Not for any other reason. They must get to customs immediately. She shouldn't have allowed Mrs. Jamshedji to persuade her to take a nap at their place. Then there was the traffic jam on the way in. Oh, how could she have been so stupid? Chandni fumed at herself. Instead of arriving early, as planned, they had arrived at the terminal a little before three o'clock. And their plane left in three hours.

Bag on one shoulder, holding Sonny by the hand, Chandni hurried out of the toilet as fast as she could and tripped. She would have fallen but for a pair of hands that steadied her. Chandni flashed a smile at the good Samaritan and, dragging Sonny, arrived at customs with just minutes to spare. This was the last step before they could board the British Airways flight out of Heathrow, flying direct to Calcutta.

With everything in order, Chandni gathered the documents; then, she turned for a brief moment.

Her intuition had sharpened to compensate for her weakening vision. She made out the tall figure of TJ. He seemed to be panting as if he had run to catch her before she passed through security. He called out to her, and several passers-by stopped to look.

“I think that woman might need help,” she heard someone say.

For a second only, Chandni hesitated, squinting at him. When she grabbed Sonny’s hand firmly within her own, she noticed TJ slump back. After all, he was not going to pursue her. In that moment, a release shook through her whole body, and she almost fell to her knees. But as she gathered herself and began to turn away, she noticed that she could see absolutely clearly the muscle bulging at the side of his jaw. With a few steps, she walked to the other side to begin the journey home.

TWENTY

Chandni
Mauchak – 1983

"I brought potato seedlings," Hari the gardener announced.

Her musings broken, Chandni returned to the task at hand. She saw the gardener patiently waiting for her to respond. She knew from the past that he wouldn't proceed unless she had personally inspected the bag of seedlings and given her permission to go ahead, just like her mother used to. Such was life in Mauchak – nothing seemed to have changed.

She took a comfortable position on the stone steps along the side of the well and said to Hari, "Please, go ahead. You know more than I about seedlings and plantings and such. I'll just sit here in the sun for a while." Having thus taken care of her immediate duties, Chandni let her mind wander again.

It hadn't been easy returning to her hometown. When word spread that she had left her husband, the townsfolk had given her a wide berth.

Those were lonely days. And yet, her vision continued to improve, and with attention to her food and regular strolls around the garden, she was becoming steadier on her feet.

When she had officially received her inheritance at age twenty-four, the first thing Chandni had done was call Mrs. Jamshedji. When no one answered, even at the tenth ring, she was forced to hang up. Two days later, she tried again. This time it was Mrs. Jamshedji herself who answered the phone. The two couldn't stop talking. Mrs. Jamshedji had been the closest to a mother she had living, and Chandni wanted to share her good news, and her plan of building a school for girls. During the course of their conversation, Mrs. Jamshedji confirmed she had received the cheque that Chandni had mailed to her. She insisted on returning it as a donation towards the school.

After much deliberation, Chandni had contacted her mother-in-law. She wanted Sonny to know his grandparents. The first time, the phone was banged down when she introduced herself. A week later, she tried again, with the same result. TJ must have spoken to his parents. This gnawed at her considerably, not knowing what TJ had said or not said.

When her fifth attempt failed, she wrote a letter, enclosed a photograph of Sonny and mailed it. The letter was returned, but not the photograph.

TJ, she had learnt to forgive, and in the process, had found release.

Forgetting, however, was another beast – this, Chandni knew she would struggle with.

Slowly, she began to make some inroads with her neighbours. And as she felt more at home in town, she noticed she was regaining her strength also. Buoyed by her steady progress, she began to make plans for the school – Kantabali School for Girls. She had chosen the name.

Obtaining a permit for construction proved the hardest. It came as a surprise, at first, when her first letter to the municipal chief went unanswered. Chandni had thought, mistakenly as she realized later, that the idea of free education for girls would be embraced by the community.

When two months had gone by, still without any sign of response, she wrote another letter. She was angry. After everything she had been through, confronting bureaucrats should have been simple. She had to go and face them.

When the black Ambassador reached a high gate made of corrugated steel a few kilometres outside the main town, Chandni told the driver to stop the car. Dictated by some perverse instinct, she wanted to walk down the long avenue which led to the yellow building where the municipal office of Mauchak was housed. The young driver stood waiting to help her out, but she clambered out on her own. This was the first step. She instructed him to wait in the car, and knowing his shy nature, told him to have lunch if she took a while.

Then she began the long walk down a gravel path, carefully placing one foot before the other, aware of the attention her entrance had garnered. But of course, that was due to the notoriety she had gained. Good, she reflected, at least that way they would know she was not to be ignored. The building, painted a soft yellow, sprawled in a haphazard manner. The original had been built during colonial times, with succeeding additions over the course of the years. Tall windows opened onto the front verandah. The long hall seemed devoid of people. Up the fourteen steps she climbed, her soft leather sandals silent on the polished cement, until she reached the top and she stopped to get her breath. She could have accepted the driver's assistance when offered. It was pride, she acknowledged with a wry smile.

At the top of the stairs sat a man in brown, the peon, the person on whose goodwill access to the inner chambers depended. Here was another hall, which, unlike the one downstairs, was buzzing like a beehive. Typewriters clacked, phones rang, and surrounding everything was a low hum of voices. Clerks had their work spread on wooden tables across the space.

Addressing the peon in Hindi, she asked to be directed to the boss's office. The man, perched atop a high wooden stool, did not look up from a magazine spread across his lap. She asked a second time, raising her voice: "Please direct me to the chairman's office." At once, the clatter of typewriters stopped. Chandni could feel eyes boring into her, but ignoring them, she now positioned herself directly in front of the peon.

The man in brown said, "What do you need the boss for? Anyway, he's busy and not even here. Come back another day." He returned to the magazine. Chandni heard a snigger which was quickly suppressed when she turned.

"Listen," she said, "I know you bring in the mail for the boss. I wrote to him two months back, but have not received a reply. Here's another letter – make sure he gets it this time," and thrust the envelope in his hand.

The man in brown turned the envelope this way and that, while Chandni waited. Her patience, which had never been great, was wearing thin, and she was about to speak when the man looked up. "*Chai-paani*…" he said, gesturing with his hand to indicate tea and food. Chandni was livid. He had asked for a bribe. She said, "If you hand it to the right person, then I'll personally give you *chai-paani*."

She turned on her heel – which proved difficult with a cane – and holding her head high, carefully made her way down. She had no hopes of her letter ever reaching the person she needed to communicate with.

When two weeks had elapsed and she had heard nothing, Chandni was prepared to take action again.

On the Monday of the third week, she reached the municipal office just as the workers were returning from their lunch break. She swept past the startled peon, who ran after her, waving his arms as though shooing away crows. She aimed for the door at the end of the corridor – somehow, it had attracted her attention the first time. Reaching it, she read the name and title on the nameplate, heaved a sigh of relief, opened the closed door, and stepped in.

The man behind a large glass-topped desk was so surprised to see a woman walk in the door, and unattended, that he forgot simple courtesies and stared with mouth agape.

Into this awkward silence, Chandni spoke. "*Namaste*," she began with palms folded, "I would like to speak to you about a proposal I have in mind."

At the sound of her voice, Mr. Dubey jolted out of his seat. Then he remembered to acknowledge her greeting. When the two had taken their seats, he rang for tea. It was brought by the same peon. Chandni thanked him with a sweet smile and accepted the cup.

Mention of her family brought a nod of recognition from Mr. Dubey. He had just started in municipal politics when Chandni's father passed; she guessed that he knew about Kunal, but was too polite to ask questions.

Chandni's esteem for Mr. Dubey rose. Now, she could talk with ease – about her plan to build a school for girls, the ones too poor to pay for education, and as she continued to explain and expand, Mr. Dubey began taking notes.

Midway, he looked up from the notebook and confessed that he had always wanted to do something more than just work for a living. He told Chandni he was ready to champion her project. In his opinion, education for girls born in poverty was of primary importance. It was clear to her that he had never received her letters.

Chandni had found an advocate.

Soon plans for the school began to materialize, from paper to construction.

There was one thing she would always remember. It was what Mr. Dubey said to her at the end of their first meeting. He said that in her he recognized a spirit, an energy not entirely physical, but one which beckoned and inspired. It was to be the highest praise she had ever received.

Now Chandni's car became a familiar sight in the town centre.

She was determined to be visible through the process, talking to suppliers, interviewing contractors, visiting parents of prospective students, assuring them their daughters would receive education for free.

Some parents showed reluctance, for this was not going to be just at an elementary level. Chandni pointed out the benefits of education for a girl; for top students, there was the added attraction of a district scholarship for higher education. Wouldn't that make a difference to their lives? Not everyone had a son to depend on in old age. Girls, if educated, could be relied upon to take care of their aging parents.

And, that was how, first in ones and twos, then in groups, people had begun to come around. Her happiness reached its zenith when one day, the peon from the municipal office came to her house. He wanted his five-year-old daughter to attend the school.

Nights were another matter. After Sonny had gone to bed, Chandni sat at her desk, sifting through paperwork until late – sleep was something that seemed to have fled. Her mother's spirit was with her at all times, encouraging and loving as always. And there was also Kanta. Just as she had come to her in Bundhpur Fort, Chandni felt her presence as a strong but mirthful energy, as if urging her to go out and embrace life. She remembered Bina telling her of how Kanta had learnt to read in secret in spite of all obstacles. As if the years created an arc, their stories had come together.

She would write about her family in tribute to Kanta and Kunjan, her grandparents. Thinking of her brother, Chandni's face brightened. She would be writing the story for him, and for Sonny also.

Chandni picked up a fresh sheet and began to write:

Moonlight, the Journey Begins

My father called me Chandni, moonlight, although I came to my parents on a dark moonless night. My father said I brought light, but of a muted kind, like a moonbeam, my smile hesitant as though unsure of the welcome. I will take you to the world I was part of, the heritage I take pride in and draw strength from. My ancestors Kantabali and Kunjan Rai stand out as beacons, guiding me, urging me to persevere until the story has been told. This then is their story, and I the weaver. From the treasure chest of memories, I pull a tapestry of those long-forgotten days.

Glossary:

Alta – traditional cosmetic used to colour women's feet

Anchal – part of a sari that is draped around the female torso and covers the head.

Ayah – maid

Baba – father (Bengali)

Babu – form of respect shown to a man

Baidyo – village apothecary

Beli – species of jasmine native to tropical Asia (*Jasminum sambac*)

Bangla – language spoken by Bengalis

Beti – daughter (Hindi)

Bhasha – language

Bhodrolok – gentleman in Bengali. *Bhodro* means cultured, *lok* means man

Bodhu Boron – a ritual to welcome the bride to the groom's home. *Bodhu* means bride, *Boron* means to welcome.

Bon – sister (Bengali)

Boroma – term used for grandmother who is also looked upon as a mother (Bengali term)

Bowma – daughter-in-law

Budhia – old woman in colloquial language

Chaukat – lintel, broad horizontal support to hold up a door or window.

Chikh – window covering made out of *khus*. Traditionally water is sprinkled on the *chikh* to bring out the fragrance of the *khus*.

Dacoit – armed robber

Dakoo – armed robber in colloquial language

Dada – elder brother (Bengali)

Dadaji – grandfather (Hindi)

Dal – lentil soup

Damaru – instrument of Lord Shiva producing spiritual sounds.

Devi – Sanskrit word for Goddess, also *debi*

Didi – elder sister (Bengali)

Didima – maternal grandmother (Bengali)

Dhoti – traditional men's garment, usually fifteen feet long, wrapped around the waist and legs and knotted at the waist.

Ghat – flight of steps leading down to a river

Ghatak moshai– *Ghatak* is marriage broker in Bengali. *Moshai* term of respect like "sir"

Gora – European person as depicted in Hindi and Bengali

Gwala – herder of cattle, also sells milk

Jaam – also known as jamun (Hindi) a small purple fruit growing in the rainy season.

Jhuri – woven basket (Bengali)

Khokababu – term of endearment, *khoka* meaning little boy, *babu* meaning older man.

Khus – densely tufted grass native to India known for its oil used in machinery and perfumes. Also used for cooling purposes.

Kurta – traditionally worn by Indian men as an upper garment

Loo – strong hot and dry wind in the summer months

Maa-go – oh my! Bengali expression

Mashi – maternal aunt. Also used to address an older woman who may not be a relation

Mataji – respectful address to an older woman. *Mata* means mother, *Ji* is a term of respect and can be gender-neutral.

Mela – village fair

Mohur – gold coin

Namaste – gesture of respect made by folding the palms together (Hindi)

Neem – tree growing in the drier regions of India. Its leaves have medicinal properties.

Nimki - savoury

Palki – palanquin

Paan – preparation combining betel leaf with areca nut and sometimes also with tobacco.

Pahar – hill in Bengali, also Hindi

Panchayat – village assembly made up of five elders. *Panch* means five, *ayat* means assembly.

Pranam – gesture of respect made by folding the palms together. Also called *Namashkar (Bengali), Namaste* (Hindi).

Pukur – lake in Bengali

Rajbari – royal mansion or palace in Bengali

Rosogolla – sweet made from cottage cheese and sugar

Saraikhana – inn

Sarkar - government

Shaal – sal tree native to the Indian sub-continent. *Shaal* literally means house in Sanskrit.

Shaheb – Westerner in Bengali

Lightning Source UK Ltd.
Milton Keynes UK
UKHW010756110821
388656UK00007B/508/J